TOO FORWARD

What Reviewers Say About
Krystina Rivers's Work

The Heart Wants

"This book is both a sweet romance and a heart wrenching tale (until the end). This book is very well written to convey the emotions of the characters."—*This Lesbian Reading*

Something Between Us

"This is a very good debut novel. Krystina Rivers uses her personal experience of being in the military during Don't Ask, Don't Tell to bring us a captivating, second chance romance. I was invested almost immediately. ...Second chance romances are one of my favorite tropes when done well. And *Something Between Us* was done very well. I look forward to reading more from Krystina Rivers. She is a new author with a bright future."
—*Sapphic Book Review*

"The fact that said relationship started while they were both in the military, had to hide because of Don't Ask, Don't Tell, and reconnect after the policy has been repealed and they're both civilians gives this second-chance romance a special flavour, all the more so as the characters' motivations to join the military in the first place are very different. All in all, it was an enjoyable read and I'll check out the author's next book. And bonus point for the characters drinking my favourite wine, Brunello di Montalcino."—*Jude in the Stars*

By the Author

TOO FORWARD

by

Krystina Rivers

2025

TOO FORWARD

ISBN 13: 978-1-63679-717-5

THIS TRADE PAPERBACK ORIGINAL IS PUBLISHED BY
BOLD STROKES BOOKS, INC.
P.O. BOX 249
VALLEY FALLS, NY 12185

FIRST EDITION: MARCH 2025

CREDITS
EDITOR: BARBARA ANN WRIGHT
PRODUCTION DESIGN: SUSAN RAMUNDO
COVER DESIGN BY INKSPIRAL DESIGN

Acknowledgments

The idea of writing a WNBA romance was one of the reasons I wanted to become a writer in the first place. I love the WNBA, and there are many queer women in the league. I desperately wanted to read these women's stories, yet there are only a handful of books that are set in the world of women's professional basketball. However, the idea of tackling a book so far outside of my own lived experience seemed too daunting a task. Although I am a huge fan and season ticket holder, I haven't ever played basketball and didn't think I knew enough about the behind-the-scenes happenings of professional athletes. I simply didn't feel qualified to try to write this book, and I put it off again and again. While I still don't feel as "qualified" as I'd hoped I would, I decided to celebrate writing my fifth book by writing the one that was my initial inspiration back in 2020 and has been floating around in the back of my mind ever since.

This book is an underdog story, and I gave Jane shades of one of my least attractive traits: imposter syndrome. I didn't even realize it at the time, but it was a tough look in the mirror when I started the initial edits. I think the feeling of not being good enough, or not deserving success is much more universal than I had realized when I started down this path. I am a badass in my day job and have had years of success. Yet, as a woman in a male-dominated field, I still don't quite feel like I belong all the time and continue to follow the mantra of fake it till you make it. And when I took up writing...my goodness. This is something I'd always dreamed about doing but have no qualifications for. I have undergraduate and master's degrees in business and finance, and the only creative writing class I've ever taken was in my sophomore year of high school. To say I don't feel qualified to write books is an understatement, let alone to feel like I even belong in the same room as some of the distinguished and amazing authors I now find myself surrounded by. I have struggled with imposter syndrome more since I became a writer than I have at any other period in my life. Yet this book became a bit of therapy for me. As I wrote about Jane gaining confidence and getting stronger, I started to feel it a little myself. I hope as you read this book, if you struggle with imposter syndrome too, that you also feel a little stronger with Jane. You are a badass, and I believe in you.

Now to my thank yous.

First, to my wife, Kerri. I would have never started writing without you. I would have never finished my first book without you. I would have never submitted that book for publication without you. And I would have never stuck with this after reading my first not-entirely-positive review without you. I also would have never realized that I enjoyed basketball without you since I didn't realize there was a world of basketball that existed outside of the NBA. You inspire me. You encourage me. You remind me that I don't have to be perfect. I am so grateful for you. Thank you for everything and I love you more than life.

To my mom, Michele, who showed me what perseverance looked like for my entire childhood. I know life wasn't easy, but I learned so much from you about doing the hard things, even when I didn't want to do them in the moment. To Mom Angel, you have always supported me, but you have shown more perseverance in the past two years than I think you even knew you were capable of. I love you to the moon and back. To Cheryl, Catherine, Malinda, Dad. I love you all so much. Thank you for all of your support in my darkest moments. You all are the best.

The writing community…I think I say this in every book, but every time I feel like I can't keep balancing everything—that maybe I don't even want to—someone reaches out and tells me how much they enjoyed one of my books or how much it touched them. Or even just checked in to see how I was doing. You all keep me going. To Kris, Morgan, and Ana…what can I say? You are my people, and I love you for it. And more recently, Fiona and Jeremy…it's been a difficult few months, but I look forward to

Wednesdays now because of you. This community is woven with love and caring and compassion. I have never known anything like it, and I am beyond grateful for every reader, reviewer, author, and friend who has taken me into their lives in one way or another. I love you all.

And last but certainly not least, to Bold Strokes Books. I sincerely appreciate you for believing in me even when I'm not sure that I believe in myself. For encouraging me when I feel lost or unsure. The fact that a publisher like this exists and creates a platform for queer voices buoys my soul, and I am so grateful to Rad, Sandy, Barbara Ann, Ruth, Cindy, Toni, the elves, the proofreaders…I know I am missing a list of people here, but please know how grateful I am to each and every one of you.

I belong to a lot of communities in my world—my physical neighborhood, my professional community, my collegiate cohorts at every level, but my favorite community is this one. Our way through uncertain times and our strength is through community. Thank you for being a part of mine and for picking up this book.

Dedication

To those who have struggled to see their own light—
may you always know you are enough

Chapter One

Sitting at a bar having a beer the night before the start of training camp was an admittedly terrible idea. Yet there I was in my hotel's requisitely fancy bar, staring into the foamy top of my fifteen-dollar Miller Lite, contemplating my life. My choices. I would have preferred a citrusy IPA with a stronger bite, but Miller Lite was barely more than water with a few antioxidants, so I justified it as health food. Silly, but it was my narrative, and I could tell myself whatever I wanted.

I hadn't been planning to go to the bar. It was an irresponsible and impulsive move—one that I sincerely hoped I wouldn't regret in the morning—but I'd just felt so alone sitting in my hotel room. I'd always been a loner, happier on my own than in a group, but something about this night made the well of loneliness that was my constant companion feel like an abyss rather than its normal insulating wall, and I needed to get out of there. Sit at a bar. Have some mindless chatter with the bartender and maybe a few lonely fellow travelers.

I was sure my stay with the Milwaukee Pitbulls was going to be brief, but I wanted to give it my all anyway. It was my last chance for a career as a Women's National Basketball Association player, after all, and thus, I was going to nurse this one Miller Lite and then head to bed to ensure I got at least ten hours of sleep before the start of camp. Undoubtedly the last training camp of my career.

Eight training camps. Eight long years of never quite being able to find the game I'd lost. I'd been planning to hang it up. Throw in the towel. I'd accepted an assistant coaching position with a division two school in Buffalo, New York. I wouldn't have even been sitting at that bar if my former college coach hadn't been the one to call me personally to invite me to camp a few days before. Convince me to come to camp, really.

Flames of embarrassment tickled my diaphragm as I thought about my pathetic excuse of a WNBA career, essentially over now. The feeling of promise when I'd been drafted. The excitement of training camp, like the first day of school on steroids. Everything in my life had been firing on all cylinders, and I'd been on top of the world.

Until the injury in my second professional game had robbed me of that entire first season, and my basketball career had tumbled down around me, burying me in a pile of rubble so deep that I couldn't even see the court anymore, no less play on it. I had no idea why teams kept signing me. They must've watched reels from my college days and thought *they* had the magical panacea to help me find my game that I'd lost that horrible May day.

I checked the Cubs game on the television over the bar and smiled as the batter hit a double and drove in a run. I wasn't from Chicago, but for some reason. I'd always pulled for underdogs—especially perennial ones like the Cubs—long before I was a cliched underdog myself.

When I looked to my beer to take another sip, I caught an attractive woman on the other side of the bar watching me. I thought it was odd that it was almost eight in the evening, and she was still in a suit, alone at the bar, but I wasn't going to judge. It was a nice distraction from the negative self-talk I'd been mired in moments before that I was self-aware enough to recognize but not strong enough to snap out of.

And the way her strawberry blond hair and pale skin glistened in the warm glow from the lights overhead...it made my chest hot. I looked away, embarrassed, though I couldn't understand why when it was her who'd been staring at me.

I picked up my phone from the bar and scrolled Twitter to give myself something else to look at. There was a lot of buzz about the new center the Pitbulls had drafted in the first round, Brittany Phillips. She'd gone to Tennessee and led them to their first NCAA championship in more than a decade and a half. She'd already signed a sponsorship with some sunglasses company at the tender age of twenty-two. I'd seen a goofy video that portrayed her turning into a dog while wearing the sunglasses. It seemed silly, but it had over a million likes, so she was clearly doing something right. I couldn't imagine having the confidence to do that when I was that young. Hell, I couldn't imagine having the confidence to do that now.

I couldn't help laughing at myself at how pathetic I was. Trying to head off another negative self-talk spiral, I looked up to check on the game. Before my eyes found the television, however, I saw the woman looking at me again. Or still? Had she ever looked away?

Her lips curved into a smirk, as though she knew a secret no one else in the room was in on. Maybe she did. I smiled back, but when her smirk turned into a true smile, my cheeks went hot, and I looked down. I was nervous, yet…intrigued.

The bubbles inexorably making their ways along the sides of my glass until they broke the surface were fascinating, weren't they? I swirled the beer, and a new round of bubbles exploded to the surface, but like a magnet, the unknown woman pulled my gaze back up.

Except this time, her chair was empty.

Even more embarrassed than before, I tried to shake off my foolishness and focused on the television, appreciating the strange mix of relief and regret that rolled through my muscles in waves.

"Is this seat taken?"

My head snapped left. When had she gotten right next to me? Those deep blue eyes that I'd thought were brown from across the room blinked at me. I belatedly realized she was waiting for a response, even though she should have been able to see that the seat had been empty all evening. "Uh, nope." *Smooth.*

"I hope I'm not being too forward," she said, leaning in, her voice silk. "But I saw you from across the room, and you were alone, and I was alone, and you seemed...interesting." She pursed her lips, and it was like my entire belly went to jelly.

"I'm probably the least interesting person in this entire bar," I said, always uncomfortable being the center of attention.

She bit her lip. "Now, I don't believe that for a second. Tall, perfect, a little mysterious. Maybe you're a spy waiting for your mark."

I scoffed. I couldn't be further from a spy. "Maybe you're an author who spins fanciful tales all day and night."

"I like the sound of that, but alas, no. Just a corporate suit in Milwaukee doing her father's bidding." She stuck out her hand, though she didn't have to reach far since she was standing so close. "Kinzie Lancaster."

Kinzie. I rolled the name around in my head, liking the way it felt against my mouth. "Jane. Jane Gray." I also liked the way her palm felt against mine. Soft. Smooth. It was almost delicate in my larger, rough, athlete's hand, but the way she shook wasn't delicate. It felt like she was commanding me to shake. Maybe she was. Little muscles deep in my belly clenched.

"It's nice to meet you, Jane." Kinzie's smile held a magnetism that I didn't understand but definitely wanted to see more of. She captivated me as she slid onto the stool and continued facing me rather than turning to the bar.

But why would someone like her be interested in *me*? Torn between wanting to talk and see that magnetic smile again or curl into my hoodie and crawl under the bar, I wrapped my arms around my torso as soon as she released my hand.

She crossed her legs, hooking one of her bold red heels on the bottom rung of the barstool, and her skirt slid up, revealing another inch of her creamy pale skin. My mouth went a little dry, and I cleared my throat, took a sip of beer.

"Who in this bar do you think could be more interesting than you?" she said, running the tip of one finger around the top of her glass of red wine.

I took another sip of beer, which had even less taste than before. I looked around the room, trying to pick out one person who seemed more interesting than me. "I bet that guy over there is," I said and nodded at a clean-cut white guy sitting at the other end of the bar, smiling—what I assumed he believed to be—a charming smile at the bartender.

She pursed her lips and looked the guy up and down. "Absolutely less interesting than you. That's Jeremiah. He's a salesperson from Lawrence, Kansas and is in town selling the plastic tips for the tops of spray cans. He's down there flirting with the bartender because he knocked up his high school girlfriend on prom night and has been tied down ever since. This is the only excitement he gets in his life. He's not going to cheat on his wife, but harmlessly flirting with women who aren't his wife while he's on the road gives him a little charge. He's a fairly decent guy, despite his flirty tendencies when out of the zip code, but he's boring as hell."

I laughed harder than her story warranted because this interaction, where a beautiful woman made up stories about other bar patrons to convince *me* that I wasn't the most boring person, was ludicrous. Surreal. This didn't happen to me. For some reason, feeling like this was happening to someone else made me a little less self-conscious. A little bolder. Fake-me said, "I don't know…plastic tips could be interesting."

"Hmm." She tapped her index finger against her lower lip. "I can't see it. But I can see that he's more boring than you by a long shot. And I still don't believe you're boring at all."

"Oh, I am."

"Prove it. What brings you to Milwaukee, Jane Gray? Why are you so boring?" Watching Kinzie's lip wrap around the top of her glass as she took a sip was a vision that I was pretty sure would live in my mind for some time to come.

"Work too."

"Wait, you sell spray can tips like Jeremiah over there?"

I choked on my beer and coughed. My chest hurt as I tried to regain my breath, and Kinzie's hand lightly patting my back was twin pleasure and pain.

"Sorry, I didn't even think that was all that funny." The twinkle in her eye was ornery. But I liked that it was focused on me, even as it made me nervous.

"It wasn't. It's been a long day, I guess."

"So if not a plastic thingy salesperson, what *do* you do, Jane?" she said when I finally stopped coughing long enough to have a sip of water.

I took a slow sip to buy time. The problem was, my job was probably the least boring thing about me, but I didn't like to talk about it. People normally had a vision of what a professional athlete should have been, and I hated being compared against that idealized vision. And it wasn't like I was any good. She wouldn't have heard of me even if she was a basketball fan. Luckily, since fake-me was at the bar that night rather than real-me, I could be flirty and evasive. "To fool you into thinking I am more interesting than I am, what do you *think* I do?"

When she took her plump lower lip between her teeth, my palms went damp, and when she looked me up and down, I thought I might slide right off my stool into a puddle on the ground. *Help.*

"Let me see." Those long fingers tapped her lips again. Did she know what she was doing to me? "You were watching the baseball game up there pretty intently, like you knew what was going on…are you a sports reporter?"

I laughed at the ridiculous notion. As if I was outgoing enough to be a reporter. Also, if she thought I was watching *intently*, she'd probably never watched a game before. "I wasn't watching intently, and that's not it. But out of curiosity, are you a sports fan?"

"Good God, no. Not at all." She shook her head wryly as she took another sip.

"Not a sports fan, got it. But I am curious, what are *you* in town for? You said you were doing your dad's bidding?" I wanted to change the subject before she actually figured out what I did. Sports reporter was a little too close to the truth.

"Me? I'm perhaps slightly more interesting than Jeremiah. I work in corporate America and, yes, for my father's company. He was supposed to be out here for this assignment that is sports' adjacent, so not exactly up my alley." She grimaced. "And I was supposed to be in San Francisco, which I find *a little more appealing* than Milwaukee—not that Milwaukee isn't interesting—but he had a heart attack a few weeks ago and isn't ready to travel yet, so here I am."

"Oh, I'm sorry."

"He seems like he's going to be fine. I hate being away from him when he's still recovering, but that's life. Okay, next guess as I'm not going to let you change the subject. You didn't actually deny being a spy earlier. Suspicious?"

"I wish. But definitely not a spy. I'm way too shy." If she knew the only reason I was able to talk to her was because fake-me had taken over, she might understand how ridiculous a notion that was.

"I don't think you're as shy as you say you are. And I'm pretty sure that's what a spy would say."

I laughed. "You're ridiculous. I swear. I'm not a spy." Something about bantering with her had me drinking faster than I'd meant to, and I tipped my head back as I swallowed the last of my beer.

"Can I buy you another drink while I work out this mystery of who is Jane Gray?" she said.

That was so much more tempting than she knew, but I couldn't. I was drunk on her, but I had a huge day tomorrow. My last chance. I checked my watch. It was getting late. Despite the surprising fun I was having, I couldn't stay. "I'm sorry, I'd love to, but I can't. I have a big day tomorrow, and I need to get to bed."

Her face fell, and I had a strong urge to break the rules for her, but I couldn't. Tomorrow was the first day of my last chance. "But it's not even that late." She checked her watch. "It's barely eight."

I signaled to the bartender for my check. As I pulled out some cash to place it in the billfold—I certainly couldn't put a beer the night before training camp on my hotel tab that the team would be paying—she laid a hand on my forearm. My skin tingled. My breath caught.

"How long are you in town for?" she whispered, her voice like honey across my senses. She stared at my mouth. I thought maybe she wanted to kiss me, but that was ridiculous.

Yet, I wanted to lean in and find out. But fear of rejection and embarrassment coursed through me, so I jumped up instead. "That remains to be seen. It was great meeting you, Kinzie. Maybe I'll see you around."

I fled from the room without a backward glance. I didn't think I'd ever been flirted with by someone so forward. It was flattering and nerve-racking and sexy as fuck. I bounced on the balls of my feet as I waited for the elevator. But it terrified me too.

"Jane, wait a sec."

Startled, I jumped like I was going up for a jump ball. I had to look like such a weirdo. Why was Kinzie coming after me? Lost in my head, I stood, still gasping from surprise, until she stepped closer.

She touched my arm again before she said, "I've never done this before, even though I'm sure this sounds like a line, but there's something about you…I don't want this to…" She finally seemed a little nervous as she looked at the ground, but it paled in comparison to the nerves racing through my veins like tiny race cars speeding out of control along a sinuous racetrack.

But she cleared her throat and steadied herself in a way I was envious of and said, "Will you come up to my room with me?" Her eyes were clear. Her voice stronger than was fair, given what she'd just asked. How did she have the confidence to be so bold? I couldn't fathom it.

Yet, it was sexy. Something about her bold question had heat flooding between my legs, and I considered her proposition more than I'd expected.

Ding.

My gaze jumped up.

"I think your elevator is here," she said and gestured to the doors opening behind me.

I stepped in on autopilot, but as the doors started to slide closed, I stuck my hand into the path. "I think your elevator's here too, isn't it?"

A pirate smile crept across her face as she joined me. "I think you're right."

CHAPTER TWO

We stepped into Kinzie's hotel room, and it shocked me to see how posh it was as she pressed a button on the wall, and sheer curtains started rolling down the wall of windows in front of us with a quiet hum. My more modest room only had a pull chain. She grabbed my hand and pulled me toward the minibar in the corner before stopping to face me.

"I was going to offer you a drink, but you said downstairs you really couldn't have another. And anyway," she said, tucking hair behind my ear and tracing a fingertip along the side of my jaw. "I'd much rather kiss you. If that's okay with you, that is."

She looked straight into my eyes, strange because I'm tall—a little over six feet—so she must have been pretty tall too. She was in heels but still. I stared at her mouth as she stepped closer and dragged her thumb across my bottom lip.

"Please," she said, barely a whisper.

That single word turned me inside out. "Yes," I said, and before I chickened out, I closed the minuscule gap that remained between us and kissed her.

Maybe it was the excitement from doing something so taboo, but our kiss quickly transformed from tentative to potent. Our tongues were dancing, stroking, stoking a fire that went from smoldering to raging in a fraction of a second, catching me by surprise with its intensity. Her fingers were under my T-shirt and hoodie, taking my arms up with them as she pulled them off, leaving singed trails in their wake.

I shoved her suit jacket from her shoulders, not caring that it landed in a heap on the floor. All I cared about was getting our clothes off before I lost my nerve. I fumbled with the tiny buttons on her silky blouse, apparently taking too long because she grabbed the hem of her shirt and pulled it over her head, tossing it inside out across the room.

Her cool fingers reaching inside my waistband made me jump. My stomach contracted as she fumbled with the button of my jeans. "Jesus, Jane, it should be illegal to have abs like this."

I chuckled and managed not to say that they weren't that spectacular when compared to many of my teammates, but I'd done a good job so far avoiding the whole professional athlete thing, so rather than saying anything, I found the zipper on her skirt and slid it down, surprised when it fell to the floor the second I released it.

Her matching purple lace underwear and bra made me wonder if she'd been planning to pick someone up in the bar that night or if she just liked pretty underwear. I appreciated getting to reap the benefits either way. I traced her areola, visible through the lace of her bra. "I like this," I said.

"I like pretty things," she said as she bit her lip and looked me up and down.

I felt self-conscious at my own black cotton bra. I was pretty sure that I was also wearing black panties, so at least I matched. To distract her, I backed her up to the desk and sat her on it. She huffed. The surface was probably cold, but I needed to taste her, and this was closer than the bed. I dropped to my knees and spread her thighs.

"Is this okay?" I said as I reached for the waistband of her panties. When she nodded, I started to pull them down. She shifted her hips to help get them free.

Her eyes darkened as I dragged the tip of my finger from her opening up to her clit, swirled it around, and back down to her opening before dipping it inside. My mouth watered, and I couldn't wait any longer. She groaned loudly when I began to lick and threaded her hands through my hair, massaging my scalp as I teased her clit with my tongue.

"Please, Jane," she said.

I leaned back to look at her, and she was so beautiful with her head resting against the wall, her fingers playing with her breast through the fabric of her bra, her nipple straining beneath it. "Please what?" I said.

She looked at me with hooded eyes. "Please don't toy with me. I need you now. Please fuck me."

I felt myself smile. "Happy to," I said and again took her in my mouth. This time, however, I slid two fingers into her and followed the rhythm she set with her hips as I thrust in and out.

Her grip tightened in my hair, and her breathing grew ragged. "More," she panted.

I slid a third finger in her and sucked her clit into my mouth. I was certain my underwear was going to be soaked by the time she came. There was something about bringing another woman pleasure that turned me on more than anything else, and every pant, groan, and heavy breath turned me on even more.

I was in awe at Kinzie's lack of inhibitions as she gave me direction, "Yes, right there, yes, yes." Her hand in my hair vibrated as her body tensed, and she cried out my name.

Her head hit the wall behind her with a *thump*, and I pressed a kiss to her outer lips before I leaned back. "Are you okay?"

"Perfect. Just need a sec here," she said, panting. She opened one eye and looked at me. "That was...I can't even come up with the right words, so I'm going to go with really, really good."

I lay my head on her thigh, basking in the moment. "Yeah," I whispered.

Sooner than I was expecting, she pushed up from the desk, nearly knocking me over.

"You're not done yet, are you?" she said.

I stood. "Nowhere near done." I was still wearing my jeans, so I flicked open the button and slid them down my legs, toeing my Adidas off just in time to keep my pants from catching on them.

"Good. Because I have a lot of plans still that don't involve sleep. If that's okay with you."

"I think we can make that work." My face felt hot, but there was no way I was leaving this hotel room yet. I was going to savor every moment of this wild, uninhibited night.

She gripped my hips and walked me back toward her bed, pushing me down. I wasn't ready for it, and my hips bounced once before sinking into her plush duvet. The sight of her standing there in just her bra and shoes made my mouth go dry. The words of that song from *The Sound of Music* about having done something good ran through my head. She was simply breathtaking.

I wanted her on top of me. Beneath me. Everywhere, until I forgot everything about the world around me. The fear and anxiety I had about training camp and everything it meant disappeared as I watched her unclasp her bra. She took another step closer and kicked off her shoes. She was finally completely naked, and she was glorious.

"You're overdressed." She *tsked*. "Let's see what we can do about that, shall we?"

She pulled my panties down my legs before climbing up my body and reaching underneath me to find the clasp of my bra.

"I think this might be easier if we just…" I tightened my grip on her hips and rolled us over.

I felt the clasp on my bra come undone, yet she still said, "That was rude."

"What do you mean? I was giving you better access." I laughed as I kissed her neck, her throat, her chest, down to her collarbone.

I gasped, surprised, when deft fingers slipped into my folds and found my clit. "Just because you're on top doesn't mean I can't find what I'm looking for."

I leaned up to allow her better access. "I was never trying to stop you," I panted. When she sat up and took my nipple between her lips as she slid a finger inside me, I knew there was nothing I would deny her that night.

I awoke in the middle of the night disoriented, but every moment came back vividly when I realized I was spooned protectively around Kinzie, the smell of her shampoo surprisingly light in my nose.

My feelings were all over the place. I was a little proud of myself for being so bold and doing what I wanted. There was something incredibly freeing about fucking someone I knew I'd never see again. It was probably why we'd both had several orgasms. I was rarely able to relax that fully with a partner, but I'd managed to completely escape my self-consciousness for a few hours.

But the high of stepping so far out of my comfort zone was wearing off, and the panic was starting to set in. How could I have been so irresponsible? That wasn't me. Instead of getting a solid night's rest, I'd been up half the night fucking a complete stranger, admittedly a hot stranger but a stranger, nonetheless. If I was exhausted tomorrow at practice and got cut on the first day because they thought my conditioning was irreparable, I'd have no one to blame but myself.

I needed to get back to my room ASAP and salvage whatever sleep I could before I had to report in the morning.

As I started to slide my arm from under Kinzie's neck, she tightened her hand over mine that I only just realized was cradling her breast. Jesus Christ. What did I think I was doing?

She groaned as I finally extricated myself but thankfully didn't wake up. I didn't know what I'd have done if she had. I crept silently around her room illuminated only by the lights of the city shimmering through the sheer curtains, collecting my clothes, my phone.

I dressed as quickly as I could, but with my hand on the door, I looked back at Kinzie, beautiful and naked in bed. I'd tucked the duvet tightly around her so the loss of my body heat wouldn't disturb her, but the expression on her face was so serene. Content. I itched to run my fingers through her silken hair one more time. Every impulse in me screamed to get back in bed, but I couldn't.

I had a big day ahead of me. Probably the last big day of my professional playing career, so I steeled myself and eased into the hallway, closing the door behind me with a nearly inaudible click and walked away without looking back.

❖

I managed to get six solid hours of sleep on top of whatever I'd gotten in Kinzie's bed. I wished it had been twelve, but all things considered, it wasn't too bad. Thankfully, our little tryst had started early.

I ordered a sensible tofu scramble with a bunch of veggies and no cheese for breakfast from room service—no way was I gonna risk running into Kinzie in the restaurant downstairs—and left my hotel at eight thirty. Report time was ten, and the training facility was only twenty minutes away, so it shouldn't have been a surprise when I got there more than an hour early. I felt like a nervous rookie rather than an eight-year veteran of the league.

I killed time by wandering around the neighborhood and grabbed an earl grey at a local coffee shop. But I started to get nervous about being late, so I headed in. An intern who looked like he was fourteen showed me to a small theater complete with stadium style seating. Each tier had several tables with two chairs at each table. I picked one in the middle on the opposite side from the door. Better to blend in when the others arrived anyway.

I wasn't sure how long I sat doom scrolling on my phone while I waited for the rest of the team to arrive. Finally, I heard some noise from the hall, though I couldn't distinguish any words until the door opened.

"Fifteen minutes early is appropriate for the team captain. But you'd better hurry everyone up. Don't want to be late for Coach Carr's first team meeting." I knew as soon as I heard her voice that I was about to properly meet Maya Norris for the first time.

I'd played against her a few times in college, and I'd ridden the bench a lot while my teams in the W played against Milwaukee, but we'd never spoken. But her smile brightened when she saw me and walked over. If she remembered me from her freshman year, she might not have been so cheerful. Though that was years ago.

"Hey, I'm Maya. Point guard extraordinaire." She stuck her hand out but squinted at me. "You look familiar, but I can't quite place you. Why don't I know who you are? You weren't on the roster?" She gnawed her lip.

"I was a late add. Jane Gray," I said as I took her hand. It stung my ego a little bit that she didn't recognize me, but at the same time, I wasn't really surprised. "It's been a long time sin—"

"Jane Gray. Duke. Of course." She smacked her palm to her forehead. "I'm still pissed at you for the final four."

So she did remember. I grinned a little. I'd picked her pocket and taken it for an easy layup that had put us up by seven with less than a minute left in the semifinal game we'd won on our way to the national championship my senior year. I'd put the nail in the coffin with that steal.

"Look, if you hadn't had the ball hanging out there like a kid with a balloon, I wouldn't have been able to swipe it. You had no one to blame but yourself for that."

"*Moi?*" She pointed at her chest, eyes wide.

Not sure where I was finding the gumption, I said, "Yeah, you. And it's not like you can complain. You simply had to wait your turn to get your two national championships. Just not that year." Something I couldn't quite place about Maya made me feel comfortable for the first time in a long time. Especially in a basketball setting.

She shoved me in the shoulder and laughed. "Fair. I was a bit sloppy at protecting the ball back then. I'm a lot better now."

I laughed. "I guess you *are* an all-star." She was a force. I could easily argue she was the best PG in the league. Not a hard argument to make; her four all-star appearances made the argument without my help.

The door slammed open, distracting us as three more women came pouring in. They took the row in front of Maya and me.

"You were on fire in the offseason, Ruby. On fucking fire. Turkey didn't know what they were getting." I recognized Vicky Vlack, the team's backup PG from last season, as the person talking to Ruby Washington, the team's fierce power forward. "A beast," she finished in a low growling voice that sounded a little demonic. Vicky sat on her table facing us, and Ruby leaned against the wall.

"Damn right," Maya said as Ruby started to protest. "Though, what the hell was that voice?" she said to Vicky. "You need us to call you an exorcist?"

"The only one who might need an exorcist is Ruby cuz she played *possessed.*"

Maya laughed. "Well, you're not wrong. Can't wait to see Ruby 2.0 in action. She held her hand up for a high five from Ruby, who pushed off the wall to reach her and Vicky.

"Fuck, yeah," Ruby said. Vicky slapped her on the ass before they both faced front and dropped into their chairs.

The rest of the players quickly followed in, and I was relieved that Maya focused on them. I really didn't want to risk having to discuss my pathetic excuse for a career.

At ten on the dot, Coach Carr and the rest of the coaching staff walked in. Maya sank into the chair next to me as Coach began. "Good morning, ladies. I'm so excited to be here as your head coach this season. Coach Brett had the building blocks for something special here before he left, and I couldn't be more enthusiastic about all the talent we have in this room. I've watched film on all of you, I've coached some of you, and if you work hard and reach the potential I know you have within you, this is going to be a really special season. I can feel it in my bones that we have everything we need to be a championship team this year right in this room."

Coach Carr's welcome gave me chills. Even when I was in college, she'd always had a manner about her that inspired me. And it wasn't just her words. It was how she said them with conviction, with her whole body. I would have followed her into the depths of hell if she'd asked. It was the reason I'd come to her training camp when I'd been ready to give up on this life. How could I say no to her when she'd brought out so much in me as a player a decade ago?

I couldn't, so there I was, letting her get me excited again despite my fear that I was still going to end up disappointed.

"I believe in unselfish basketball with good ball movement leading to the right shots, in an up-tempo offense. Bring one hundred and ten percent to every game and every practice, and I think you'll find that you'll fit right into my system." She looked around, seemingly making eye contact with everyone in the room. "All right, now that the boring part is over, let's get out on the court and run some drills. Today is mostly diagnostic. I want to see how your conditioning is. I'm sure you've all been training like fiends in the offseason if you haven't been playing overseas and are in peak conditioning." She grabbed her clipboard and clacked it on the desk. Everyone stood. "But we've only got a scant three weeks before the season starts, so it's time to show me your hustle."

What she hadn't said—what she didn't need to say—was that only twelve of the fifteen of them in the room were going to get roster slots. My nerves returned in full force. I knew most of them were returning from last year's team, and then there was Brittany Phillips, this year's number three draft pick. The fear that I was going to embarrass myself and get cut seized me, and for a second, I couldn't move.

"Guards and small forwards with Coach Brandy. Centers and power forwards with Coach Josh," Coach Carr said. "I'll be floating between."

"Hey, you okay?" Maya shouldered me, apparently noticing my statue impersonation.

I nodded. Took a deep breath. *Get yourself together, Gray.*

"Well, let's go." She grabbed my hand and pulled. I shook my head to snap out of my stupor. "Coach Brandy is amazing. And not just because her name is my favorite drink."

"I loved watching her play. Her footwork was lit."

"For sure. I've gotten so much better because of her. I've really learned to create more opportunities on the ball and off. You're gonna love her."

Maya was right. I did love working with Coach Brandy. She was really encouraging when someone made a mistake, even me. Several hours went by quickly, alternating with shooting drills, defensive drills, penetration drills, three-on-three half-court scrimmages, free throws, and the final half-court shot exercise until Coach Carr blew the final whistle, and everyone gathered around her.

"Great job today, everyone. I'm loving what I'm seeing. If you all keep playing like this and bringing this intensity, you're going to make our jobs very difficult in two weeks. Every single one of you has a chance of making it onto my final roster this year." I swear, she was looking at me specifically when she said that. I swallowed hard. "So rest up tonight and be prepared to show me what you've got tomorrow."

I fell into line as everyone headed to the locker room to change, and I waited until a few people started to trickle out before I headed back out to the gym. I'd always tried to end every practice with shooting drills, but this season, I'd decided to up my numbers. I'd end every practice by hitting one hundred free throws, fifty jumpers from each elbow, and thirty three-pointers. I was old with a bum knee, so I knew I had to make waves somehow, and materially increasing my shooting percentages from every spot on the floor felt like my chance this season.

The door to the gym opened, and Maya boomed, "I was wondering where you'd gotten off to after practice. I wanted to see if you wanted to grab dinner, but I couldn't find you before my session with the shrink."

"The...shrink?" Since when did they have shrinks on staff?

"Have you met the mental performance coach, Brigitte?" Maya grabbed a ball from the rack as she walked toward me and started dribbling it.

"Oh right. She was at the team meeting, but she wasn't at practice, was she?" I was still in my three-point rotation, so I dribbled three times and went up. *Swish.* Twenty-three from beyond the arc. I'd only actually missed two from back there, so I was feeling pretty good about myself.

Maya passed her ball to me as she went to grab the one I'd just sent through the basket. "She was in the bleachers. She just blends in well. She doesn't want to be noticed during practice so she can notice everything happening on the floor."

Great. Something to make me even more self-conscious. Two between-the-leg crossovers and I took my next three. *Swish.* That felt pretty damn good.

"Nice shot. How many more you got?" Maya passed me the ball again so I didn't have to get my own, which was nice.

"Six more makes."

"Want to grab a smoothie with me when you're done?"

"You didn't come out here to practice yourself? You're just going to watch me?" I felt a little self-conscious, but we played in front of thousands of people, so it wasn't like I was truly uncomfortable with an audience.

"No. I like to do my shooting drills before practice. I came out here looking for you. So we could grab a smoothie."

I took a higher stance in my dribbles that time, feigning that I wasn't planning to shoot in an attempt to lull the defense. *Swish.*

"Sure. I think you're good luck. Five more makes and we can head out."

I miraculously drained my next five in a row, packed up, and we were on our way. It felt like Maya was taking pity on me and had decided to be my first-day buddy since all her friends from the team were still here at camp. It was probably because she was the team captain. Since I was the newbie and she was the leader, the vet, welcoming new players was probably part of the job description.

Regardless, she was nice and fun, and I'd appreciate her camaraderie while I was with the team. I figured I'd make real friends again once I got to my coaching job.

"You looked good out there today when you were defending Abby. That steal reminded me of why I almost hate you." Maya snickered as she unlocked the doors to her Rivian truck. "You've got fast hands."

Embarrassed at the compliment, I said, "Not fast enough, really."

"Hey." She paused until I looked at her. Her gaze was intense, and I struggled not to squirm. "Don't do that."

I swallowed with intention. "What?"

"Downplay it when someone gives you kudos."

"I don't—" But I couldn't continue the lie under her stare. It was intimidating as fuck.

"I knew you weren't that oblivious." She laughed as she threw the truck into reverse, and I sighed in relief when she stopped staring and looked at the backup cam instead. "You played really well today. Your roll action off the pick that Ruby set for you was beautiful."

"I missed the shot," I protested.

"First day nerves. That's going to be a great play for you this season."

"If I'm around this season," I mumbled. Or thought I did.

"I'm going to need you to stop talking like that." She punched me in the shoulder without taking her eyes from the road. "Because I'm calling it now. You're going to make the team. And we're going to go to the finals."

Her words had my eyes burning, and I prayed I didn't cry. I couldn't remember the last time someone had shown such blind faith in me. I worried it was misplaced. "How do you have such conviction? I haven't done shit in the league, and I was playing in France—barely—during the season last year because I didn't even make a team here."

Maya stopped at a light and pursed her lips as she leveled her gaze at me. "I just know things. I can't explain it, but I have a feeling about you. This is your breakout year."

I let her words sit with me as we rode in silence. Part of me felt more stressed because if I failed now, I'd be letting Maya down too, but the rest of me wanted to wrap myself in her blind confidence. I wanted to believe she could see that spark that I'd lost eight years ago. I needed to believe it.

She seemed to know I needed time to sit with it and changed topics. We talked about the Bucks and how horrible they were this year. As we got smoothies, I found out she was from New Mexico, and I told her about growing up in Vermont. The time passed quickly, and before I knew it, the slurping sound of air mixing with the last vestiges of my green smoothie filled the air.

"This place is good, huh?" Maya said.

"Delicious." I'd never been a smoothie person, but I wondered if maybe I'd just never had the right one.

"It's my after-practice routine. But don't you just want to sing, 'He's a smoothie operator…smoothie…operator'," she belted out to the tune of Sade's *Smooth Operator*.

I couldn't help but laugh. I couldn't believe she'd make such a spectacle of herself in public, especially given she was a *much* better point guard than she was singer. Hell, she probably would've been a better center than she was singer, but she really owned it.

"I want to sing that every time I come in here," a Latinx person in a Cubs baseball hat said from where they were waiting in line.

"I would like to make a motion that we all do from now on," she said.

"Yes, let's start today."

The entire place broke out into song. Apparently, Maya had the ability to make a roomful of strangers like her so much, they'd sing for her. It was wild, but she was incredibly charismatic. I was pretty sure I was blushing on her behalf.

"On that note, you ready to head out?" she said.

"You don't want to stay and sing with your new besties?" I said with a giggle.

"Nah, I'll sing with them next time." She shrugged. "Are you in the team apartments?"

"Not yet. I just got in yesterday afternoon, so I'm at the Hyatt a few blocks from here, but they said I'm moving in a few days." I couldn't stop myself from mumbling, "If I'm still here."

"Stop that right now." She shoved me in the shoulder, and I stumbled a step. "You will still be here in two days. Technically, the whole team will still be here in two days, at least until the first preseason game. But I told you. We are going to be le-gen-dary. A dynamic duo. I can feel it in my bones." She shimmied her shoulders.

I wanted to kick myself. I didn't really know Maya or if I could trust her. My gut instinct was that I could, but I didn't need to make my chances worse by having her tell Coach that I didn't have any faith in myself. "I guess we'll see."

"Now, do you want a ride home? You're on my way."

"You don't live in the team apartments?" I rolled my eyes at myself since most successful players out of their rookie contracts had their own places.

"No, I have a condo in the Third Ward. I sublet it in the offseason when I'm playing in Europe, but I like having my own space when I'm here. Plus, it's a great investment. And a nice tax break."

I sighed. Maybe someday. But more than likely, it would be a modest house in Buffalo. Maya's words came back to me, however, and a little flicker of hope whispered, "Maybe sooner than you expect and not Buffalo."

I must have been zoning because Maya said, "Not to rush you, spacey, and I'd love to hang out more, but I do have to get home to my pup. Francesca gets antsy when she's home alone for too many hours."

"Aww, you have a dog? What kind?" My heart melted. I'd wanted a dog for so long, but with my life, it'd been impossible. I'd get cut or traded midseason and end up back in France or wherever sooner than expected. And then what would I do with a puppy? I promised myself that one way or another, I was going to have more stability that year and get a dog.

Her face went soft. "She's a little terrier mutt. Some yorkie, chihuahua, westie, who knows. She's adorable and a perfect princess."

"I'd love to meet her."

"For sure. I'll have you over soon. We'll celebrate you making the team."

I rolled my eyes.

"Fine, fine. I won't make you wait that long, but we *will* celebrate together when you make the team."

"It's a deal," I said as we pulled up to my hotel. It was so close, I probably could have walked from Smoothie Operator, but it was nice to find out that we had a love of dogs in common. Having the captain and starting point guard on my side would be nice.

"Rest up, and I'll see you in the morning," she said as I got out of the car.

I put my hood up and hiked my duffel higher on my shoulder when I walked through the lobby, terrified I was going to run into Kinzie. God, she was hot, but I couldn't stand the thought of having to face her again, and we'd never gotten around to discussing how long we were both staying there. I hadn't thought of her all day, but now that I was back in the hotel, everything came rushing back.

What a whirlwind the past twenty-four hours had been. I'd had my first one-night stand and the best sex of my life, I'd had a fairly decent opening day at training camp for the first time in a long time, and I'd had a smoothie with a new friend.

When I got to my room, I stripped and got into a steaming hot shower. It felt amazing on my limbs that were achy now that the adrenaline from the last day was wearing off. When I'd hopped on a plane the day before, I could have never predicted how the next thirty hours were going to play out, but I was proud of myself.

I'd stepped out of my comfort zone, and it felt like the world was starting to change around me. Or maybe I was starting to change in it. And I was cautiously excited about it. Very, very cautiously.

Chapter Three

The next three days of practice went surprisingly fast. And surprisingly well. I still made a few boneheaded plays. Maya stole the ball from me three times, but I stole it right back once, which wasn't as easy to do as it was when she was a college freshman. As the day was nearing an end, Coach Carr said, "All right, ladies, everyone circle up on the baseline."

I was exhausted because Coach Brandy had been running us ragged, but I tried not to show it. At my age, I couldn't show weakness if I wanted to make this team, still a dicey proposition. I saw a group of people talking with Coach, but I had tunnel vision in grabbing my water bottle and falling in next to Maya. She was something of a security blanket, which felt pretty pathetic for a veteran player approaching thirty, but Maya had taken me under her wing, and even if it was out of pity, it felt like we were still becoming friends. Real friends.

She elbowed me and jutted her chin toward the group of people standing with Coach. "What do you think is going on there?"

I shrugged, still too busy gulping water to actually look.

"I think that's the team's marketing person, but I don't remember her name. Jade? Janean? But I don't know any of the others."

Maya seemed concerned, and as she was the captain, that worried me, so I looked over. There were several suits clustered together and another suit standing next to Coach and the rest of the coaching staff. None of them looked familiar, though there was a woman in a dark charcoal pantsuit with long, strawberry blond hair facing away from me whose silhouette seemed vaguely familiar.

Maya snapped her fingers. "Oh, Jada. She's definitely the head of marketing. She's the one talking to the coaches, but I have no idea who the others are. So I guess it's something to do with marketing?"

"You'd know more than me. I don't know any of them." I took another swig. How was my mouth so dry? It'd been a tough practice, but nothing that should have made me feel like I'd run a half marathon after drinking an entire bottle of tequila the night before.

Coach clapped her hands.

"I guess we're about to find out. Want to grab a smoothie again after? I'm like Niagara Falls here with the sweat. I need some electrolytes." She swirled her hand around her red face.

"At least I'm not the only one whose ass has been kicked by this practice."

She barked a laugh. "Are you fucking kidding me?"

"Nice practice, everyone. I'm loving the effort. Brittany, that was a fantastic block earlier. Your progress so far in camp is exceeding my expectations. Jane, that was an amazing steal. Great anticipation. I'd really like to see that same energy on some of those drives and see you get a block or two as well."

Nice of her to not mention the multiple times Maya had taken the ball from me, but whatever.

Coach went through a few more shout-outs to nice plays before she got to the reason for the early huddle. "We wrapped a little early today because the team's marketing group is here to talk about a few things. A lot of you probably already know Jada Morrow, the VP of marketing, but over the offseason, they also brought on Owen Park as the VP of sponsorships. And in order to help grow the team's fan base as a whole, they partnered with Lancaster Consulting. Kinzie Lancaster is…"

I missed the rest of what she said. At the name Kinzie, I started scanning the rest of the group. It wasn't a terribly common name. In fact, I'd never met a Kinzie until the other night, but there was no way...

Holy fuck. It was Kinzie from the hotel bar. Kinzie who had seen me naked just a few short days ago. Kinzie who had given me more orgasms than my last girlfriend.

Oh my God. I couldn't breathe. I had no idea what Coach was blathering on about because I was staring at Kinzie as though she'd turned into a unicorn. Thankfully, it appeared that she hadn't noticed me, so I tried to shrink down. It would've been better if I'd been standing next to the centers rather than in between two guards, but there wasn't much I could do.

Kinzie had been looking at Coach but started to scan the crowd. It looked perfunctory until her gaze caught mine. And everything stopped. She stared at me while I stared at her. Her eyes went wide. I was sure mine already were. Those full lips parted just a little. Although I'd stopped sweating after Coach had blown the whistle, it felt like my entire body was breaking out in a sweat all over again.

Maya elbowed me in the ribs hard enough that I looked down at her. "What are you doing? Why are you staring?"

I shook my head. I didn't want to call more attention to the fact that I hadn't been paying any attention to Coach. I jutted my chin back to Coach and tried to focus on her, but I couldn't keep from glancing at Kinzie. She looked a little different. She was in her full pantsuit with the jacket buttoned, unlike at the bar. The blouse underneath was a deep burgundy that coordinated perfectly with the dark charcoal of the suit. She was in the same heels, and I had a quick flash of her walking toward me in nothing but those and that sexy as fuck lacey bra before she kicked them off.

I swallowed hard at that image.

Coach handed the reins over to Kinzie, and she stepped forward. "Good afternoon. It's great to meet everyone, and I look forward to getting to know you all a little better as I work with Jada and Owen to strengthen the brand that the Pitbulls have already built."

She took a few steps, and the peek I got of her ankles as her pants rode up a bit with every step was ridiculously enticing. Why were her ankles so perfect? Why were her hips so perfect? I envisioned running my fingers over her shoulders and knocking that jacket to the ground again. Running my fingers over the soft skin I knew lay beneath. I needed to keep looking at her since she was the one talking, but I also needed to quiet my brain. Stop these images. Focus.

"I'm based in New York, but over the coming weeks, I'll be bouncing back and forth so I can attend practices and games and meet with many of you to get your thoughts and ideas. My goal is to assist Jada and Owen to strengthen the current bond between you and the community, forge new connections and partnerships both locally and nationally, and bring more awareness as we look to grow women's professional basketball as a whole."

"I can't believe the team is paying for someone like her to come out here," Maya said under her breath.

I nodded again. I was afraid of saying anything. Even a whisper or mumble might draw more attention to myself, and I'd been way too conspicuous already. But it was pretty impressive. None of my other teams had more than one full-time person and *maybe* an intern or two in the marketing department.

"I don't want to take any more of your precious time today. I'm sure you all want to hit the showers or whatever." She let out a nervous chuckle that reminded me of her saying something at the bar about not being a big sports person. Why would the team hire someone who wasn't a sports person as the brand manager for a professional team? "But don't be surprised if you see me circling practice or pulling you aside for one-on-ones. Thanks, everyone."

The team clapped when she finished, which was weird. I wondered if the front office knew how much of a sports fan she *wasn't.* Regardless, it was nice that they were spending money on her, even if she didn't know a field goal from a free throw. But maybe she didn't need to know the sport to sell it?

As Coach wrapped up practice and reminded us that we had a late start the next morning, I glanced at Kinzie again. Her cheeks had a hint of pink, and I wondered if she'd been red the whole time she'd been talking, and I'd missed it or if something had embarrassed her once she'd finished. It was a similar color to the flush in her cheeks after she'd come.

Fuck.

I needed to stop thinking about that. It would be *completely* inappropriate for me to pursue anything with her. And I was fairly certain she'd only pursued me that night because I was the only woman alone in the bar. She was probably a player and liked to pick up women in every city. It had to be why she'd played my body like a violin.

Someone pulled my arm. Maya. "Come with me," she said, her voice so low I could barely hear.

"What?" I asked.

She dropped my wrist once we were out of hearing range from the group. "What is going on with you and the brand woman?"

"Nothing," I said, but I knew I'd said it too quickly.

"Bullshit. You two were practically fucking with your eyes while Coach was introducing her. I doubt you even heard anything Coach said."

"Nothing was going on." She wasn't wrong, but there was no way I was going to admit anything. I opened my mouth to try to make up some excuse, but the way she was staring at me, I couldn't do it. I waited a beat. Then another. She still just stared with expectant eyes. "Okay, fine, there's a story, but I'm sure as hell not going to get into it here with you. Can we talk later?" I was surprised to find myself not hating the idea. I'd never really had platonic girlfriends who I could talk to.

"Smoothies?"

"How about I come to your place—or vice versa—tomorrow evening? I'd rather not talk about any of it in the open. It isn't particularly professional. And I need to pack tonight because I'm moving to the team apartments tomorrow." And I needed time to really consider how much I wanted to share.

"Fine, but I can't believe you're going to make me wait another whole day to dish." She rolled her eyes.

"Maya," Coach called from the other side of the gym. "Do you have a sec?"

"Coming, Coach." To me she said, "I'm not letting this drop, so don't think you're getting out of it by pushing it off until tomorrow. But still, smoothies in a bit?"

I nodded, but as she jogged away, she pointed two fingers at her eyes and at me. She was weirder than I thought she was when we first met. Probably the reason we were becoming friends.

I looked around, and most of the team was already in the locker room. I didn't see Kinzie or any of the other suits, so I grabbed a ball and started my post-practice shootaround routine. I practiced some footwork, dribbled between my legs, and spun as I made my way over to the free throw line.

I made my first dozen free throws no problem, but as I was shooting lucky number thirteen, I heard, "You didn't mention you were a professional athlete when we met the other night." The ball rolled for an eternity but rimmed out. Of course she'd seen that, I thought, rolling my eyes. The miss was absolutely her fault. She'd distracted me on my release. "Though I can't say I'm surprised, given your physique." She swirled a finger at me, and I felt like I'd taken a sharp elbow to the chest, knocking me to the court and ripping the breath out of me.

Somehow, I managed a snappy retort. "As I recall, you claimed you didn't even like sports and somehow forgot to mention that you were working on branding for the city's WNBA team, which seems a little more than *sports tangential* or whatever you called it. There was clearly a lot we didn't talk about. Though I guess we didn't spend much time talking at all."

She smirked. And God, it was sexy. "Well, there's truth to that. And please don't tell anyone that I don't like basketball." The ball rolled to a stop in front of the toe of her pump. Watching her squat in those heels to pick it up was a beautiful thing. She handed it to me, standing closer than was necessary. My body instantly responded, and I was afraid she could hear my heartbeat accelerate. When our fingers touched as I took the ball, it looked like her breath caught. She closed her eyes. When she opened them, she said, "I was sad when I woke up alone the other morning."

I shrugged but couldn't bring myself to make eye contact. I was too embarrassed about everything. The fact that she'd seen me naked, the fact that I'd had a one-night stand, how uninhibited I'd been that night, how close she was in that moment, how much I liked all of it.

When I didn't say anything, she said, "I've been looking for you in the bar every night since, but you haven't been there."

I swallowed. "Yeah, training camp keeps us really busy."

She stepped closer, and it felt like my heart rate tripled. She touched my arm, and I finally looked at her. "I—" She was cut off when the door to the gym slammed open, and Maya barged in.

I stepped back, hopefully before Maya saw us.

"Are you still not done with your...shooting drills?" Her words slowed as she approached us. I took another step back.

In a low whisper, Kinzie said, "Are you still staying at the hotel? Can I buy you a drink tonight?"

I wanted to say no and run away, but the mature, adult half of my brain knew we needed to talk about what had happened between us and how the next few months would look as she *worked closely with the team. Fuck my fucking life.* "A very quick one, and I can't meet until later. I have stuff now."

"Eight o'clock, lobby bar?"

"Fine," I said, feeling reluctant and afraid but also a little excited. Kinzie reminded me of the boldest moment of my life, and although I was embarrassed about it, it also made me a tiny bit proud.

She plastered on a smile that looked totally fake. "Thanks for walking me through that, Jane," she said loudly enough for Maya to hear. "I look forward to getting to know you better over the next few weeks."

"Anytime. Happy to be of service." I dribbled the ball as I moved back to the free throw line to finish shooting, a complete cluster because I was ridiculously distracted. I took so long that Maya went and got her phone and started playing on it.

I wanted to beg off smoothie time, but it had kind of become our thing, so after my terrible shooting and Maya's teasing, we went, though we kept it short because I did need to prep for the big move. Most assuredly *not* because I was excited to see Kinzie again and needed to get cleaned up. I probably looked like a drowned rat from the sweat and my sad, limp ponytail. I wanted her to think I was pretty, to *not* regret having slept with me, even if we couldn't do it again.

When I arrived in the bar at eight sharp, I was relieved to see her already sitting at a cozy table in the back corner. She was sipping red wine and wearing jeans and a soft-looking navy sweater, more comfortably dressed than I'd seen her before. Well, other than without any clothes at all. She had seemed *surprisingly* comfortable sans clothes in front of a stranger. Apparently, she was comfortable in everything.

"Hi," she said softly as I slid into the seat, but before I had a chance to reply, the bartender walked over.

"What can I get for you?" she said. "Or I can give you a little more time to think about it."

I thought about ordering a decaf, but that didn't feel strong enough. Same with a Miller Lite. "Can I get a Heavenly Haze IPA?" I'd had enough games in Milwaukee to know that was my favorite local IPA without checking the menu.

"Sure thing," she said and walked away.

"Hi," I finally greeted Kinzie. This felt so weird. I wished I already had my beer for something to do with my hands other than wringing them in my lap.

"Thank you for meeting me. I—"

The bartender again interrupted us when she sat my beer in front of me.

Kinzie ran her fingers through her hair and looked a little nervous, her eyes wider than normal. "Sorry, as I was saying, thank you for having a drink with me. I think we were both a little surprised today. It wasn't that I didn't want to see you again. I had a great time the other night. I've had a drink down here every night on the off chance that you were still here, but I never expected to see you at work."

I thought about saying I'd been avoiding this bar because I was afraid of running into her, but that felt needlessly cruel. And it had nothing to do with her. It had to do with me and my embarrassment and my need to focus on my game. In the basketball sense not the dating sense, obviously.

But that was too much to explain, so I laughed and said, "I never expected that either. I'm only on a training camp contract, so I didn't—and still don't—know how long I'll be here. I'm moving to the team apartments tomorrow, and practice is exhausting, so I haven't been down. And if I want to make the team, I need to focus on my physical conditioning, so I've been going to bed early, and I can't indulge in these very often." I lifted my glass in case my implication wasn't obvious. "I mean, I had a great time too. One of the best nights, really." I looked into my glass, unable to look at her as I said, "But I just can't..." Yet, as I trailed off, I couldn't help but look up in time to see her shoulders slump.

"I get it." She nodded and took a sip of wine. "It's unfortunate. For me, anyway." She ran her index finger up and down the line of her neck, and all I could see was that finger all over my skin just a few nights ago. Across my chest, between my breasts, teasing my nipples.

I clenched my jaw, hoping she couldn't see my desire all over my face. *Unprofessional. Unprofessional. Unprofessional.*

"But I get it. It wouldn't be appropriate for us to repeat. *I've* been known to be a little unprofessional at times, but…" She looked at me with a heat I'd never felt before the other night.

But it was impossible. I wanted to salvage my career. And to do that, I needed to not do something stupid like get involved with someone who distracted the shit out of me and was associated with the team. I couldn't be that foolish. Reckless. "I'm…not. Ever. Walking the straight and narrow. That's me." My nervous giggle that followed made me feel like a fool.

"Hmm." She ran a finger around the rim of her glass. "Judging from the way you screamed my name a few nights ago, I'd beg to differ on the *straight* piece of that statement."

I swallowed wrong and was pretty sure I'd inhaled some of my IPA. My throat burned, my eyes watered, I gasped for air.

"Are you okay?" She placed a hand on my forearm, real concern in her eyes.

I nodded. But how could I keep myself together because all I could think about was how many times she'd made me come. How much I *wanted* to be unprofessional with her.

"Seriously. Are you okay? I'm sorry if I offended you."

After what felt like an eternity, I was able to manage, "I'm fine. Not offended."

"Oh good." A smirk played across her lips, and God, it was hot.

I took shallow breaths through my nose. She was going to kill me. It didn't matter that practice started late tomorrow because I was going to have a heart attack sitting in this bar, so I wouldn't be there anyway.

"So anyway, I'm hearing you. Nothing unprofessional or untoward can happen between us. I'm glad we got that cleared up," Kinzie said and cleared her throat. "We probably should pretend that nothing ever happened, huh? Even though we didn't know then, it still might look inappropriate."

I laughed. "I've never had a one-night stand before, but I don't think walking around advertising it is normal, so, yeah. Let's keep this just between us."

"I hadn't thought about it that way, but, yeah. Who would go into work and talk about the person they picked up in a bar?"

Calling me just someone she'd picked up in a bar stung a little, despite how foolish I knew I was being. I *was* just someone she'd picked up, but…I was being ridiculous. I needed to shake this off. "Totally. I'm moving out of here, so at least there won't be a chance of running into each other. We'll pretend we don't know each other when you're in town with the team."

"Because we don't know each other, right? One night does not create any type of relationship." When she looked at me, the draw that had been there the other night was still there, but I needed to pretend it wasn't.

"Exactly. And on that note, I'll take the rest of this drink up to my room. I still need to pack." The need to run was too strong to resist. I couldn't decide if she had a thing for me or not, but I wanted her, and that was impossible.

I tried *impossible and unprofessional* as a mantra, running it through my head and even saying it out loud while I packed, but as I lay down to sleep between the cool crisp hotel sheets, all I could picture was Kinzie's eyes sparkling as she leveled that sexy as fuck smirk at me. This was not good. Not good at all.

Chapter Four

O
h my God, she's so cute," I said as a little terrier puppy with pink bows over her ears and a matching collar came scrambling toward me. I dropped to my knees and let her run full force into me. Not that there was much force behind her little body. She lapped at my wrist, and I almost died of cuteness.

"Clearly, I'm chopped liver when Miss Francesca is around," Maya said as she stepped around me.

"Sorry," I said, trying to scooch to the side to let her pass because I wasn't done loving on the perfect pup yet. "But she's just so cute. And I needed a dog fix."

"Ugh." She sighed playfully. "Well, fine, while you're getting it, you want a drink? Mocktail? I've been feeling bougie as hell with a Sodastream I bought while engaging in retail therapy. I'm in love with this strawberry mint concoction."

"That would be great, thanks." I needed something, and a mocktail was the best I was going to get to fortify myself. I'd been dodging Maya for a few days after what had happened between Kinzie and me. It was easier because we had our first preseason game the night before. While "I need to focus on the game not my personal life" was a perfect excuse, Maya told me in no uncertain terms that my time for delaying was up. Not that it was all that big of a deal, but everything that had happened with Kinzie was so out of character for me. I was trying not to feel embarrassed, but I'd never done something like that before, and I was a private person. Sharing what had happened with Kinzie didn't come naturally.

"You can also move to the couch for cuddles. The princess will come with you. No need to sit on the floor. Our bodies take enough abuse as it is." She laughed as she walked into what I assumed was her kitchen.

I did move because she was right. My knees had been abused enough, and the cold hard tile of her entryway was something my tender joints really didn't need. Sitting on the couch, I took stock of her living room. It was nice. Settled. Mature. Like a genuine home rather than a temporary home base, which was the best I could say about anyplace I'd lived since college. She had shadow boxes with pieces of the nets from her two NCAA championships, along with pictures of her cutting the net, as well as the official team photo. I had something similar, but it sat in a box in my parents' basement, waiting for me to have some semblance of permanency to retake ownership.

I was trying not to get my hopes up, but we were a week and a half into training camp, and I was surprised at how well I'd been playing. When I'd come to Milwaukee, I'd been convinced I'd be the first player cut. But I wasn't. Coach had already cut one guard and one forward, and she had one more cut to make before finalizing the roster before the start of the season. She still had almost a week to make that decision, but after my meeting with her earlier that afternoon, I thought I *might* have a chance.

"What did Coach want to talk to you about after practice today?" Maya said as she came back carrying two low ball glasses containing something light pink and garnished with a strawberry and what I guessed was a mint leaf. She flopped into the corner of the couch, mostly facing me, and pulled her knees to her chest.

"She damn near gave me a heart attack today when she asked to see me. I thought for sure I was getting the ax." The only players she'd met with one-on-one were Maya and the two players she'd already cut.

"*Psh.* No. She hasn't made her final decision yet, but I'm pretty sure you're safe based on what she's said to me. And I know from watching you play that you should be on this team. Especially after last night."

For our first preseason game, I'd been solid. No, I didn't set any records, and I wasn't perfect, but it was the best I'd played in years. Admittedly, preseason games were about finding the right combinations of players on the floor. I wasn't playing against what would likely become their starting lineup, and those players might have never played together before that rotation, but still. There were so few moments in my professional basketball career that had made me feel genuinely good about my game and myself, and I was going to bask in it.

"Wait," I said. "What did she say?"

Maya looked away. "I'm the team captain, and Coach likes to debrief with me after practices with what I'm thinking about player development, camaraderie. She's the boss, but she knows I have an eye for talent and can feel the team chemistry better on the court than she can from the sidelines, so we talk about the team as a whole as well as individual players."

I wondered if they talked about how uninspired my play was sometimes. I wasn't sure why the thought bothered me. Maybe because Maya was a friend, and I didn't want her convincing Coach not to cut me because she liked me. I swallowed, knowing I needed to ask, or I'd always wonder. "Are you just keeping me around because we're friends?"

She poked me in the thigh with her sock-covered foot and laughed. "Are you kidding? Firstly, I don't have that much power. Secondly, I want to win and wouldn't do that. And finally, your play is keeping you here. And that's Coach's decision. That being said, I told her honestly that I think you bring something to this team, and I think you're getting better as you get more relaxed and more confident."

"But—"

"And Coach agrees. Get out of your head about this, have a drink, and tell me how your chat with her went today."

I knew I needed to work on my confidence, which, funnily enough, was related to what Coach had talked to me about. I really didn't mean to be down on myself all the time, but it was hard. I didn't feel like I'd done much to be proud of in years. To buy time to get my head straight, I took a sip. "This is fantastic. What else goes in it?" The light fruitiness combined with the bubbles and the sweet, delicious smell of the strawberries and mint. *Maybe I should invest time into learning how to make drinks like this.*

"I make my own syrup. I'll show you how some time if you want, then just the fizzy water and some fresh fruit and leaves. But there's no guilt, just a perfect, refreshing drink after a long day of practice."

"I'm going to take you up on that syrup lesson," I said after I took another sip.

"Now tell me about Coach. And don't think I've forgotten about Kinzie either." She chuckled as she leveled her gaze at me.

The more I thought about it, the less important the Kinzie thing was, and I wasn't trying to hide anything. "The meeting with Coach was good. We talked about the game last night."

"That fast break you had was beautiful. When that defender came out of nowhere, I was sure you were going to pull up, but that feint and hard drive to the basket was fire." She fanned herself, and I could feel myself start to blush.

"Coach was impressed too, and she asked me why I didn't play as dynamically as in college anymore." I sighed, hating that damn knee, the reason I'd never had a real career.

"I've wondered that too. After I saw you on the first day of camp, I looked up some of your old film. I remembered our final four game, but I didn't really see many of your other games back then. We were in different conferences, and you graduated when I was a freshman, so we didn't play other than that one game. I watched your tapes from college and then some from here and your overseas play, but you were a different player after college."

The thought of her seeing how terribly I'd played for all those years embarrassed me, and I looked away so I didn't have to see her face. I focused on scratching Francesca's neck. "I'll tell you what I told Coach. I've never felt like my knee was one hundred percent after the surgery and rehab, and I'm afraid to test it in games for fear of blowing it out again."

"Yet since joining the Pitbulls, you've made some amazing plays that are reminiscent of how you played in college. I had a good feeling when we first met, and watching your play over the last ten or twelve days affirmed that I was right. Do you feel like your knee is getting better? Is it a mental thing?"

"Well, that's just it. I don't know. My knee doesn't feel any different or more stable than it has over the last few years, yet sometimes, in the moment, my instincts take over, and I just do whatever without thinking. But if I try to do it on command, my body doesn't always respond. Which is what I told her too." I didn't tell Maya that I wished I could take it back. That certainly wasn't going to help my case to make the team. Why would Coach want to keep someone who could only occasionally play well and who had no control over when that was?

"When you're in the zone—really in the flow—your subconscious takes over, and it knows your knee can take it. What did Coach say to that?"

"She wants me to work with the trainer more to confirm my knee is good and to increase the overall strength in my legs to help me have more confidence. She also wants me to talk to Brigitte because she thinks it's more mental than an actual physical issue."

"That's a good idea. Aaron can make sure you *can* trust it, and Brigitte can make sure you *will* trust it. And spoiler alert, that sounds like she's planning to keep you around because another week of PT with Aaron isn't going to make a massive difference in your game."

"I guess," I said, hoping she was right. I knew my game was getting better. I just worried it wouldn't be enough.

She poked me in the leg again. "Now tell me what's up with you and Kinzie."

"Cone of silence. You cannot tell anyone." I emphasized every syllable of anyone to make sure my point was crystal clear.

"Yes. Now. Spill. The. Tea."

I felt my face grow hot, but I closed my eyes and blurted, "We met in the hotel bar my first night here and fucked. And then didn't see or talk to each other until the other day after practice."

When Maya didn't say anything or react, I pried one eye open a sliver and looked at her. She was gaping at me.

"Well, say something," I demanded.

"Wow," she said, her eyes still comically huge. "I was expecting it to be something a little personal, but not, like, one-night stand level. Do you normally...do that?"

"No! Never. I've never. I still can't even believe I did it. And now, of all the people, it's someone I'm going to be working with on and off for months. If I make the team." I closed my eyes and shook my head.

"We've already discussed that. But this is...wow. She's fucking hot. I would've never guessed she played for our team." She fanned herself again.

"She doesn't..." I trailed off until I realized what she meant. "Oh, you're gay too."

"Yeah, Gay, bi, pan whatever. I don't put much into labels. I like who I like, but do I appreciate the pure perfection that is the female form? I most certainly do." She nearly sang the words, and I laughed at her description.

"Pure perfection sounds right," I said, thinking of how exquisite Kinzie looked lying on her back with her hair fanned around her face, seemingly completely unselfconscious, which I was in utter awe of.

"That dreamy sigh of yours is very telling, Jane Gray."

I threw a pillow at her, which she, of course, caught, though Francesca huffed as I accidentally jostled her. "Shut up," I said without any heat.

"Is she as good in bed as she looks like she'd be?"

"Oh my God, yes, she was fantastic. In a different life, I would totally want to see her again. But that can't happen. She is—would be—way too distracting. And it would be totally unprofessional."

Maya *tsked*. "Not sure if any of that's true, but *okay*."

"If it's no big deal, why don't *you* date her?" I said and felt a strong stab of jealousy at the thought. I tried to suppress it. It wasn't like I had any claim to Kinzie.

"Oh no. Not me. First, I don't date people my friends have had any sort of relationship with—that's way too messy—and second, I have sworn off dating for now. And for sure with anyone to do with the W. I've had a rather horrible on-again, off-again thing with Paris Turner."

I tried to picture Turner but was drawing a blank.

Maya must have noticed my confusion as she continued, "You know, Indiana's shooting guard? She's lethal on the court but also lethal to my mental health off it." She blew out a loud sigh as she shook her head. "And I need a break. She and I are combustible but like bleach and ammonia. Sometimes, you want that explosion, but most of the time, it's just toxic. And I can't do it anymore."

I grimaced as I remembered who Paris was, a beautiful woman with dark brown skin and nasty range from beyond the arc. I didn't really know her, but she'd always seemed stuck up when our paths had crossed. "That sucks. I'm sorry." I was a little surprised that bubbly Maya could have something toxic with someone, but I was also surprised that I'd had a one-night stand myself, which I guess proved the point that no one ever knew what went on behind closed doors.

"It's fine. It's over. I'm just still giving myself a little space. But back to you. You're so shy. I still can't believe it. Did you pick her up in the bar?"

I scoffed. "God no. She picked *me* up."

I gave her the high-level details about how we'd met and then chatted for a while longer before I'd called an Uber back to the team apartments. The car situation was getting annoying. I had a car, but it was in Vermont in my parents' driveway. If I made the team, I'd fly up there and get it, and if I didn't, I'd fly up there and drive it over to the coaching gig in Buffalo.

But I was going to make the team. Maya's words always gave me confidence. I was going to try to be less critical and negative. Maybe I'd bring that up with Brigitte when I talked to her about the rest. So far, our conversations had been relatively superficial because I didn't fully believe that she was going to be helpful. However, with Coach and Maya endorsing her, I wanted to do better at giving her a shot.

I also couldn't help but think about Kinzie. Maya was right. She was fucking hot. But I had too much on my plate. I couldn't carve out time to date. I didn't imagine there was a policy against dating someone involved with the team, especially not someone who was an outside consultant, but it just wouldn't look right.

Yet, I found Kinzie's face bouncing around in my head for the rest of the evening. When I finally gave in and slid my fingers into my already wet folds, deciding that an orgasm might help me fall asleep, it was the vision of her body over mine, her hair surrounding my face that sent me over the edge.

My first appointment with Aaron, the head athletic trainer, was the next morning before practice. I'd seen him around, but I hadn't worked with him yet. While he'd always been friendly, I doubted he'd do anything my previous trainers hadn't already tried. To make the team, though, I was willing to try anything.

After we exchanged pleasantries, he quickly got to the point. "Coach mentioned you tore your ACL and had reconstructive surgery quite a few years ago. Eight or so, right?"

I nodded.

"And you did the full rehab and worked with physical therapists who were experts in those specific recoveries?"

I nodded again.

"Tell me what it felt like when you first tried to come back? Did you have problems immediately?"

"Yes, looking back, I was probably trying to come back too soon. My knee never felt fully stable. Even when I was in a brace, it always felt like it wasn't really there anytime I'd try to pivot or cut."

"Do you still feel that it gives out when you play now?"

"No, but I still feel like if I plant and cut, it isn't going to hold." It was hard to describe because it wasn't like my knee hurt or anything. I just didn't feel like I could trust it.

He pursed his lips. "When was the last time you felt it give way when you were making a cut?"

"Um. Technically never." I shifted uncomfortably on the training table.

He chuckled. "Okay. Let me check it out, and I'll have you do some diagnostic exercises to check that the ligament is still holding as it's supposed to. Once we have that, we'll get you into a training plan, okay? Later, we can also consider an MRI if there are any indications of continuing instability."

I really hated MRIs, but this plan sounded reasonable. Hopefully, there wouldn't be a need for one. "Perfect."

He made me step off a box and then back onto it, then jump on the box, then lateral lunges, and single leg jumps, and what felt like one hundred other tests, all the while staring at my knees. At the end of it, he declared that it seemed to be in good shape, but that he'd come by and watch me in practice too. That was a relief and also scary because what if my knee had been healthy this whole time, and I'd wasted years? What if even with a healthy knee, I just wasn't good enough anymore?

I tried to push those thoughts out of my head as I walked to the court to join practice, already in full swing. I jogged over to Coach to see where she wanted me and saw Kinzie standing and talking to Brittany, who was likely going to be the starting center. Brittany appeared relaxed with her hands in her pockets as she said something that made Kinzie laugh loudly, touch her arm, and shake her head.

The flair of jealousy that burned in my gut was not attractive, so I tried to push it down. Kinzie looked at me and gave me a small smile. A smile she'd give a stranger, no doubt. Which I was. We'd agreed upon that.

"How'd it go with Aaron?" Coach Carr said as I approached.

I shoved all feelings about Kinzie out of my mind. "Good. He seemed happy after our diagnostic tests. He's going to drop by practice later to watch, and we're going to meet again tomorrow to work on a conditioning plan with the strength and conditioning coach. It'll be good to have a new plan."

Coach smiled big. "I'm glad to hear that. I know the player you are, Jane, and I keep seeing flashes of her when you're out on the court. I want that momentum to continue until she's always out there. Are you warmed up? Ready to jump into the scrimmages?"

"I should probably warm up more. Aaron told me that it was important for me to do even more dynamic stretching, so he gave me a whole new pre-pre-workout routine. If it's okay, I'll run through all of it and jump in?"

"Of course. Once you're done hop in there with Coach Josh."

As I warmed up, I was acutely aware of where Kinzie was at all times. After her talk with Brittany, she had private sideline meetings with Maya and Mercedes, another guard who seemed nice, though we didn't know each other well yet.

Kinzie was clearly going for the stars of the team. Not that I wanted her to talk to me, but why didn't she talk to anyone other than the players who generated buzz all on their own? I felt indignant on Vicky's behalf. She was still an excellent point guard to back Maya up. She could have been a starter on a weaker team. She just had the misfortune of being drafted by the Pitbulls in the second round. Though having Maya as her mentor would only benefit her.

I worked myself into a bit of a lather about Kinzie slighting the rest of the team before I joined my half-court scrimmage, but luckily, that let me work off some of my aggression. I possibly went a little too hard, but at least Kinzie was gone by the time practice was over.

I still felt on edge. I knew I wasn't in the head space to have a productive shooting session, so I texted Maya to let her know the weight room was calling me, and I couldn't do smoothies. I worked out the rest of my aggression lifting. However, as I was heading back to the training room, I realized that although my head felt better, my old lady—by professional athlete standards—body wasn't handling the punishment I'd just doled out.

I wished I could have rewound and did fewer lunges or dialed back the weights as my legs and shoulders were starting to tighten up painfully.

I hated—hated—the ice bath, but I knew it was what my body needed to recover. Dammit. Ice baths were the fucking worst, though my dread of them was nearly as bad as the experience itself. I marched with determination into the training room and asked one of the athletic training interns to get one ready. He told me it wouldn't take long and ran to get some more ice while I used the restroom. Nothing like frigid water causing a sudden need to pee that would become as painful as the water itself.

"It's ready for you, Jane," he said when I walked back into the room.

"Perfect, thank you," I said, happy I didn't have to wait. I also appreciated that he'd laid a stack of towels to dry off and warm up with afterward, the key to making this unpleasant experience bearable.

As he walked away, I pulled my hair into a messy bun on top of my head and stripped off my warmup jersey and gym shorts, leaving me in my sports bra and spandex shorts. I took three hard exhales to pump myself up, started Billie Eilish's "Bad Guy" as my timer, and stepped into the tub.

The first brush of the water against my ankles was excruciating as always, but I'd done a million of these, so I knew I needed to just get all the way in and not prolong it. That would only make it worse. My determination didn't keep the water from stealing my breath as I sank my abs below the surface.

That first breath after the water hit my collarbones was always the hardest to find, but that was why I liked using "Bad Guy" as my timer. I would typically be trying to take a breath just as her voice joined the beat, and for some reason, it always helped me.

My skin felt like it was being pelted with tacks, but I always tried to envision the tacks releasing all the tightness from my muscles, like a really intense dry needling session or something. It helped a little as the cold sank beneath my skin and into my very core.

Someone had once told me to focus on my breath and sing the words to whatever song I decided would be my ice bath timer rather than thinking about how much time I still had in that torture device. "Bad Guy" didn't have a lot of words to it, but I still hummed along as I breathed in for five, held for five, released for five, and held for five again before starting the entire process over, fighting the impulse to shiver or hyperventilate.

Around the time my body started to relax as much as it could, I heard the latch of the training room door release. I resisted the urge to whip my head around to see who had joined me because any quick movements sloshed icy water against my skin.

"Thanks, Jada. No, I think I left my jacket in here. I'll see you tomorrow."

That was definitely Kinzie. Perhaps if I stayed perfectly still in the torture tank, she'd walk right by. Unlikely, but a girl could hope.

Her heels clicked in a rapid staccato as she approached, and as she turned the corner, her eyes locked on me, and she jumped. "Jesus, Jane! I thought everyone was gone. You scared me."

"Sorry," I said, endeavoring to keep the shiver out of my voice that was now wavering from a combination of the freezing water as well as the chill that ran down my spine at how amazing she looked today. "Just doing a little active recovery. And trying to not freeze to death." I tried to smile, but that took energy I was using to prevent shivering.

She appraised me, and I swear, even though my entire body was so numb, I could feel it to my bones. "How does a tank of ice help with recovery? Your lips are blue."

"They are not," I managed, though I didn't really know. I'd never looked in the mirror while I did this. But it was only three minutes. I could do anything for three minutes. "But it has something to do with blood vessels and inflammation. I don't know. Google it if you want, but it helps. I've done the research. I wouldn't subject myself to this shit if it didn't work."

"Hmm," she said and laughed, playing with the large pendant on her necklace that looked like a knot of diamonds. Of course, the movement drew my attention to the hint of cleavage her button-up shirt revealed like a coy smile. When I pulled my gaze back to hers, she was biting her lip, and I swear, the air in my lungs fled faster than it had when I'd first gotten into the water.

We stared at each other for a weird moment until I realized Janelle Monáe was serenading us rather than Billie. And it wasn't the opening lyrics, either. My time was well past. I jumped up on instinct and stepped out of the tub without thinking of how little clothing I was wearing until I realized my towels were on the other side of her, and I was standing there dripping in spandex underwear.

She cleared her throat, and the heat of her stare warmed me nearly as much as the towels she was holding hostage would, but I still wanted them. I felt like a swimsuit model who'd just been doused in water while posing for a cover shot. Being on display made me uncomfortable as hell.

"Um, do you mind?" I pointed at the pile of towels behind her.

She looked back and said, "Oh, of course. Sorry." She stepped to the side, but rather than letting me grab my own, she picked up two. She handed one to me but wrapped the other around my shoulders and ran her hands up and down the tops of my arms a few times before seeming to catch herself and stepping away. "That arctic blast really helps with inflammation?"

"Yeah, I'm like a dinosaur in professional athlete years, so I need every bit of help I can get. Though lots of the kids these days take them too." I pulled the towel she'd wrapped around me from side to side across my back a few times before wrapping it around my chest and tucking it into itself. I wrapped the other around my shoulders.

"Oh, stop. You're what? Twenty-eight? Hardly a dinosaur."

"Thirty, actually. Damn near thirty-one if you're counting. But other than the legends, not a lot of athletes play much past their early thirties." It was a hard fact, and I was nowhere near a legend. It was why I was throwing in the towel as a player as soon as my stint in Milwaukee was over. Whenever that ended up being. Though Maya had me believing that maybe—just maybe—that wouldn't be next week. "Did you see most of the kids you talked to today? They're babies. And don't be judgy about my age. You're what? Barely thirty?"

"Thirty-three, which I don't think constitutes barely."

I scoffed as I grabbed another towel and propped my foot on the chair as I dried and warmed my leg. "Are we really arguing about who is older here? Based on the abuse I've put my body through, I'm nearly ninety."

"Yeah, but you also probably eat healthy, almost never drink, at least based on my knowledge from our limited interactions, stay in shape—"

"Are you trying to imply that you're not in shape? Because I have fairly personal knowledge that you are." Shit. I hadn't meant to bring that up. We'd agreed that we would pretend it had never happened. Yet my brain had a really hard time with that course of action. *Fuck my life.*

Kinzie laughed. "You're sweet. And I'm not saying I'm in bad shape, but compared to you and those rippling abs? Fuck. I've never seen anyone in that good of shape."

I stood from drying my leg with my foot still on the chair and stared at her, looking for a clue as I wasn't really sure what she meant. I was average in every way.

"I don't know why you're looking at me like that. Look down. You have an I-don't-even-know-how-many pack."

I looked at my abs. Sure, they looked better than normal because every muscle in my body was flexed in revolt from the ice bath and frigid air in the arena, but they weren't anything special. Picturing Kinzie naked in her bed, standing in front of me, in our interlude in the shower? She was perfection in every single way. I knew I wasn't unattractive, but I wasn't perfect like she was. "I'm fine. But not remarkable."

"Oh my God. It's true what they say. No matter what we look like, all women think they aren't attractive enough." She smiled as she looked at me, but it looked sad. "Please hear me when I say you are very, very remarkable. You have left a lasting, remarkable imprint on my brain."

She looked sincere, but I worried she was just being nice. "I appreciate that," I finally said when I realized she wasn't going to let it go. I did appreciate it, even if I didn't fully believe it.

"I should probably grab my jacket and get out of here, but I'll see you tomorrow. You'll be here tomorrow, right? I was hoping to chat with you, but you looked so damn intense today, I didn't dare interrupt."

"Yeah, I'm here all day. I'll see you then."

She took a step back and looked me up and down. "Yeah, I'll see you." She shook her head, a half-smile gracing her lips before she turned and walked away, the sound of her heels echoing again.

I was completely bewildered by that entire exchange. I would have sworn she'd looked at me with desire, but for someone as amazing as Kinzie, an old, washed-up, never-been basketball player like me could never be anything more than one-night stand material, could I? There was no way. She was Park Avenue. I was Podunk, Vermont. I had nothing to offer her.

Chapter Five

G ray," Coach Brandy yelled, and I spun on instinct. "Coach wants to see you."

My heart dropped. We'd won our final preseason game the night before, the roster had to be finalized by tomorrow, and Coach had one more cut to make. I hadn't had a great game, but I hadn't played poorly either. But in the best league in the world, with slots for only one hundred and forty-four women, average wasn't good enough. It was the story of my career.

"Coming," I said and pulled my warm-up shirt over my head.

Maya caught my eye and smiled. She mouthed, "You're fine," but it was hard for me to believe that.

I walked down the hall, my feet dragging like a prisoner heading for execution. I'd been trying to prepare myself for this, but it still felt like shit. I knocked on Coach's door even though it was partially open and swung in farther at the contact.

She looked up. "Come on in, Jane. Close the door, if you don't mind."

I tried to school my face as I sank into her guest chair, knowing I must not have done enough. Not wanting to draw this out if the situation was hopeless, I said, "I'm the last cut, aren't I?"

She tipped her head back and laughed. "Oh God, no, I'm sorry I scared you. That's not it at all. I just finished talking to

Brenda Hobbs, the last cut. You are a part of this team. If you want it."

I must not have heard her right. "Wait. Did you say I'm staying?"

Her smile grew bigger. "Yes, that's the gist."

"But…why?"

"Because you earned a spot. Your growth has been exponential over the past two weeks, and I'm excited to be seeing more of the dynamic player I coached eight years ago. You're coming into your own again, and I'd be a fool to cut you."

My body felt numb with relief and disbelief. I'd made the team. I didn't really understand how, but this was going to happen. I mean, I'd hoped, but I certainly hadn't believed.

"You look shocked," she said, still smiling.

"That's putting it mildly. I hoped my play was enough, but I just wasn't sure." I released a shaky exhale.

"How have things been going with Brigitte?"

"Good, I think. We've been talking a lot about my injury and what it did to my confidence that has always been a little lacking. I'm…working on it."

"Good. Because believe me when I tell you, I believe in you. Your play is fantastic when you find the zone. I want you to keep working with Brigitte and Aaron so you continue to gain confidence and trust your knee. In the beginning, your minutes are going to probably be limited, but I don't want you to feel discouraged. Your ability to earn playing time is unlimited, and as you prove to me that the player I can still see is the one normally on the court, you'll spend more and more time out there, okay?"

"Of course. I wouldn't expect anything else. And I am working. I spend at least an hour after practice working on my shooting. My percentage in at least the first two preseason games was higher than it's ever been," I said as though I was making another case for her to keep me.

She arched an eyebrow. "Do you think I'm unaware? Your three-point percentage is also higher than ever, and you're taking more shots from beyond the arc. Your future is brighter than you know. You just need to keep putting in the work and keep believing in yourself, okay?"

At thirty, I didn't think my future could possibly be that bright. Or at least not bright for all that long, but I still took a moment to bask in her praise. And confidence. "I will, Coach. I promise." I'd never spoken truer words.

"I know. Now get out of here and go celebrate with Maya and the rest of the team."

I floated on a cloud back to the locker room.

"*So?*" Maya yelled, stretching the one syllable when I opened the door.

"I'm in," I said, unable to lessen my smile even a little bit.

"Woo-hoo." She grabbed me in a bear hug and swung me around in a circle. A feat, given I was about six inches taller than her. "I was sure that was going to be her decision, but I'm super happy for you." She nearly sang the words as she finally put me back on the floor.

"Nice," Brittany said and held up her hand for a high five. "Congrats. I'm happy for me too."

"As if there was any doubt about you, Brit. You've been killing it," I said.

"Yeah, but I'm a rookie. There's no guarantees. The league is fucking strong, and I'm unproven against the best of the best. We all know lots of first round draft picks don't get picked up by their teams." It was odd to see Brittany, who was six-six, a fucking force in the low post, and already had multiple sponsorships have self-doubt too. With her normal swagger, I thought she was immune to feeling like that.

"Well, I never had any doubts about you making the team," I said.

"And *I* never had any doubts about *you* making the team," she retorted.

I'd chatted with her plenty in the locker room about inconsequential things, but I'd never had a real conversation with her. Yet, her words warmed me to the core. My first instinct was to deny or deflect, but maybe some of the things Brigitte and I had been talking about in our sessions were starting to sink in. Instead, even not fully believing her, I said, "Thank you. That means a lot."

She shook my shoulder. "Seriously. I went to Tennessee, but I'm from Raleigh, and I grew up cheering for Duke. My dad and I were in the stands when you won the national championship. I wanted to be like you when I grew up. Regardless, I was amped when I saw you on the first day of camp and am super stoked that we both made the team."

I was totally speechless. Self-doubter Jane whispered furiously, but Brittany looked truly genuine. "Uh, wow," I finally said. "Seriously?"

"I started that entire fangirl mini-speech with the word 'seriously.' Don't make me say it again." She laughed. "Hey, can we take a pic for me to send to my dad? He'll love it."

"Sure."

She slung her arm around me, making me look almost miniature. We both smiled big like fools. I couldn't help myself because I kind of believed her.

"Do you mind if I post it on Insta later?"

"Of course not. I was a fan of yours all season when I could catch your games while I was in France. I'm excited to play with you too." I had to fess up to being a fan too since she really had gone fangirl on me.

"For real?"

"Yeah." I chuckled.

She grabbed me into a hug tight enough to knock the wind out of me and spun me around, which was an altogether different feeling since she was five-ish inches taller, but because of her height, she was able to jump up and down, and I felt a little like a five-year-old.

"All right, all right. Enough of this love fest," Maya said. "Let's go celebrate, huh?"

I started to say I couldn't, but Maya cut me off. "No excuses from you. Or anyone." She got louder as she said anyone. "We've got our team, and we need to celebrate. Tomorrow is our first off day from practice since camp began. We've got media day in the morning." The entire room groaned. Media day was always horrible since they glitzed a bunch of tomboy girls in more makeup than we'd ever worn and took thousands of photos and promo video shots while asking hundreds of questions. Missing media day would have been the best part of not making the team. "And then, we're watching film in the late afternoon. And you know all that makeup will cover any bags under our eyes. So. We. Are. All. Going. Out. Tonight. No excuses."

"Where we going?" Ruby said.

"Paydays."

Half the locker room groaned.

"What's Paydays?" I said to Vicky, who'd been one of the groaners.

"The diviest of dive bars. It's on Third Street, and Maya loves it for some reason. It's fine but not where I'd choose to celebrate anything. It's the kind of place where if you stand still for too long, your shoe is going to get stuck to the floor, and you'll walk right out of it."

"Gross. Sounds like college," I said.

"It's a little like a college bar, but it isn't. It's small, it's woman-owned, the dive bar aspect is a total choice, and no one other than the owner ever recognizes us there. It's a perfect spot to get a little drunk," Maya said, defending her choice.

"Look," Abby Gibbs, another forward on the team, said. "We can start there, but I am not staying there all evening. Once all the finance bros who also love that place start getting wasted, I'm out." She was nice, though she seemed a little high maintenance for me. And not because of her bro comment. I was hoping I might also be able to leave before the night got too rowdy.

I had a lot more fun than I'd been expecting out with the team. But I did end up having to sneak out with Abby around the time Paydays started getting more crowded.

Even though we didn't have a true practice or a game the next day, we were professional athletes, and we couldn't abuse our bodies too much, particularly during the season. And since I'd turned thirty, my hangovers had been lasting for days. I certainly didn't want all my promo photos to look haggard. But it felt good to celebrate. I wasn't sure if it was Maya herself or the atmosphere that Coach cultivated, but this team felt more like a family than any team I'd ever belonged to. I was excited to get this season started.

❖

Media. Day.

Those two words always lodged dread in the pit of my stomach. I did not enjoy being the center of attention. Ever. I knew I was an anomaly as a professional athlete. Most were outgoing, but I preferred flying below the radar. Too much attention made me nervous. I was always sure I was going to say the wrong thing. Say something ridiculous. Or embarrassing.

It did not help that I had a *slight* headache from the night before. I didn't get drunk or wild, but I'd had more than a single drink for the first time in eons, and the three glasses of water I'd had before bed had me up peeing all night but did not seem to help with the headache. Hopefully, the ibuprofen I just took would.

It was fucking jarring. And to make matters worse, there was Kinzie standing to the side observing everything, her arms crossed and looking like a badass in her delicious pantsuit and heels. How could I focus on what the capital of Austria was for their silly trivia games that they'd show in the arena during TV time-outs when Kinzie was radiating nearby.

Fuck.

At least I'd remembered Vienna was the answer.

A few questions later, I finally finished that segment and moved onto some Pictionary challenge before they split us up into two groups for a rousing round of *Family Feud*. That one was fun. I had to have an interview with Bo Reid, the sports reporter from *The Journal Sentinel*. He asked me all about my journeywoman status and if I thought this was the year I was truly going to break out.

What was I supposed to say to that? There were no good answers. If I said no, I'd look like a loser, and if I said yes and it didn't happen, I'd look like a fool. I tried to be noncommittally positive when I said, "I hope so. I've been feeling great in practice, and I'm just excited to be here and keep improving my game overall with this team's great coaching and training staff."

"Congrats on making the team, Jane. Though I'm not surprised at all."

I knew who it was before I turned around. Kinzie. I hated that I couldn't stop the smile at the sight of her. Thankfully, she was smiling too. Though her smile always had that sexy smirk to it, and I had no idea how to channel something similar into mine.

"Thanks, Kinzie. I'm excited. There's something special about this team that I've never had. I haven't been able to put my finger on exactly what *it* is, but it just *feels* different." Needing to fidget with something to release some of the nerves I felt talking to her, I pulled out my ponytail holder, shook my hair, and pulled it up again. In a game, I would normally have had it in a bun, but for media day, the ponytail apparently looked better. They'd tried to get me to wear my hair down, but they still had us in our uniforms, and I'd never worn my hair down while wearing a basketball uniform, so that just felt silly.

Kinzie stared at me weirdly before clearing her throat. I wasn't sure what that was all about. "Yeah, you all seem very family-like. It's why we're playing off it a little bit with the *Family Feud* stuff."

"Ugh. That was *your* idea, wasn't it?" I said, joking because I had actually enjoyed the game. It had been my favorite part of the day. Probably because I was playing with my teammates rather than being solo.

"Don't lie. I saw you out there laughing and having fun. Clips from that are going to make great promo videos, and we're going to put the full game on an episode of our new behind-the-scenes show on our YouTube channel." She looked so casually sexy standing there with her hands in her pants pockets. Was that look the reason they didn't put pockets in women's pants? Because it was too suggestive? Also, how did she find the only pair of women's dress pants with pockets? She'd probably done it on purpose to torment me.

I rolled my eyes. "I might have been acting."

"No." She smirked, and my stomach fluttered. *Fuck my life.* "I would have been able to tell."

"Based on how long you've known me?"

"Yeah, you don't have much of a poker face."

"Oh really? What am I thinking about right now?" I crossed my arms, trying to look tough, and glared.

She tapped a fingertip against her lip as she studied me before sliding that hand back into her pocket. "I'm not a mind reader, but you're annoyed that I'm right about you having fun in *Family Feud*. You're also stressed at having this much attention on you all day. You try to pretend to be outgoing, but you're shy at heart."

Did she read my owner's manual while I slept in her hotel room?

"You think I'm sexy in this suit of mine, but it annoys you because you've told yourself I'm off limits, even though I've admitted I'm willing. How am I doing so far?" She looked smug, which just irritated me more because I did, of course, find her sexy. In every suit. Probably in anything, though I'd never seen her in anything other than a suit, a sweater, and nothing at all, but she was an eleven out of ten each time.

"Not even close," I said with as much bravado as I could manage. "And now I have to go pretend to be fierce and intimidating as I make random basketball moves in front of a green screen for their pregame video. As if I can look intimidating in this ridiculous amount of makeup. I look like a clown." I snarled.

"For what it's worth, I think you look really nice. I'll admit to preferring your normal look." She stepped in closer, not close enough to touch but close enough that no one could overhear. "But you look fantastic. You make me wish you'd reconsider your stance on us." She stepped back and cleared her throat. "But I don't want to stand between you and tossing the ball in the air or whatever for the camera, so I'll go make myself useful elsewhere." She winked and walked away, leaving me speechless.

I watched as she walked to where Jada was standing with Coach and said something that made them both crack up. I was pretty sure she flirted with everyone. I wasn't jealous. Watching it was simply a reminder that even though she flirted with me, it didn't mean anything. It was who she was. I wasn't anything special.

"How are you feeling about tonight's game, Jane," Brigitte said, her tone as calm as always.

Our first regular season game was that night, and I was trying not to be nervous as hell. "Ah, well, a little stressed but handling it."

Brigitte leveled her gaze at me, and it made me squirm. It was like she had an embedded lie detector.

"Okay, I'm nervous, but I'm trying not to be. It's not like this is my first professional game or something."

"Some nerves are normal before any game. Is this your normal level, or do you think higher?" She wasn't taking notes, which felt weird to me, but she never did. Weren't head doctors supposed to take notes or something?

"Higher, I guess. But I feel like my expectations are higher for myself because I've been playing better, you know?" I realized I was bouncing my right knee incessantly and placed my hand on my thigh to still it.

"Tell me more."

"After the injury, I've always had low expectations for myself because I've never trusted my knee and was playing like shit. But now, it's like I expect to do better. I don't know why. And it's scary. What if I get my hopes up and play like shit again?"

She pursed her lips. "Let's start with the why and move to the what-ifs."

"Okay," I said, unsure how she knew the whys if I didn't.

"You've told me how much more supported you feel with this team than you've ever felt before. Coach Carr is someone who was one hundred percent in your corner the last time you feel you really played well, right?"

I nodded.

"And you've said Maya is perhaps your biggest cheerleader? Which is new for you?"

I nodded again.

"And you've been doing more exercises with Aaron to work the knee, and you're seeing me, not to toot my own horn, but it's still all different."

"Yeah."

"So everything is different than it's been at other teams where you've never had that level of support, especially not since your injury. Do you think maybe that's helping you? Contributing to your better performances?"

"I guess. Knowing that I have people who believe in me and who are cheering me on because they believe in me...I mean, it adds more stress too because I don't want to disappoint anyone. Coach always says something good about me even if I have a shitty practice." I picked at a thread in the seam of my track pants.

"So you have unconditional support now. How does that make you feel?"

"Like it's okay even if I'm not perfect," I said without thought.

"And what if you go out there and play and make a mistake or don't trust your knee and miss an important shot? Is the world going to end? Are you going to get cut? Are you going to lose your friends?"

"I guess not." She stared at me with brows raised, and I adjusted in my seat and tried to be more honest. "No, but what if I play bad today and next game and the game after that? I'll eventually get the ax."

"And what if a meteor crashes into Earth tomorrow and wipes out all human life?"

I scoffed. "Now, look, that's not comparable. We'd know if a meteor was going to crash into the planet."

"Why is that not comparable? It's tomorrow. Anything could happen. We don't know, and that's the point. If you're always thinking about tomorrow—or even the next possession—rather than today, this moment with the ball in your hands, you're always going to have a chance to mess up. Sports is an area where you can't think about the last possession or the next. It's not chess or pool. Focus on what you *can* control. Which is you in that exact moment. Does that make sense? I'm sure this isn't new advice."

"Not at all." I laughed and was relieved that she did too. I didn't want to offend her, but staying present in the moment was, like, cannon sports motivation. "It's just a lot easier said than done."

She chuckled. "Of course. We'll start on some mindfulness meditation next week, but for tonight, if you feel yourself starting to get stressed about playing, try bringing your focus back to your breath. Focus on the feel of your breath. The sound of it. The count of it. Use that to shut everything else in the arena out. The crowd, trash talking, your own internal narrative, whatever. It doesn't faze you. Because all that exists is you, that basketball, and your team."

It sounded like bullshit to me, but I'd been trying to rely on the advice of the experts who were around me. It was my last chance. I was trying a different approach, and so far, it seemed to be working. I resolved to give Brigitte's breathing woo-woo stuff a chance. "Okay."

"I can see on your face that you aren't convinced, but just try it. Establishing a regular meditation practice is going to make it work better, but even on its own, I promise you, you'll feel different. More at peace. Promise me you'll try it."

"Okay," I said. I would try it, and I'd try to have an open mind, but I didn't have a lot of faith.

❖

I got my first chance to play when there were about two minutes left in the first quarter. We were up by seven over Dallas, and Coach decided to give a few of the starters a break. I subbed in for Abby Gibbs, but I was relieved that Maya was still out there. For my first regular-season minutes in the WNBA in nearly two years, having my best friend on the court felt like a safety blanket. I wondered if Coach knew it.

She went with a smaller lineup, with the tallest person on the floor our power forward, Ruby, who inbounded the ball to Maya. Greyson, one of Dallas's smaller forwards, was guarding me, and I had her by about two inches. She was playing right on me, which was strange since I was so far beyond the arc, but it might give me a chance to lose her. I jogged closer and paused like I was watching the play on the other side of the court, then cut hard to the left and caught Greyson off guard. I looked back to Maya, not sure if she saw the separation I'd just created, and without breaking stride, she sent a no-look bounce pass my way. I grabbed it, spun and went up all in one motion, nailing my short jumper.

Our lead went up to nine, and Maya ran over, slapping my hip as she said, "Nice shot, Jane."

I grinned. "Nice pass."

She shrugged as she ran back to guard Dallas's point guard as their center inbounded the ball to her, and I ran up the court, staying with Greyson. I gave her some room as I knew she didn't have much range beyond the arc but was dangerous off the drive.

Their point guard stopped just before the top of the key, and I read the pass coming Greyson's way and picked it off. Maya already had a head start toward our basket. I passed her the ball, and she made the easy layup.

Damn. Two points and an assist in a half minute of game time. That wasn't bad. But I couldn't stop my mind from wondering if my luck was about to run out. I couldn't possibly expect to play well on every possession, could I?

I stayed on Greyson again as we jogged back up the court, but she got me off-balance when she feigned right and cut left. She got around me just as their PG passed her the ball. Shit. I tried to get back into position, but it was too late. She pulled up and shot. Luckily, it rimmed out, and Ruby got the board.

Ruby passed the ball to Maya, who slowly brought it back up the court while the rest of us set up our half-court offense. I found my favorite spot on the right wing while I waited for Maya to signal what she wanted us to do. As I waited, I began to wonder if my knee was hurting. Had I damaged something on that last play? When I'd made that last cut? Shit. Was I going to tear something again? I felt a little nauseated at the thought.

Stop.

I reminded myself to focus on my breath like Brigitte had told me. I took a deep breath in through my nose and paid attention to the feel of the cool arena air inside my nostrils as I inhaled and the feel of the warm air as I exhaled. I was able to focus on how the team was moving, and I knew what I needed to do. I cut in at an angle and tried to lose Greyson on a pick from Ruby, and Maya passed me the ball. I'd been expecting Dallas's defense to collapse in on me and thought I would end up passing the ball back out to Maya or Mercedes, who was standing at the corner, but they didn't. I drove hard and fast toward the basket before anyone else could react and hit the reverse layup. Guess not having played well enough to have film in the modern era was working to my advantage since they didn't have a clue how I played.

Then again, *I* barely knew how I played anymore.

Ruby blocked a layup, and Mercedes scored another quick two, and Dallas's coach called for a time-out. I jogged to our bench, and Coach hit me on the ass with her clipboard with a, "Nice, Jane," as she and the other coaches stepped onto the court to huddle. I sat as adrenaline coursed through my veins, and Maya sank into a seat next to mine, bumping me with her shoulder.

"Damn, girl. You played for less than two minutes and were responsible for an eight-oh run. *You* made them take a time-out."

"That wasn't just me. It was the whole team."

"It was the whole team, but who was the spark? That was all you. You tapped into a next level."

I took my water bottle and swallowed deeply before handing it back. I tried to respond, but the coaches came back and outlined the strategy for the last thirty seconds of the quarter.

I ended up playing almost nine minutes and impressed myself every time I was on the court. And Maya wasn't my only good luck charm as I did well when Vicky was running the point too. I couldn't believe it.

Even running into Kinzie after the game didn't make irritation flash through me as it normally seemed to. "Nice game," she said when I passed her in the hallway heading to the locker room.

"Thanks...no disrespect, but how do you know? You don't even watch basketball." I smiled as I said it so she would know I was just giving her a hard time, but at the same time, I didn't really believe she knew if I'd had a nice game or not.

Her lips curled into a cocky smirk that was far sexier than was fair. "I may not get all the strategy, but I know that when you shoot the ball and it goes through the hoop, that's a good thing, and I saw you do that quite a few times today."

She was right. I'd scored twelve points in just under nine minutes, which was pretty darn good. "I didn't know you were here. Where'd you watch from?"

"I was in a suite with Owen and Jada and a couple of companies we're courting for sponsorships. I couldn't help but keep an eye out when I heard them announce your name." She shrugged, and my pulse raced at the idea that she was telling me the truth. My instinct was to not believe, but at the same time, as far as I knew, she'd never lied to me. She cleared her throat. "Well, anyway, I'd better let you hit the showers. Or the ice bath," she said as she looked away.

I thought her face turned a little pink, and I wondered if she was thinking of seeing me a couple of weeks ago. My body flushed hot as I thought about it. I was still surprised at how bold I'd been standing there in front of her nearly naked as I'd dried off. I deflected before either of us brought it up. "Yeah, my old lady body is going to need ice after tonight. But it felt good. I felt like I found a groove that I forgot I had."

"I'm glad. You looked good. I mean it," she said cutting me off from another deflection. "Anyway, enjoy the ice, and I'll see you in the gym soon."

Watching her walk away, my head was a jumbled mess. I could have sworn she was flirting with me, but it just didn't seem real. I knew she had been interested in me the night we'd slept together, but at the same time, it seemed like she flirted with everyone.

Chapter Six

The next two games flew by as we were on a quick road trip to the northeast, and my minutes steadily increased game by game. I scored in double digits each game, despite limited minutes, and I had as many steals as I had assists. It was a little wild, but I was just trying to make a nuisance of myself against the opposing team and not get ahead of myself.

I'd just finished my first session with Brigitte since the day of the first game, and I was excited. I'd been using her breathing technique, and it had been a game changer, so I was eager to spend more time working on the meditation and mindfulness that she walked me through today.

I was on a high as I pushed open the door to the gym and tried not to sigh when I saw Kinzie in there again. She was watching from the sidelines with Jada. She smiled and waved when she saw me, and I wasn't proud of the flutter of excitement it prompted in me. I tried to tell myself she was nothing more than a distraction. For me, for the team.

Okay, she was working on growing our brand, which was great. But she was always pulling people out of practice. And it wasn't like she'd *done* anything yet. At least I hadn't heard of any new sponsorship deals. But I smiled and waved back before I started my warmup. I thought for a second she might walk over and talk to me, but she didn't, which was a relief. However, I felt her eyes on me as I moved up and down the sideline, warming up with different dynamic exercises, and it made my skin prickle. I tried to tune her out, but I still found myself glancing at her over and over, confirming my suspicion each time. I could feel my cheeks heat as I wondered if anyone noticed. Jesus.

With the extra attention, my warmup felt like it took hours, so I used my breathing to center myself as Brigitte had been teaching me. It was helpful, but I was still relieved when practice began, and I had something else to focus on.

At some point, Kinzie and Jada disappeared from the sidelines, but like a bad penny, they reemerged just as practice was wrapping up.

"Your crush is back," Maya whispered as she elbowed me and nodded toward them.

I rolled my eyes, not dignifying her ridiculousness with a response.

"Roll your eyes all you want, but I saw her watching you while you warmed up."

"Shut up. You did not."

"Oh, I surely did."

"Okay, fine, I noticed it too, but I think that means that she has a crush on me, not the other way around," I said, surprisingly bold. There was no way Maya could argue with that next-level logic.

"I would believe that except that I saw you checking her out right back. A lot."

Deflect. That was the only choice. "Why were you watching us so intently and not focusing on your own warmup? Do *you* have a crush on one of *us*?"

Maya barked a laugh. "Bullshit. You're beautiful, but I'd never ruin our friendship by crushing on you. And I'd never crush on Kinzie because she's your ex, and you're my BFF."

She shrugged like it was no big deal, but I felt so warm and fuzzy at her calling me her best friend that I forgot to call her out for calling Kinzie my ex.

"All right, ladies, bring it in," Coach yelled. Once we'd all gathered, she said, "Great practice today. I'm loving the chemistry that's getting stronger and stronger each day. Now, before we wrap, Kinzie and Jada have an exciting partnership that they want to talk to you about."

Kinzie stepped forward. "One of the things we've been focusing on is creating tighter bonds with the local community. In that pursuit, we're going to get more face time with high school players and their families. Over the next few weeks, we'll be sponsoring some skills competitions at the local high schools for all levels of players, male and female. And to help establish bonds with the community, some of you are going to provide mini-clinics on skills while others will be the judges. We are going to get everyone involved in this one, and we'll shoot some footage to stitch together and push on social media."

That actually all sounded really good, except for the socials part of it. Of course they couldn't just do a good thing for kids. They had to make sure everyone knew it.

"Also, we were able to negotiate with the Bucks and some of the players' agents, and we are going to have several of their stars throughout the season here for some halftime entertainment. We'll be having one of you playing Horse during halftime."

Watching Coach's face as Kinzie said that mirrored my own horror. How were we supposed to concentrate on the game and rest up for the second half if she was going to trot us out like ponies for a playground game? It was a dumb idea clearly drafted by someone who didn't understand sports.

Thankfully, Maya spoke up and was a little more diplomatic than I would have been. Just one of the many reasons she was our captain. "Um, I love that idea, and I'm sure having the NBA players at the games participating will be amazing, but I'm not quite sure that halftime entertainment makes sense. Firstly, everyone is getting concessions during halftime, so this might hurt that income. Secondly, the team is fairly busy at halftime. We are strategizing, making adjustments, taking a few minutes just for a breather. Our season is short. Every game is important and could make the difference between making the playoffs or not."

Surprisingly Kinzie nodded as she spoke and looked like she was really thinking about her words. "Those are good points, Maya. Thank you for speaking up. Let me chat with the front office and see what we can do to make this make a little more sense."

Well, that was an annoyingly reasonable response. I couldn't even be irritated with it unless she ended up sticking to her guns.

❖

It was a beautiful mid-May morning and a rare day off for us. Maya and I decided to meet at Cupertino Park to go for a bike ride along the lake. I'd finally gotten my bike—along with my car—from my parents' house when my brother had taken pity on me and driven it out, and I'd been dying to get out on it. The car was great for getting around, but that was a tool of utility, whereas my bike was both a means of fitness and travel but was also simply fun.

There was nothing like getting out on the road or a trail early in the morning before the world woke up. Just me, the fresh air in my nose, the wind whizzing past my ears. And apparently, Maya felt the same. At some point, I wanted to head away from the city and find a more remote trail, but for today, we decided to enjoy the lake scenery.

"Morning," Maya called as she got out of her Rivian.

"We couldn't have picked a better day for a ride." I swept my arm in a circle as Maya unhooked her bike from the rack on the back of her truck.

"For sure. I love Milwaukee at this time of year."

We mounted up and rode in comfortable silence for the first ten or fifteen minutes. I was still assimilating into the new day as I'd only been awake for about forty-five minutes and was working on feeling like a human. But the power of fresh air to do that for me couldn't have been overstated. I wasn't sure if Maya had the same reason or not, but it was nice.

The earthy yet fresh scent of the lake riding the slight breeze was reminiscent of my youth growing up near Lake Champlain, and I smiled, remembering long summer days spent at the beach and looking for Champ with my brother. I didn't think Lake Michigan had a mythical creature living in its depths, which was a real shame for the kids growing up along its shores. The sound of the waves lapping against the wall below us was peaceful and caused a level of contentment to bloom in my chest that I wasn't terribly familiar with.

"What else you planning to do today?" Maya said.

"I'm going to hit a yoga class. Aaron suggested it a few weeks ago, and I've really been enjoying it. He said the movements are designed to work on strength and flexibility in a way that will really help with my knee."

"That's cool. I've only done it a time or two, but it seemed nice. Peaceful. God knows I could use some mental relaxation with our game looming this week."

I furrowed my brow. "Our game? Oh right, Indiana. Well, do you want to hit up some yoga with me? Mind, body, and all that. I really think it's helping my physical knee condition as well as my perception of it."

"That's awesome. I'm so amped with how you've been playing. This season has been a dream come true for me so far."

I looked at her, disbelieving. "Dream come true for *you*? Why? I mean, it is for me. I feel like my old self for the first time in eight years. It's wild. But you always play like this."

Were her cheeks rosy from the rush of cool air, or was she a little embarrassed? "I'd be embarrassed, but I'm going to tell myself not to be. I *might* have had the tiniest ice queen type crush on you after that first time we played each other, and you sent me packing from the tournament. But like in a hero worship kinda crush. And then, you showed up here, and you've quickly become my best friend like we've known each other forever, and I just dig it. I adore playing with you. You're amazing, and I love being a part of you finding your game again."

I was at a loss for words. I never would have thought Maya had had a thing for me. Incomprehensible. And she was cute, but I'd never gone for the athletic type. But I was beyond grateful for her friendship and encouragement. "I don't know why on Earth you'd have a crush on me, but I'm glad you collected me like a lost puppy on the first day of camp."

Maya hit her brakes so hard, her tire squealed as it slid across the concrete.

I stopped, worried something was wrong. "What is it?"

"Just come here," she said as she hopped off her bike, kicked the kickstand down, and walked over. She wrapped her arms around me in a hug so tight, I could barely breathe, but I thought I saw her eyes glisten before she pulled me too tight to see.

"Whoa," I grunted.

"I'm just happy we came into each other's lives."

"Aren't you friends with the whole team?" I said when I was able to eke out a few words around her vise grip.

"I'm friendly with all of them, but that doesn't mean we're friends. And I just clicked with you. You felt the click too, right? From the first day?"

"Well, yeah, but I just..." I didn't know what to say. I'd been trying to work on my self-esteem issues but kind of couldn't believe she'd felt it too.

"Just nothing. We were born to be best friends starting right now. I know it. And these besties are going to win the WNBA championship together. I can feel it. Just like I felt you were going to make the team and be important. Sometimes I just know things." She shrugged one shoulder before hopping back on her bike.

And although it might have been Maya forcing her will on the world through sheer determination, I really hoped her feelings were premonitions about all of it. We were already friends, but I hoped we'd win a championship, and I hoped I'd be important in that run. Rather than sidelined because I wasn't playing well or hadn't earned my spot or I'd injured myself again, the image of which haunted my thoughts when I let my guard down, especially in those last few moments before drifting to sleep. But dammit Maya made me feel like we *could* will this to happen.

❖

It was the second to last game of May, and we'd been on the road for six days already. Luckily, we were flying home tomorrow morning, and we had two days to recover from this brutal road trip before we played again. I could feel the whole team's exhaustion around me, so it wasn't just me. We'd split our games so far—lost in New York and won in Connecticut—and were hoping to take this one against DC tonight to make us two of three on this road trip.

Maya flopped in the chair next to me halfway through the third quarter. "Jesus, it shouldn't be this hard. Why am I this tired?"

"Our grossly delayed flights? Or shitty hotel food? I don't know, but I can't wait for steel-cut oatmeal and a smoothie."

"Oh my God." She groaned. "I *need* a detox smoothie. My life might depend on it."

"Get the hotel restaurant to make you one."

"It won't be the same. Smoothie Operator just knows what they're doing."

We both settled our forearms on our thighs and leaned forward to watch the game. It was closer than it should have been. Probably because most of us were feeling the fatigue of travel. It was also more physical than we were used to. Likely because it was closer than we'd been expecting, and DC was fighting as though their lives depended on it. That made us punchier too. Brittany had just gone to the ground after an elbow to her solar plexus that the refs somehow missed.

Coach had nearly lost her mind and got teed up after she screamed at the ref for missing it.

"Get ready, Maya," Coach said, signaling that she'd be going back in at the next whistle.

"Enjoy the rest while you can, Jane Gray," Maya said and slapped me on the shoulder as she popped up with a surprising amount of enthusiasm. That was one of the many things that made her a fantastic team captain. She might have played at being tired for a minute, but I think it was so she could make the rest of us feel like she was commiserating, but really, she had the power to flip back to beast mode in a breath. But honestly, it worked for me. I felt a little peppier about my rotation that should have been coming soon.

As I looked at the court, however, I watched Abby take an elbow to the neck and come down hard—really hard—on her right foot, which bent at an angle that looked awful from my perspective. I hoped I was wrong, but as she landed on the ground, the cry that radiated through the air had me flashing back to the moment when I tore my ACL eight years ago. Which felt like it also might have been eight minutes ago.

Her scream sliced through the air like a scalding, straight-out-of-the-dishwasher knife through butter, and I felt it viscerally. It was like my ACL was tearing again, and I wanted to turn and throw up. Our trainer ran out onto the court. I looked to Coach, and she looked as green as Abby did. I looked the other way, and Maya was still crouched in front of the scorers' table. She might have also been a little green, but I wasn't able to tell for sure.

Aaron and his team were on their knees beside Abby, who had stopped writhing but was still visibly in pain.

"Jane!"

I spun my head at Coach's voice. I'd been focused on Abby, and I wondered if I'd missed her first call. *Fuck.* This felt like my worst nightmare. My soul ached for Abby because I'd been there. Based on her scream, I was fairly certain she'd torn something. It happened so fast, I wasn't sure what had happened, but I knew it was bad.

"Jane," Coach said again but much sharper. She jutted her chin to the court.

Oh fuck.

She wanted me to get in there. Holy fucking fuck. I wasn't ready. I was tired. My emotions were all over the place at Abby's likely serious injury. I took a few breaths and focused on the sensation in my nostrils. It was weird as fuck, but it worked. In. Out. In. Out.

My legs moved on instinct. Despite the nausea coursing through me, I put one foot in front of the other until I was on the court. I went to Maya because she was my rock. My security blanket.

My legs were rubbery. My chest was on fire, yet ice sloshed in my stomach. I was trying to focus on anything that would anchor me.

Maya shouldered me, "You okay?"

I nodded, trying to look nonchalant, but Maya grabbed my arm and pulled me two steps away from the group.

"Hey. Listen to me." She shook my arm harder. "You're the next woman up. It's up to *you* to step in. We need to win this game. Injuries happen. We've all had them. I hate that Abby is hurting, but this team needs you. You are ready for this moment. Your game is ready for this moment. Shake it off and step up."

I still wanted to throw up, but her words helped settle my jitters. I hopped up and down a few times to release some nervous energy. I couldn't look at Abby. I looked away before Aaron and one of his staff could help her up. I probably looked like a cold bitch as they helped poor Abby off the court while I clapped yet stared at my feet. But I couldn't look. I couldn't make eye contact, or I knew I'd never be able to hold myself together.

They upgraded the foul against Abby to a flagrant two, so the other player was ejected. Maya took Abby's free throws and made both, which put us up by four.

"You with me?" she said.

"I'm good." It wasn't really true, but whatever.

"Inbound to me."

That was never my job, but I think Maya knew it would help settle me. And it did. Thankfully. My fear somehow evaporated that night. I felt like I was playing on a cloud. It didn't feel like I could do anything wrong. I wasn't sure what my shooting percentage was, but in my mind, it was one hundred. We ended up winning by fifteen points.

That obviously was the whole team, not just me, but by the time the game ended, I was on a basketball high I hadn't felt since college.

I did an interview for ESPN, so I was nearly alone when I jogged down the tunnel.

"Nice game," came a familiar voice from behind me. My stomach dipped at the sound of Kinzie's voice, but I couldn't decide if it was a good dip or a bad one.

I slowed to a walk and spun. "You're coming to our away games now too?"

"I was in DC for business and thought I'd swing by. I got here a little after halftime. You had a fantastic game."

"Yeah, because Abby got hurt." I hated that I'd capitalized on her bad luck, though we didn't know yet how bad her injury was.

"You didn't play well *because* of her injury. You had more playing time because of it, but I think you played well because you're a good player."

"Please don't say that. It's bad luck." Athletes were a superstitious bunch, and I was even more than most.

She laughed. "I didn't realize telling you that you're good was bad luck, but I'm sorry. I'll try to keep that information to myself going forward." She looked me up and down before she said, "You look like you need a shower." But she didn't look repulsed by it. She looked…hungry, and it sent a jolt straight to the apex of my thighs.

I took in her skirt suit and heels for the first time since we'd been talking. I couldn't help myself. And fuck, she looked good.

She wore almost the same thing every time I saw her—a dark suit with heels and a blouse—but she changed it up between skirt and pantsuits, the color of her blouse, the jewelry she wore, and my God, why was I noticing all of that? But that was better to think about than the impulse I had to unbutton the single button holding her suit jacket closed and slide my fingers under her silky blouse to see if my memory of her smooth skin was accurate.

I finally cleared my throat and made eye contact. I could tell from her smirk that she had at least some hint of what I was thinking about. "Ah, yeah, you're right. I'll probably shower and take a dip in the ice bath. It was an intense game, and it's been a long road trip."

Kinzie took a step toward me and dropped her voice. "You take care of you, Jane. It would be a shame if you gave yourself frostbite on any of your delicious appendages. I'll see you soon."

I felt the lightest brush against my pinkie as she was passing, and I wasn't sure if I'd imagined it or not, but the heat in her eyes told me it was real and wasn't an accident. My finger fluttered without my consent, seeking more contact, but Kinzie was already walking down the tunnel, the click-clack of her heels echoing off the concrete surfaces surrounding us. I cursed myself, but I stood and watched her fantastic legs carry her away.

As I got into the ice bath a little later, hoping it would cool my over-revved libido as much as help my achy muscles, I lamented how badly I needed to get this schoolgirl crush under control. It was getting ridiculous.

We'd had our one night. And I needed to focus on my game. I was far too old to be sidetracked by a woman, let alone one who would be completely inappropriate for me to have a relationship with. And who lived halfway across the country. I had to be able to will the physiological responses I had to her mere presence away. I envisioned that the pins and needles of the icy cold against my skin were creating holes to let my attraction to her leak out.

I could barely breathe as I found the bottom of the tank, and water sloshed up my chest to my neck. It felt a little like I was in a vise, and I focused on my pinhole visualizations. As I exhaled, I forced the attraction out in extra strong bursts.

I was just starting to get my breathing under control when the door opened. I worried that it was going to be Kinzie again, but it was Coach Carr. Odd. She didn't usually seek me out after games.

"Hey, Jane. You mind if I join you for a minute?" Coach asked.

"It might be a bit of a tight squeeze here in the ice tub, but I guess we can conserve body heat." I focused all my effort on not letting my teeth chatter as I spoke.

"Ha ha," she deadpanned as she dragged a chair over and sat. Apparently, she was staying awhile. Once she was close, I realized how tired she looked too. "Great game today. Really. You stepped up big time."

I gave her the smallest nod I could to keep from disturbing the water around me. "Thanks."

"I just got off the phone with Aaron. I wanted to talk to you first because I thought you'd take the news hardest. And we need to discuss how it's going to affect you." She sighed.

"Okay."

"Abby ruptured her Achilles when she landed. She's out for the season."

"Did you tell me this while I'm in the ice tank because my brain is too numb to panic?" I made a feeble attempt at a joke, but my brain really did feel like it didn't work right for these three minutes. And although I felt horrible at the news that Abby had torn her Achilles, I wasn't having flashbacks to when I'd torn my ACL. Which was kind of a miracle.

She let out a real laugh that time. "No, but if I'd thought of it, it would have been intentional. I wanted you to hear it from me. Also, you're going to start in our next game."

"What?" That time, I did slosh in the water, sending another icy burst against my skin, as I turned to look at her.

"You're starting in our next game in two days. Also, your music changed. So please get out before you hurt yourself. I need you in top form."

I hadn't even realized Billie had stopped singing, which only spoke to my shock. "Oh, right." I swiftly got out of the water and wrapped towels around my torso and shoulders before I used another towel to vigorously dry and warm up my legs. "Are you sure you don't want to start someone else? Faith or Brooke or whomever?"

"Seriously, Jane. You've been pretty much splitting minutes with Abby for the last few games. Have you not noticed? Every game you've been getting better and making a case for yourself to be a starter. You earned this spot. I feel like I've been coaching the same player I coached in college." She chuckled. "If a little less confident. You *are* talking about that with Brigitte, right?"

"Yeah, we're working on it. Some days are better than others. I just thought I'd missed my chance to be a starter in the WNBA." I shook my head, still in disbelief.

"Well, believe it. And spend some extra time with Brigitte this week, okay? I need your head in the right place."

After Coach left, I sat and tried to process all the news. The knowledge that Abby had ruptured her Achilles shook me deep down. Intellectually, I understood that it was a rough sport and that injuries were going to happen, but seeing it happen reminded me that it could happen to me again. I was afraid that it was going to make me get in my own head and revert to playing scared basketball.

I closed my eyes and took a few deep, meditative breaths and focused on the sensation of the cool air in my nose. In and out. Visualized a candle with the flame swaying slightly with the force of my breath. Just like Brigitte had taught me to do. Within minutes, my mind quieted, and I was able to let go of the fear of another injury as well as the excitement of starting. And the fear of starting too. The fear of not living up to Coach's expectations. Or my teammates'. I resolved to check in with Brigitte in the morning and get a few more sessions lined up before our next game.

Chapter Seven

As practice was drawing to a close, I caught sight of Kinzie standing on the sidelines. "What new annoying and distracting things do you think she has for us today?" I said to Maya out of the corner of my mouth.

"Don't be crabby because you find it inconvenient that you're attracted to her. Our school clinic the other night with Vicky and Mercedes was pretty damn fun."

"It was fun, but all of the staged videos got old. Fast." I was really happy that I'd been paired with Maya, Vicky, and Mercedes. They'd made the experience—even the never-ending videos—better.

"Well, that's fair. But all those tweens and teens who are that into basketball? It was cool to see. And I hope we inspired some of them to keep working at it."

"Me too. It warmed my heart. It's hard to remember when my love of this sport was so pure. And I'd kind of been expecting the boys to be resentful of having women teach them basketball skills, but they seemed really excited."

Maya tossed my water bottle to me, and the cool liquid was heaven. "A few told me they'd been to some of our games. And I think they'll come to more. Especially now that they know us. Kinzie created a good event. And it was good for the team."

"Yeah, yeah, yeah." I rolled my eyes just on the principle of the thing. But Maya wasn't wrong.

"Maya, Jane, Brittany," Coach yelled and motioned us over to where she was standing with Kinzie, Owen, and Jada. *Great.*

"Ladies, thanks for giving us a few minutes," Owen said.

Brittany and I half smiled and nodded, but Maya said, "Of course. We're always happy to help with whatever the marketing group needs from us." She smiled broadly, and I couldn't tell if she was being genuine or facetious. Knowing her, probably genuine. She was like Pollyanna.

"Through Lancaster's relationships, we were able to secure a partnership with Chaos Automotive. As you're probably aware, they're a rough-and-tumble local startup EV company, and they've been around since before Tesla but only recently achieved success. We want the three of you to shoot some promos with them tomorrow. The new kid on the block, Brittany, because they have a new SUV that's taking the market by storm. The journeywoman, Jane, because they've been working at it for years and are now achieving success."

Owen kept talking, but that spin made my stomach hurt a little bit. It wasn't like I didn't know that was my truth, but the fact that they were going to blast my life story as a marketing tagline...I didn't like it. At all.

"We'll meet here tomorrow morning at nine and head down to the Chaos manufacturing facility together. Does that work?" Owen said.

I assumed it was mostly rhetorical since it didn't seem like we had a choice, but I nodded. Maya, however, in her normal bubbly manner, as though she'd been holding the day free just in case this opportunity came up tomorrow said, "Sounds great, Owen. Looking forward to it."

As we dispersed, Maya whispered, "Smoothies?"

"Sure, but I need...uh...shooting practice first." That was my second objective, but it was the one I was willing to share.

"Of course. I meant after. I've got to go meet with Coach now anyway to discuss the schedule and make sure we don't miss the film session tomorrow afternoon."

"I don't know why I thought you might forget my extra practice. I'll be around when you're done." I was superstitious as hell, and I'd never change up my routine when I was playing well, which included my post-practice shooting drills, but I had a bone to pick with Kinzie about tomorrow's debacle, and I wanted to track her down. I really needed to focus on my game, which did *not* include missing an entire day of practice. Plus, parading around my journeywoman status made me incredibly uncomfortable.

"We live and die by our routines, don't we?" Maya laughed as she walked backward. "I'll catch up with you in a bit."

I looked for Kinzie for a few minutes before giving up and heading back to the court to shoot, but about ten minutes in, the door to the gym clanged open behind me. I hoped it wasn't Maya really early, but when I turned my head, it was Kinzie who walked toward me. Perfect.

"I thought I would find you here," she said, looking every bit the sexy businesswoman as she walked to me.

"I'm a creature of habit. You can pretty much always find me here after practice. I looked for you before I started, but you weren't anywhere to be found."

Her lips curled into a knowing smile. "You were looking for me, huh?" That smile did things to me, and to keep from ogling her, I turned, dribbled twice, and shot the ball. It sliced through the hoop and the net with barely a sound.

Without looking at her, I said, "Yeah, but you go first."

She chuckled. "Sure. I wanted to apologize for blindsiding you back there."

Shocked, I spun back to her. "What?"

"I know you don't exactly love the limelight, but Chaos asked for you specifically. Their CEO is a former college basketball player, and she is a fan of yours. Your story also fits in with the way they consider themselves a journeyman sort of company, so it was a natural request. I thought of it myself when I started talking to them, but I might have given you a few more weeks before pulling you into it."

"Why a few more weeks?"

She rubbed the back of her neck. Was she nervous? "Just to relax into your new role. Get comfortable."

Ah. Because I'm a bundle of nerves, and now everyone knows it. Embarrassing but true.

"Anyway," Kinzie continued. "I'm sorry if it makes you uncomfortable, both being in the limelight as well as emphasizing the journeywoman thing, but it's for the greater good, so I hope you can forgive us. What were you looking for me for?"

I went up for another jumper. Swish. I was still annoyed, but her words took the wind out of my sails. I sighed. "I'd wanted to track you down because this sort of thing is such a distraction, and I'm not sure why the players keep having to do all these extracurricular sessions. I certainly don't have time for it in my training plan. And I hate my eight years of failure being trotted out and overshadowing my current successful year. Though I feel a little guilty now because you came over here to apologize. And I understand why it's a popular storyline." I chuckled. Why did I just admit that? "But still. This is frustrating? And on such little notice. I had a whole day already planned."

"I'm sorry to horn in on your other plans, but marketing and branding is important. It's what gets butts in seats that, at the end of the day, pay your salary and my consulting fee. It also helps the team get more money for facilities, chartering planes. I know it's annoying, but it's good for you in the long run. But I *am* sorry it's such an imposition."

I knew she was right, and she actually looked chagrined, but it was just fricking irritating. I huffed and dribbled the ball. "I get it. These are all things I know, but I just don't want it to mess with my game. But I know that's me, not you."

She pursed her lips, and a hint of a smile appeared at the corner. "Good."

I dribbled the ball out of habit and to have something to do with my hands while I wondered why she was still staring at me. My curiosity got the better of me. "Why good?"

"Because I like watching you play. I'm enjoying all this a lot more than I thought I was going to, and I think pretty much all of that is because of you. I'd hate it if you blamed me for anything that annoys you."

She had a heat in her gaze that I wasn't sure if I'd missed at first or if it was her confession that put it there, but my mouth went dry as recognition dawned. "Maybe not annoying, but I find you distracting," I said without much thought.

She stepped closer. "Is that a good thing or a bad thing?"

"I…"

She tapped me on my collarbone before she took two steps back. "You know what? Don't answer that. I know what I want the answer to be, and I don't want to walk away with hurt feelings. I'll see you in the morning, Jane. Sleep well." She flashed a smile that I swear looked vulnerable, but for someone so confident, that didn't make any sense at all.

It made me feel guilty for being a little cruel. I hadn't meant to be but realized my irritation for tomorrow's *adventure* had made me uncharacteristically so.

I arrived at eight fifty-five sharp the next morning with a venti coffee in hand and a venti level of aggravation in my soul. I'd gone for a run that morning which was fine. I'd been hoping for seven miles, but I only had time for five, which had me frustrated. But it was all fine. I was fine. I was going to smile and remind myself that this dog and pony show was good for the team and for me. And I'd get revenue share from this partnership that my agent had negotiated so that was a real win. But this was *not* how I wanted to spend my day.

"Good morning," Maya said as she bounced up. Was she *actually* excited for this?

"Morning," I answered, unable to attach a good to it. I just felt crabby about losing my day. And having to focus attention on the fact that I hadn't been a decent player in a long ass time, but now I was. Was there a better way for me to invite my play to fall off a cliff? I really didn't think there was.

"Oof. Someone woke up on the wrong side of the bed, huh?"

I suppressed a growl and flashed a toothy smile. Okay, it might not have exactly been a smile.

"Are you grumpy because you missed your workout this morning?" She giggled, and I scoffed. "Brittany texted to tell me she's running fifteen minutes late. We could shoot around some while we wait if you want. Maybe a game of Horse?"

Before I could answer, Kinzie walked up. "Good morning. We ready to get going?"

Maya sighed. "Brittany is running late. Jane and I were going to hang out in the gym till she gets here unless you have something you want us to do instead?"

"No, that's fine. We have time. But do you mind if I watch? Maybe…ask some questions? If I wouldn't be in your way?" Kinzie said, eyes wide in what appeared to be sincerity.

"Of course we don't mind. We love to share our love of the sport. Especially when we can convert someone to fandom," Maya said.

"What do you mean convert? Why do you think I'm not a fan?" Kinzie asked, the speed of her words the only signal that she wasn't totally calm about that information being made public.

I'd forgotten that no one except me knew she didn't like sports, and I wanted to say something to tell her I hadn't betrayed her confidence, but I couldn't figure out what to say without giving it away. Though Maya seemed to know already.

"Just a feeling," she said. "And fans normally wouldn't need to ask questions about two people just shooting around to kill time. But I won't tell anyone. I promise."

Kinzie bit the side of her lip. "I'm not admitting to anything, but thank you."

Maya went to get the key to the storage room while I turned all the lights on in the gym. The team would be here in about forty-five minutes, but I always loved being the first person to arrive on a court. There was something so pure about the click of the big switch and the industrial sound as all the lights flickered on. The gym smelled like whatever woodsy smelling cleaner the custodial staff used but with a faint smell of sweat and rubber always lingering. It was odd but comforting.

Kinzie's nose wrinkled.

"Don't like the smell of a gym?" I asked.

"It's just...a little off. Kind of bad but not completely bad. Like gasoline."

"I always thought they should make a cologne based on that smell."

"Eau de gasolina?"

"It would be...combustible." Such a dad joke.

"Nerd," she said but chuckled as she said it, so I took it as a win. Even if it was a dumb joke. Yet despite being called a nerd, her eyes caught mine. Held. Neither of us seemed able to look away until the metal clang of the door opening and slamming into the wall reverberated throughout the gym.

I took a subtle step back, hoping Maya was too distracted with the equipment she was bringing in to notice that she'd just interrupted something.

"We get the whole cart, Jane. Because practice is starting soon, we can just leave it in here," Maya said, wheeling the ball rack in. "Do you just want to shoot, or do you want to play one-on-one?"

I felt nervous with Kinzie watching, but... "Let's go one-on-one. It's been a while, huh?"

Kinzie peppered us with questions between every point, and Maya and I ended up calling it a tie when Brittany arrived as we went back and forth in the lead until the very end. I was surprised when I realized Kinzie was cheering, though I would have liked it more if she'd just been cheering for me instead of both of us. Ridiculous.

The commercial shoot was surprisingly effortless, even though I felt ridiculous the whole time. However, when we were preparing to load back into the big SUV, Maya threw a curve ball.

We'd stuck Brittany in the back because even though she was the tallest by far, she was the youngest. With the youngest knees. We decided she could climb back into the third row. On the way down, Maya and I rode in the middle row with Owen driving and Kinzie in the passenger seat, so I was really surprised when, just as I was sliding into my seat, Maya said, "Hey, Kinzie, would you mind switching seats with me? I was feeling a little carsick on the way down here, and after such a long day, I'm worried I'll actually get a little sick on the way back if I'm not in the front."

Kinzie stood straight from where she'd been leaning into the passenger seat in the open door. "Of course, Maya. No problem. I wish you'd said something on the way down. I'd have swapped then."

As Kinzie slid into the middle row next to me, the seat felt a lot smaller. Weird because the SUV was wide enough that we were nowhere close to touching.

"You were good out there today," Kinzie said to me.

"Thanks, but I felt like I was playing dress-up or something."

"Nah, you're a natural in front of the camera." She tapped her lips. "We might need to use that to our advantage going forward."

"Please, no more ideas."

I didn't like Kinzie's noncommittal "Hmm," but after an uncomfortable silence, I pulled out my phone and lost track of time doom scrolling. I normally hated all social media with *brave* keyboard warriors who felt entitled enough to make all the vile comments they wanted behind the anonymity of their screen names, but I needed something to distract me. I skipped past all the politics crap and focused on the cute animals and the basketball posts. I was surprised to see myself as a topic of conversation. I'd been starting for a few weeks, and since then, we'd gone five and oh, and none of the games had even been that close.

And now WNBA influencers were calling for me to be an all-star. No freaking way. I swiped the app closed as panic seized me. I wasn't sure why I'd used that for a distraction. It wasn't really good for my mental health. I should have stuck to the animal videos on TikTok, but I hadn't wanted the noise of videos in the car since I forgot my headphones.

"What's wrong?" Kinzie asked, her voice surprisingly muted.

"Why do you think something's wrong?"

"You just huffed and slammed your phone down on the seat."

I looked around and realized that Brittany and Maya both seemed to be asleep. Owen was driving, but I was pretty sure I'd seen him put earbuds in, so I didn't think he was listening either.

"All of this attention makes me uncomfortable. I just saw three posts calling for me to be voted an all-star. It's a bit premature—I've only been a starter for less than three weeks— and the whole idea stresses me out." I sighed.

Kinzie bit her lip, and God help me, I couldn't look away. "Don't take this the wrong way, but have you always struggled with confidence? I wondered for a while if you were just fishing for compliments, but I think you just have a really skewed self-image."

"I…" I wasn't really sure how to answer that. "Probably," I finally said. "I don't know. It's kind of up and down, I guess. I haven't often felt like I fit in anywhere in my life other than basketball, and I've been so bad for so long…" I took a deep breath unsure why I was being this candid with her. "I think the last time I was playing well was back in college, and I had people who believed in me, and it helped me channel a confidence I never truly felt. But I was playing well, which fed the cycle and led to more people believing in me, and I was able to fake a confidence that was never there. But the second I got injured, it was like the entire house of cards of my confidence was blown over. Onto a candle. Now those cards are burned to hell, and I'm trying to patch them up and rebuild the house."

"That is quite the imagery. Have you considered that, rather than building a house of cards, you should build a more permanent house of confidence? Maybe one made of brick to keep it from being blown over by the Big Bad Wolf of self-doubt or burn down as easily?"

I scoffed. "Of course it's occurred to me. I'm trying to work on it. I've been spending a lot of time talking to Brigitte about it. But it's hard." We sat in awkward silence for a beat, then two. Eager to change the subject, I said, "How are you settling into this sports role?"

She pressed her lips together and shook her head, and I wondered if she wasn't going to let it go. Thankfully, she said, "I'm finding it...more rewarding than I'd expected. I hope you couldn't tell when I got here, but I was a little bitter."

I shook my head. I hadn't noticed anything that looked at all bitter, other than her words at the bar but nothing with the team.

"I'd been courting this up-and-coming AI firm, but just as they were about to sign, my dad had his heart attack. That was scary as hell. It's just been me and Dad for as long as I can remember, and there isn't anything I wouldn't do for him. Including passing up that assignment I'd been working to land for months and take this one for him. He's hoping we can convert working with you all into a wider WNBA partnership. But..." She dropped her voice even lower. "I've been loving every second of this. Helping raise brand awareness for women is amazing. I love watching you." She cleared her throat. "I mean, the collective you. The team. And I've been watching a lot of YouTube videos on basketball to learn."

I couldn't help laughing.

"What's so funny?" Kinzie said, her brows drawn.

"Just the image of you sitting at your hotel room desk watching YouTube videos of basketball lessons to learn the sport. When you work every day with professionals who could tell you anything you wanted to know. Such a geek."

"Wow. Name-calling now, huh? That's beneath you." But her smile let me know she was kidding.

I rolled my eyes but circled back. "Is your dad okay now?"

"Yeah, he's on the mend. Thankfully. It was a small heart attack, if there is such a thing, and he'll be back in the swing of things soon." She ran her hand through her hair and shook it out. It was a cute nervous tick and did things in my middle that I wasn't comfortable with.

What about Kinzie captivated me? Drew me to her in a way I'd never felt before? I could barely see her in the dark vehicle, illuminated only by the occasional flash of headlights from passing cars, yet just being near her had my skin tingling. "That's good. Is he thinking about stepping in here now that he's almost back to full strength?" The idea made me feel a little nauseous, but I refused to examine that reaction.

"No, it's still too much traveling for him right now. But I wouldn't give it up anyway." She laughed. "I've been having a great time working with the team and with Owen and Jada to forge new alliances with other sports teams," Kinzie continued. "We have lots of exciting things that should be final soon that are really going to give you all great exposure."

"Wait, all of us? Like, I'm going to have to do more of this?" I twirled my finger in the air.

"I'm not sure why I'm the one informing you of this, Jane, but you're a hot commodity these days. Everyone is excited for the journeywoman's return to the limelight. It sells itself. You're bringing a lot of attention to the sport. In the best way."

I squeezed my eyes shut. "Attention is all well and good, but it's such a distraction. I'm a basketball player having success for the first time at the professional level. I need to focus, and all this stuff does is take my focus off what really matters. My play. My chemistry with my team. Our play as a whole and whether that leads to wins or losses."

"I hear all that, and I understand as much as someone who has never played sports can, but without fans, without a growing fan base, the game as a whole stagnates. But if people like you, if they can relate to you, they want to buy what you are selling. And what you're selling is tickets, merchandise, airtime. But for people to feel like they can relate to you and to your experience, you have to be visible to them."

"But why *me*?" I felt like a huge whiner, but seriously? Why couldn't they just focus on the entire team?

Kinzie chuckled as she laid her hand on my forearm that was resting on the back of the seat and squeezed briefly. "You are the underdog that everyone counted out. You're a Cinderella story that everyone can relate to. Plus, you're gorgeous and flirt with the press and the public in a way that makes everyone feel like the center of the universe. You're the whole package. A marketer's dream, really."

I didn't believe what I was hearing. It sounded sincere, but I'd never been called a *whole package* before. I didn't feel like it could be real. Yet Kinzie had looked earnest when she'd called me gorgeous and a marketer's dream. None of it made any sense. Okay, yeah, she'd picked me up in a bar, so she had to have been attracted to me then, but I wasn't *gorgeous*.

"Jane." She squeezed my arm until I looked at her. "I can see the thoughts rolling in your head. I swear to you, everything I'm saying is the truth. Please stop adding qualifiers—that I neither said nor implied—to all of it. I promise, I'm not lying to you. I won't lie to you. Please take my words at face value."

I squirmed under her intense gaze that I could feel more than see in the dim vehicle.

"If I woke either of your teammates in this car up, they would both agree with me. I'm not going to. I know that would embarrass the shit out of you, but I wish you could see yourself the way we see you. And when I say 'we,' that is every person in this car."

I had a hard time verbalizing any response, so I think I managed a sound of assent as Kinzie's words tried to sink in. Or as I tried to let her words sink in. My natural instincts were to discount them, but maybe there was truth in them that I needed to get out of my own head about. We were silent for the rest of the drive home as I, of course, obsessed. My forearm tingling the whole time from Kinzie's brief touch.

Chapter Eight

It was official. I was a meme. And I was going viral. We'd done some damn promo event with our starting five, along with five players from some local professional sports teams: the Milwaukee Bucks and Brewers, the Chicago Red Stars, and the Green Bay Packers. It was all for charity, and we'd raised over two million dollars for girls-in-sports initiatives through ticket sales and a silent auction, but for the players, it was a field day of sorts, with lots of games that made us all look silly.

Okay, admittedly, it was also a lot of fun. We played kickball and beer pong, though I only used Miller Lite since I was in season, even if most of the men weren't. But then came the inflatable sumo suits and the demise of my reputation.

That was probably a slight exaggeration. It wasn't my entire reputation.

I was going up against the Brewer's star pitcher, Bryce Landon. He was about an inch taller but had at least thirty pounds of muscle on me. To keep things fairer, the organizers of that little event spun us around ten times before entering the ring so we'd both be unsteady on our feet. It was a best of three competition, and we split the first two games, but I was determined to take him down in the final round. He seemed like a nice enough guy, but I had remembered what it felt like to win, and I liked it. And I didn't care if he was an early front-runner for the Cy Young Award. I *was* going to win.

So after I spun, I bounced into Bryce in the middle and backed up, catching him off guard. I used that moment of confusion to plow into him with all my momentum, and not only did I knock him out of the ring, I also knocked him on his ass. Well, okay, onto the back of his sumo suit.

The sportsman like thing to do would have been to give him a hand up, but instead, I gloated. Just a little. I stomped my feet like a sumo wrestler and yelled in victory. Based on the memes, I might have yelled something like "Stay down there," but I blocked the memory in the passion of the moment.

But me stomping like a fool and trash-talking took over the socials. Anytime someone had a win, there was my meme. The Pitbulls got a win? There was my meme. Hell, *I* made a great shot? Twitter lit up with my meme. And honestly, I'd been making a lot of great shots lately.

I was feeling like my old self. For real. I still had a hard time believing it, but I felt *good*—hell, great—when I was playing. I wasn't sure I'd ever felt this confident on the court. It was wild. And even though I was embarrassed about the meme, I wasn't even letting it get to me. Not most of the time anyway. Not the way I would have in the past.

"Watching this never gets old," Maya said as she stared at her phone and giggled.

Sometimes, I hated her a little bit. "Do you really have to keep watching it? Come on. We just finished a game. We just lost—"

"Yeah, but you played fantastic. The whole team did. And it was such a close game—that we weren't supposed to win—so the fact that we lost on a buzzer beater that put New York up by one? It's frustrating, but I think we'll get them next time. It's... invigorating."

"What the fuck? We. Lost. At. Home." I emphasized the words because I really didn't understand how Maya wasn't pissed about it. I couldn't believe Stewie had hit that three-pointer with Ruby's hand in her face.

"Sometimes it's better for growth to lose well than to win bad. We played like a championship team today. And we're about to watch the announcement of the starters for the all-star team, and I have a really good feeling about it. Really good. Ooo. Look, it's halftime in Vegas. Announcements incoming," she yelled the last two words and pointed to her laptop that was live streaming the game on a chair.

The stream left Rebecca and Ryan courtside and moved to Morriah Pace and Regina Walsh in the studio. They recapped the first half of the Vegas game, then moved to ours. I cringed when Morriah said, "I think I speak for all of us when I say Jane Gray has been the surprise of the season, and she did not disappoint at all tonight, even though Milwaukee didn't pull out the win. Can you believe that a year ago, she didn't even make a WNBA team, and now she's leading Milwaukee in scoring and is third in the entire league? And that's after coming off the bench for the first seven games."

Ugh. I wouldn't have minded if she'd left off some of those details.

Regina said, "A total surprise, but I'm here for it. Her play has been inspired, and I'm really hoping America agrees. She certainly got votes from me, so without further ado, let's get to the announcement everyone's been waiting for. Morriah, do you want to announce the captains?"

"I'm sure this will come as no surprise, but Stewie and A'ja led all voting and will again captain their respective teams."

I was not at all surprised. A'ja was playing out of her mind and was probably on her way to another league MVP award. Morriah and Regina bantered for a while and read out a lot of the usual suspects. I was not at all surprised when they announced Maya had been voted as a starter. I jumped up and hugged her and swung her in a circle while the whole team cheered.

Morriah's tinny voice didn't waiver when she said, "Regina, you are going to be very happy to hear that the world has voted, and Jane Gray will join her teammate Maya Norris at the WNBA All-Star Game."

Maya screamed and started jumping, and I was sure I hadn't heard Morriah right. They had to have meant Mercedes or Brittany or someone else, but I couldn't think as Maya wrapped me in a huge hug. The rest of the team followed, and I felt like I was being smashed into an overfull suitcase as everyone collapsed in. Yet, even as my brain rebelled, my heart absorbed the love of my teammates.

I was a fucking all-star. Holy fucking shit. I was embarrassed as my eyes welled up, and I squeezed them tight hoping no one else would see.

Regina said, "I'm surprised by this next name, not because she isn't deserving, but because three players from one team, especially one sitting at sixth in the standings, is surprising, but Brittany Phillips is the third star from Milwaukee who will be joining us in sin city."

The room broke out into another huge round of applause, and everyone swarmed Brittany, who was openly crying. I maneuvered my way in to hug her, excited for this big win in her first year in the league. I wished I could spin her around like she'd spun me a few weeks ago, but everyone was jumping and spinning.

"This just goes to show what a good thing Shelby Carr is putting together in Milwaukee," Morriah said. "It's her first year in the W, but her coaching is top-notch. She brought an unselfish style of basketball that emphasizes the whole over the individual but still allows the stars to shine that is delightful to watch. And drafting Brittany number three overall was a fantastic choice because she's been amazing this year."

I couldn't pay attention to the rest of the broadcast because I was flabbergasted. Maya and Brittany and me. It was fucking overwhelming. I snuck out when everyone seemed involved in their celebration, and I hoped they wouldn't notice, but I needed a second to breathe. To let it sink in that all of this was real.

Of course, as I stepped out into the hall, the sound of heels echoing let me know that I wasn't going to be alone for long. I thought about finding somewhere to hide but decided to face the owner of the approaching heels, whom I assumed had to be Kinzie. I was starting to recognize her gait, though there weren't a lot of people down here who wore heels.

I turned just as Kinzie said, "I hear congratulations are in order." She was beaming.

"You heard already?" Not that I should have been surprised.

"I had some meetings in town today, so I stayed tonight for your game and hung around to watch the selection with a few people from the front office. I'm excited for you." She squeezed my shoulder. "I voted for you in the fan voting." She went a little pink, and I loved that she'd both voted for me and was embarrassed to admit it. It was adorable.

"Well, thank you. It feels surreal, you know? I thought my career was over, and now, my manager is getting sponsorship offers, and my agent is getting a lot of inquiries about where I'm going to play overseas this offseason. I was planning on coaching in the fall. Hell, I'd be coaching already except Coach Carr called me. She's the only coach I would have come back for, and now she's helped transform me into *me* again. I…" I trailed off as my throat got tight with emotions. I swallowed hard, trying to clear it.

"It's almost like you've got a second lease on life. You thought this part of it was over, but as it turns out, it was just a little break. I think that's why you resonate so much with fans. They love you because everyone loves the underdog. The journeywoman. And it helps that you're well-spoken, and the camera loves you." She shrugged.

I'd always rooted for the underdog myself, reminding me to be a little more understanding to everyone's renewed interest. "I'm not getting away from the extra press stuff anytime soon, huh?"

She shook her head. "Sadly, no. Well sadly for you, maybe, but honestly, I'm ecstatic. Because you're easy to sell. It's one of the first lessons my dad taught me in this business. If you find something people want, giving it to them helps, no matter what your marketing objective is." She bit her lip. "You want people in the stands? You want people to cheer for you? Isn't the crowd a big advantage in games? When people cheer, it helps you find a groove or something, right? It makes it easier for you to get into the zone?"

"Look at you talking about 'the zone.' It's kinda hot," I said without thought. "Shit. Please ignore that. I'm sorry."

The sly smile on her face said she didn't hate it. But I couldn't go there. Kinzie had nothing but options. She flirted with everyone. It was her personality. Her flirting with me was nothing special. "I'm…glad to hear you enjoy my new love for basketball. I wouldn't say it extends to other sports. Or even men's basketball. But there's something about athletic, powerful women battling for rebounds." She stared, and I lost my breath at the intensity until she laughed and looked away. "Sorry, I should leave you to celebrate with your team. Especially Maya and Brittany." She took a step backward. I hadn't realized how close we were standing until we weren't that close anymore, and I missed it.

Kinzie looked sad and not as lighthearted as she'd been when she walked up. I didn't know what to say to undo whatever I'd done wrong. Instead, I said, "Uh, yeah."

Her sad smile made my chest ache. "Please give them my congratulations. Oh, and if I don't see you before then, I'll see you in Vegas."

I sighed. "More media stuff?" I was starting to get used to all the extra stuff, and it wasn't as distracting as I'd thought it would be, but I didn't want Kinzie to know it.

She chuckled. "I'm not one hundred percent on anything yet because we weren't sure who would be selected, but rest assured, we'll have plenty going on for you all and anyone else who heads to Vegas to cheer you on to make sure we're keeping you in the limelight." The look on her face was pure excitement.

"How'd you go from not being a sports fan at all to looking ready to burst at the idea of selling us in Vegas?" Kinzie laughed, and I realized what I'd just said. I lightly punched her in the arm. "Not like that. You have a dirty mind."

She bit her lip and shook her head. "To answer your first question, I am a woman of many mysteries, Jane. Many, many mysteries." She smirked as she walked away, and I was relieved that she seemed to have recaptured some of the buoyancy she'd had when she'd first walked up.

As I watched her walk away, appreciating every flex of the muscles in her calves, my emotions warred with themselves. I was surprised that she'd cared enough to watch the selection show. It made sense with her job being to grow our brand and fan base, but had she really come down here just to congratulate me? It didn't seem like she had another purpose.

Why would she do that if she didn't care? If she didn't have feelings for me? Despite my best efforts, my attraction to her had been growing. But I had to be misreading any genuine interest on her part. And regardless, I couldn't afford to get distracted. Everything was firing on all cylinders, and the last thing I wanted to do was screw that up.

Chapter Nine

The weeks between selection and the all-star game blew by in a breeze of games that we won more than lost, and before I knew it, I was preparing to board the private jet the team had chartered for us. I was still in a little bit of shock that they'd done that.

"I don't know about you, but I'm feelin' a little fancy," Maya said as she slid onto the seat next to me in the back of the plane.

I opened my eyes to look at her. I'd been trying to zone out a little as I'd never flown on a plane this tiny before and was feeling nervous. She was holding a champagne glass, clearly in the mood for the huge party that was all-star weekend.

"Take this." She handed me a second flute. "You can't let me drink this mimosa by myself."

I rolled my eyes but took it. It probably *would* take the edge off. "Thanks." I took a small sip. I really didn't like orange juice, but it had only a hint. "This is good, thank you."

"Yas!" She clinked her glass to mine. "I'm beyond excited for this weekend of debauchery. And having you as my wingwoman."

Her enthusiasm was catching, and I found myself smiling back. Though debauchery was not what I was planning.

She leaned forward and looked out the window. "Oh, I need to talk to Vicky. I'll leave you to your meditation now that I've got you living on the edge with me." She lifted her glass and smirked.

Vicky wasn't an all-star, but she and several other team members were flying out to support us, which was awesome. I loved how we all loved each other. I hadn't been on a team like this before. Normally, there was more rivalry, with everyone jockeying for more playing time, but that wasn't this team, and it was amazing.

I took another sip of my mimosa and leaned my head against the headrest, though it was only a moment before I was disturbed again.

"Is anyone sitting here?" I knew it was Kinzie from her first word, even without opening my eyes. "Sorry to disturb you, but this seems to be the only open seat."

She actually looked uncomfortable. I smiled before saying, "I think it's yours, then. I didn't realize you'd be flying out with us. I figured you'd be heading right from New York."

"I had a meeting with the Milwaukee school board president this morning about what a partnership might look like, and the team suggested I hop on this flight. It's why you're a little later than anticipated. They held the plane for me. I guess that's the advantage to flying chartered, huh? I was trying to hurry."

I finally took in her appearance. She looked a little out of sorts, as though she'd run across the tarmac. Her hair was up in a twist, but I'd never seen so many hairs out of place. Okay, other than *that* night, but we weren't going there. I resisted the urge to tuck a few behind her ear.

Which was good because Maya arrived and said, "As the designated booze pusher today, have a mimosa, Kinzie."

"Oh, I really don't think—"

"Nope. Take it." She looked her up and down. "You look like you need it."

"What?" Kinzie said, sounding more shocked than offended, and I just laughed.

"You need it." She swirled a finger in the air. "And buckle up. We're about to start taxiing."

"Well," Kinzie said when Maya went back to her own seat. "I'm not sure how to take that. But I guess if even you're drinking, I'll join in."

"She's a little much today. I'd wonder if she had a mimosa before she left, but that's just excited Maya." I'd never seen her this wound up, either, but it was all-star game weekend after all.

As Maya had promised, the plane started moving, and I took a big swig. I drank so rarely that I could already feel the effect of the alcohol loosening my muscles. I closed my eyes, leaned my head back, took a deep breath in through my nose and out through my mouth, and visualized sitting on a beach.

"Are you okay?" Kinzie asked. I felt her warm breath on my ear.

I nodded without opening my eyes. "Just don't love flying."

She laughed, which was incredibly rude. "Isn't that a little strange for a professional athlete who travels all the time?"

I rolled my head toward her before I opened my eyes, and the closeness of our faces jolted me. It wouldn't have taken much for me to bring our lips together. "The size of the plane and the size of my fear have an inverse relationship. When I fly a jumbo jet to Europe, I'm barely even afraid. Though the Xanax that I take shortly before takeoff might have something to do with that as well."

Neither of us moved back, and her lips curved into a smile.

"However," I continued. "This is the smallest plane I've ever been on, so my anxiety is probably the highest it's ever been."

"Hmm." She ran a finger over where my hand was gripping the armrest between us. "I don't think small planes are any more dangerous than big ones, but I'm happy to hold your hand. Just let me know." Her tongue flicked out, and she bit her lip. I was still staring at her mouth because why wouldn't I be? "Anytime."

I nodded, but I'd lost track of what she'd been saying. The engines revved, and I squeezed my eyes shut as I pushed myself back into my cushy leather seat for the second worst part of every flight.

I hadn't realized I'd moved my hand from the armrest and was gripping her thigh until she laid her hand on top of mine and squeezed. "Everything seems normal thus far," she said, her voice not as close as before. "We're in the air. Everything is smooth. There's a great view of downtown and the lake if you want to open your eyes."

I didn't really want to see, but I also didn't want her to think I was too huge a wimp. I forced my eyes open. "You're right, it is beautiful. I do love this city. It's one of my favorite places I've lived."

"I've always been a New York girl, but Milwaukee is growing on me. Like women's sports." She mumbled something that I couldn't hear very well.

"What?"

"Oh, nothing. Life just surprises you sometimes, doesn't it?"

We moved on, and she distracted me for the rest of the flight, other than when Maya was dancing up and down the aisle topping off our drinks, but I couldn't get the words I thought she'd mumbled out of my head:

Like you.

Stepping outside onto the tarmac took my breath away. It was fucking hot, but I always forgot how beautiful the mountains were around Vegas, and this time was no different. We were whisked away in a black SUV to check in before we had to head to some VIP meet and greet with fans. I'd planned to take a nap, but instead, I spent nearly the entire two hours between check in and the event staring out my window and replaying my interactions with Kinzie.

In hindsight, something had been slowly shifting between us for a while, but that shift had sped up on the plane. Or I was misreading everything. We'd held hands off and on during the flight. We'd stopped the first time Maya had come by with refills, but I'd frantically grabbed her hand every time we'd hit a patch of turbulence. It was a pretty bumpy flight, so I think I started holding her hand about halfway through and didn't let go until we'd landed. Was she holding my hand because I needed a little support or because she wanted to?

I know Maya saw us on a round of refills before the turbulence kept her in her seat, and she'd ask me about it at her first chance. In fact, I was surprised that she hadn't already come to my door, though she was probably napping as a responsible athlete rather than staring out the window admiring the red mountains as an excuse to obsess over what was going on with Kinzie. Fuck.

What I *wanted* to happen with Kinzie was another question I didn't know the answer to. The night we'd spent together months ago still lived rent free in my head. God, she was fucking sexy. And our chemistry had been off the charts that night.

I was certainly still incredibly attracted to her, but I didn't understand why she'd still be interested in me. She was so far out of my league. Beautiful, corporate job, seemingly rich…and I was in no position to allow any distractions for myself. My game was fragile, and I worried any distraction, no matter how minor, might throw me right back off my game.

Ugh. After that depressing thought, I finally lay down, but even as I napped off the mimosas, my brain didn't give me any peace from Kinzie as I dreamt of that one amazing night we'd had.

I awoke to a pounding at my door. Shit. In my delirium, I'd forgotten to set an alarm. I jumped out of bed with my heart in my throat, my limbs rubbery as the adrenaline coursed through them, and I stumbled to the door.

I opened it to Maya.

She laughed at me. "You don't look quite ready to head downstairs."

"Give me ten minutes." I left her standing in the open door and rushed into the bathroom, starting the water as I grabbed my toothbrush.

I was always more comfortable in a track suit or jeans and a hoodie, but in recent years, athletes had gotten more into fashion, so I wore one of the outfits my business manager had sent me from a new sponsor, a designer of athleisure. Nine minutes and fifty-eight seconds after I left Maya in my doorway, I dashed out of the bathroom and said, "Okay, let's go."

"Wow. I saved you from being late, and this is the thanks I get?"

"What?" I said, missing something.

Maya laughed as she stood. "I came over early to pump you for info about that hand-holding between you and Kinzie, but now we don't have time." She sighed heavily. "You disappoint me."

"Let's go." I opened the door and gestured to the hall. When she pouted, I said, "And if you stop moping, I'll tell you all there is to tell in the elevator. Come on."

Maya rubbed her hands together like a movie villain. "Tell me, tell me."

"You want the truth? The whole truth?" I pressed the elevator call button.

"Yes!" She jumped and clapped.

The elevator door dinged. "I don't have a fucking clue what's going on with her. That's the entire truth."

Her arms dropped to her sides, and she leveled her gaze at me. As much as she could given the several inches I had on her. "Seriously. You got me excited for *that*?"

"It's all there is to say. I haven't a fucking clue what's going on." Part of me was trying to fuck with her because I knew she'd be excited for the deets, but I also really didn't know what else to tell her.

"Come on. There's got to be *something* else." Her tone was whiny as we stepped into the empty car.

"I don't know. It feels like something might be happening, but I don't understand what she would see in me."

"Just stop there." She placed a hand on my arm. "You're super sexy. I would've made a play for you, but I learned my lesson with Paris." She shuddered as she said the name. "You're a fucking rockstar. You're an all-star *starter*. I love watching you play."

"You're biased because you're my friend, but Kinzie is from NYC. She's got to be surrounded by hot, successful, rich women. Why would she want a nomad like me?"

"Has she ever said any of this to you? For example." She switched to a high-pitched voice that sounded nothing like Kinzie as she said, "'Jane, you're smoking hot, but I'm surrounded by hot rich women in New York, a city I choose to not spend much time in these days because I'm too busy spending time in Milwaukee with you, but I'm still not interested in you because of those ladies'?" She turned and put her hands on her hips as she stared at me. I hadn't had her intimidating stare leveled at me since college. It worked now, unlike back then.

"Well, no. I guess not."

"Then why would you think she isn't interested? From what I can see, she's ridiculously into you. She barely takes her eyes off you when you're in the room."

My jaw went slack. "Really?"

"Yeah." She scoffed. "I think you're the only one who doesn't see it."

The elevator dinged, and the doors slid open. Who else would be standing there other than Kinzie? Jesus. "The only one who doesn't see what?" she said as she stepped in.

I just stared, unable to come up with something and prayed Maya didn't tell her the truth.

"What a fan favorite Jane is. Everyone loves her. Don't you think, Kinzie?"

Kinzie's lips curled up into a sultry smirk. "I absolutely agree. The Pitbulls are lucky to have you." Her smirk transformed into a real smile, and she laughed. "You're helping me build the shit out of their brand. Do you know how many new followers you have on Insta?"

"Uh, no." I'd turned those alerts off eons ago and rarely posted anything. "Who has time for that. All I do is train, sleep, and have smoothies with Maya. I have nothing interesting to post."

"Well, the team and some of your teammates have been posting for you. You're up to almost half a million followers. If you started posting about your journey, which is what everyone is interested in, you'd probably gain even more. Though as a plug for making my job easier, I'd ask that you tag the team too." The way she smiled, I would've given her a kidney if she'd asked.

Before I could respond, the doors slid open again, and the calmness of the elevator was overtaken by the cacophony of casino chaos. Digital slot machines spinning and the cheers of gamblers around a craps table happily prevented me from promising Kinzie anything.

"Does anyone know which way the convention center is?" Maya said. "I think that's where we are supposed to be heading."

"Yeah," Kinzie said. "I've been down there getting everything set up. I just ran upstairs to refresh myself. It's this way." She headed out into the smoky haze, and Maya and I followed.

The afternoon of smiling for photos and signing jerseys—who knew so many of my jerseys even existed—went surprisingly quickly, and before I knew it, Jada was grabbing us to get dressed in truly fancy athletic duds for some fundraising dinner.

It hadn't even been a full day, and already, my poor introverted soul was exhausted. Though every time I thought of holding Kinzie's hand on the plane, my chest warmed, and I had a small surge of energy.

It was weird. I hadn't ever been drawn to someone the way I was drawn to her. No one had ever given me the energy she gave me without even trying. I didn't know what the fuck I was going to do because I was starting to realize that I had it bad.

And it was ridiculous. I didn't have anything to offer Kinzie, and pretty soon, I'd be living in upstate NY or some other state in a college town, well off the beaten path...

"Stop zoning out, Gray." Maya elbowed me.

"Sorry," I said, remembering that I really couldn't sit around in my own internal monologue, agonizing about my pathetic life. Because although I'd been playing basketball pretty damn well, nothing lasted forever. "I'm ready."

"Well, stop dawdling." She grabbed my elbow and pulled me to the private dining room of the restaurant in front of us.

"What would I do without you, Maya? You force me to ignore every introvert instinct within me."

She laughed. "You'd have to dig deep and force yourself to take one step in front of the other because you couldn't miss this event. They say Reyna Ray might even make an appearance. There's no way even your introvert heart would let you miss that."

"True. And, I've heard that Coach knows her. I'm not sure if that's why she might make an appearance, but it's cool either way."

I stumbled as we walked into the lavishly decorated dining room, taken aback by how gorgeous it was. The room felt really dark, in typical Vegas fashion, the walls a deep navy, with shiny brass light fixtures hanging from the ceiling and brass accent trim on everything from the curtains around faux windows to the edge of the tablecloths.

The star power in that room was a little wild as well. I was pretty sure the mayor of Las Vegas was standing near the wall talking to Coach Carr and our GM. There were three women who I thought were actresses on a police procedural; the WNBA commissioner; several other players who would be playing in the all-star game in two days, including Maya's ex, Paris Turner; and even a former secretary of state. No sign of Reyna Ray yet.

Maya elbowed me in the back. "Stop embarrassing me just standing there. Even if you haven't seen that many famous people in one place before, you need to act like it's just another old day," she hissed.

"Oops. I've seen this many famous people in one place before, really, I have," I mumbled, lying.

Brittany bounced up to us with a grace that shouldn't be possible for a woman over six and a half feet tall, her bright blue locs that reached her low back swaying behind her. "I'm so glad you're here. Let's take a selfie for the socials, huh?" She squatted to bring herself down to our level and nearly reached around both of us with one arm. It was no wonder she was tied for second in the league for blocks in the first half of the season. I took a second to be grateful we played on the same team, though we wouldn't be on Sunday since Stewart had drafted her, whereas Wilson had picked me and Maya. Luckily, no one ever seemed to play defense in the all-star game. At least from what I'd seen on TV.

Brittany and Maya both made appropriately sexy faces, and I didn't know what to do, so I just smiled like a doofus.

"Come on, Jane," Brittany said. "You can do better than that."

"Yeah, make pouty lips like this." Maya made duck lips, and I tried to mimic it. I felt foolish, but she said, "Yeah, exactly like that. Now give me sexy bedroom eyes."

I stared at her, not sure what that meant.

"Like, a little sleepy but hungry. Like you do when you look at—"

I hit her in the arm to stop her from saying Kinzie's name.

"Come on, Gray. The whole team knows you and Kinzie have a thing for each other. If you can't recreate how you look at her on demand, try to imitate how she always looks at you."

Okay, so the whole team knew? Maybe not that we'd slept together, but at least that we had some kind of flirtation going on? Jesus.

"Did you think your little mutual crush was a secret?" Brittany said. I nodded, and she laughed like a hyena. "No offense, but we have eyes. You can't hide that hunger, sweets."

As I just stared at her, Kinzie walked up. Of course. Just to add to my embarrassment. Further compounding my humiliation, she said, "Good evening, ladies. You all are looking amazing." She said it to everyone, but she was staring at me, and I understood the hunger Brittany had mentioned. I wasn't sure how I'd missed it before, really, but if I finally saw it, I'm sure Brittany and Maya did too. "Did I interrupt you talking about me or something?" she said as no one greeted her.

Heat flooded my cheeks, and I had a hard time forming words as I stared at her in that deep turquoise, one shoulder dress that skimmed her curves in a way that made my mouth water. I knew exactly what the skin along her exposed collarbone tasted like. I knew how smooth the skin of her leg felt where it was exposed by the slit in the dress that ran to just above her knee. I had grazed my lips along nearly every inch of her and couldn't banish those images as I saw her in something other than a suit for the first time since *that* night.

Maya reaffirmed her position as team captain, however, when she said, "No, we were just working on our selfie faces for Brittany's Insta feed."

Kinzie smiled, and I was grateful for Maya's half truth. And her *not* saying we were working only on *my* selfie face. However, I couldn't help but wonder if Kinzie fully believed her. "Please, don't let me stop you," she said and took a half step back.

Feeling foolish still, I made my pouty duck lips and tried to channel sexy eyes as Brittany pulled Maya and me in close again and snapped what looked like twenty shots. "Perfect," Brittany said.

I wondered how she knew it was perfect since she'd taken dozens, but I hoped I didn't look ridiculous. I'd learned the trick of looking at the camera on the phone rather than the screen, so it didn't look like I was staring off into space. But it also meant I couldn't be sure if I'd nailed the face they'd tried to coach me into or not.

"Well, I need a drink, and Brittany, I think I heard Coach was looking for you before," Maya said.

"Really?" Brittany's brows furrowed, and Maya elbowed her in the ribs. "Oh yeah, I think you're right. Catch up with you two in a bit." She flashed me a knowing smile, and I was left alone with Kinzie.

She sucked half her bottom lip into her mouth before rubbing her fingers along the silky lapel of my blazer just below my collarbone. "This outfit is something else."

I'd felt ridiculous putting it on. I knew people like Sue Bird could pull off fancy gym shorts paired with a black blazer with nothing other than tape holding their boobs in place, but I wasn't sure I had enough of Sue's panache. Thankfully, it was a double-breasted blazer, so it was a little more modest than hers was at the ESPYs a few years ago. Yet, the way Kinzie was looking at me had me wondering if I had more swagger than I believed. A lot more.

"My agent finagled something with an up-and-coming designer for this faux tux outfit, and Adidas sent out a stylist team for hair and makeup and to bring me these fancy dress sneakers. I feel a little silly, but it's better than being stuffed into some cocktail dress that makes me feel like I'm in drag."

"Well, it works. It really works. But I can't help but wonder what's under this delicious blazer."

"I think you already know." I laughed because she'd seen exactly what was under it a few short months ago. Nothing but skin.

Her jaw slackened. "Really?"

Her reaction gave me confidence the way a successful pump fake getting the defender to commit and giving me an open shot that floated through the basket did. The revelation was surprising, but like in basketball, I pushed forward, stepping out of my comfort zone. "Really." I leaned closer. "This dress of yours is also...something." I looked her up and down, hesitating on her legs before making eye contact again. "It has me fantasizing about those thighs wrapped around me when I had three fingers in you." Apparently, dreaming about having sex with Kinzie all afternoon had prompted the return of fake-confident sexy Jane.

Her eyes went wide, and I imagined she was wondering where those words had come from. Where that boldness had come from. She'd never seen it. Hell, I'd never seen it, but she brought something out of me, and my God, I wanted to take her by the hand and lead her right out of that event and up to my hotel room. In that moment, I loved fake Jane, who, for the first time in my life, made *me* too forward for a change.

I started to reach out, but Jada Morrow shattered the moment. "Sorry to interrupt, but, Jane, can I grab you for a second? I have someone who wants to meet you."

I felt like I'd been doused in cold water. Had Jada been able to feel the tension radiating between Kinzie and me? I hoped not. "Of course, no problem."

Kinzie was able to slip back into business mode. If I hadn't known what I'd just said to her, I would have thought we'd been talking about the weather. "Thanks for filling me in on that, Jane. I'm glad you're still thinking about it." I coughed to suppress a laugh. "I'll catch up with you later."

As Jada pulled me away, Kinzie winked and gave me a sexy smolder that I knew I wouldn't be able to wash from my mind, and my entire body nearly combusted. A few moments later, when I shook the hand of former secretary of state, Brenda Collins, I worried that I'd burn her, but if the heat existed outside of my own mind, she didn't seem to notice.

As starstruck as I'd been by her when we'd walked in, even Brenda Collins couldn't pull my mind completely from Kinzie. I'd had a lot of doubts about myself and where I stood with her, but I found myself wondering, did she truly want more than the one night we'd shared? Watching her watch me—her eyes filled with longing and lust—I knew she wanted at least another night.

And as I watched her work the room for the rest of the night, I couldn't remember why exploring something more with her was such a bad idea. The low buzz I'd been holding on to all night likely contributed to my missing inhibitions. Regardless, I'd never been so turned on in front of so many people in my life. It was embarrassing as hell but also fucking hot.

Chapter Ten

The next two days passed in a blur of team practices that were more like playground basketball games with friends; the two-person skills challenge that Maya and I took second in, missing winning by less than a second; the three point challenge; walking the orange carpet; charity events; and fan meet and greets. Through everything, Kinzie was always nearby looking at me in a way that made my skin prickle with desire.

When not daydreaming about Kinzie, I tried to savor every minute since it was my first all-star appearance, but it just felt like so much was going on. When they called my name and I came charging out of the tunnel to applause like I'd never received before, I was filled to the brim with pride. All I could think about were my parents, who had flown all the way from Vermont with three layovers just to be in the audience cheering for me. I wished I could take a picture, but our phones always stayed in the locker room. I didn't think I'd believe the next day that all of it had even happened without photographic evidence.

After the game, which Team A'ja won in another surreal moment in a weekend of surreal moments, I took my parents out for a late dinner before they had to hop a red-eye home. I tried to get them to go to someplace fancy—they weren't wealthy and didn't splurge much—but they insisted they just wanted to have Johnny Rockets, so burgers it was.

I teared up saying good-bye to them as they hopped on the airport shuttle, but they were so practical, they didn't cry at all. I consoled myself with thoughts of the evening ahead. I was going to meet up with Maya and the crew, and I could only assume Kinzie would be there too. I was excited and nervous because tomorrow was an off day until the late afternoon, when we had to catch our charter home. I had a feeling tonight was going to be wild.

Every night in Vegas had been successively wilder, but with a travel day the next day, plus one more free day before practice started back up, it felt like the need to really let loose had been building in everyone.

I texted Maya to ask where they were, and she said one of the Vegas players had a connection at the Hakkasan nightclub at the MGM and had scored a reservation for all of us in a VIP section. I hadn't spent much time in Vegas, but I had learned that everything there looked close, yet took forever to get to. I tried to take a taxi since it felt like it was a zillion degrees outside, but the cab line was about twenty people long and wasn't moving quickly, so I decided to walk. I wasn't surprised that even though the MGM seemed to be a block away, it still took fifteen minutes to walk there. Luckily, it was less miserably hot than expected.

When I gave my name to the bouncer, someone escorted me to a cordoned off area of the mezzanine. I normally found nightclub scenes a little overwhelming with the number of people gyrating nearby, especially given how sweaty they always were and how few clothes they had on, but Vegas was worse than normal. So I was particularly happy to see that VIP really meant VIP. The skybox was tucked away from all the sweaty people, and I felt like I could take a deep breath for the first time since I'd entered the club.

"Jane," Mercedes screamed as she ran over to me. "You're here. I've missed you." She pulled me into a hug, and I could tell she'd had a few drinks. While we liked each other, we weren't hugging friends. At least, not until that moment.

Vicky was next, and she screeched my name as she approached, her arms outstretched. Okay. Apparently, this was going to be a very huggy evening. She squeezed me tighter than Mercedes had, and I could smell the tequila on her, which made me laugh. It was nice to see them taking advantage of the chance to truly unwind. I just hoped they didn't get sick. As athletes, we rarely drink, especially because we played nearly year-round between the WNBA season in the US and overseas the remainder of the year and lacked an offseason to relax in. Vicky and Mercedes hopped back into the crowd, and I scanned the room for Maya. Or Kinzie.

I couldn't decide who I wanted to find first.

Maya. Definitely Maya.

Maybe she could talk some sense into me about Kinzie. Though, I didn't *really* want her to talk sense into me about Kinzie. Since our flirtation at the cocktail party, I hadn't been able to stop thinking about her. Whatever had been simmering felt really close to boiling over, and I was having a hard time reminding myself to turn off the burner.

However, it was Kinzie who came over next. "Hey, you. I've been wondering when you were going to get here. Maya said you were having dinner with your parents. They didn't want to come celebrate with you?"

"Ha ha, no," I deadpanned. "I love them to death, but they aren't partiers. I think they'd be scandalized at how little clothing most women are wearing down there."

Kinzie chuckled. "Well, I'm not a prude, but I felt a little scandalized myself. Vegas is like that sometimes. I'd hesitate before touching much in this club. Seems like everything might have…grossness on it."

"Well, I'm clean." I couldn't believe I'd said that. It was like I was inviting her to touch me. Sure, I'd been fantasizing about her for days, but now that we were in front of each other, I remembered how unprofessional it would be. Plus, it might be bad luck. I was afraid to introduce something new that might fuck up my head. Yet, she looked fantastic in the black camisole that emphasized her toned arms and high-waisted black pants so I couldn't make myself regret the comment.

She traced a finger from my shoulder to my elbow. "I'm clean too, so I'm safe." She smirked. "At least for now."

I realized I was starting to lean in when movement over Kinzie's shoulder caught my attention. Maya was waving. It was odd because it was at her hip level, but I realized she was standing next to her ex, Paris Turner. And they were standing close. Maya didn't look like she was trying to get away, but when she caught my eye, her jaw looked tense.

This was horrible timing, but I wouldn't have been able to live with myself if I didn't check in. "Um, I need to check on Maya. I'm sorry. I'll catch up with you in a bit, okay?"

She blinked at me, hurt in her eyes.

"I'm sorry, I want to continue this conversation, but Maya is over there with her ex, and their relationship has been... tumultuous." I didn't want to betray her trust, but I also didn't want Kinzie to think I was blowing her off. "I think she's trying to get my attention, so I need to check." I squeezed her hand. "I'm not playing games, I swear."

Her face softened. "No explanations needed. Go check on your friend."

She looked earnest, and the hurt was gone. "Thank you. I *will* catch up with you later, okay?"

Her smile bloomed fully. "I'm going to hold you to that, and I'm not going anywhere." Her words were light, but they felt weightier for some reason. Was there a hidden meaning I didn't understand?

I kissed her on the cheek. I wasn't sure what compelled me, but I had to. She looked a little surprised, but I squeezed her hand again and walked away.

Maya didn't look like she was having a bad time, but something was off. I plastered a bright smile on my face as I walked up to them and said, "Sorry to interrupt, but I've been looking all over for you, Maya. I thought we were going to meet up?" I was hoping she knew that if she wanted to blow me off, she could, but I was here as a lifeline if she wanted it.

"Oops, you're right, Jane. I lost track of time." She looked back to Paris. "I'm sorry, I'll catch you later, okay?"

Paris's face looked pinched as she said, "Okay, sure. I'll be around."

Maya hooked her arm into mine as we walked. "Thank you," she whispered.

"I wasn't sure if you needed a bail out, but I wanted to give you the choice. You looked like you were into the conversation and also looking for an escape."

"It's possible to be doing both at the same time." She sighed. And pulled me to the bar. "This is why I shouldn't drink when I'm around her. Because I am *so* into her. Still. But it always breaks me when things fall apart. It's...so lesbian of me. God, I hate it. And I hate myself a little bit because I still want to fuck her. Fuck me."

She ordered us two tequila shots. I wasn't planning to drink anything other than beer, but this was the first time I'd made it to the bar. Since Maya seemed to need it, we clinked shot glasses, tapped them on the bar, and tipped them back. I tried not to wince at the burn and wondered why Maya hadn't asked for salt and lime. Or even orange and cinnamon. But, no. She seemed unaffected as she held on to the edge of the bar and sank into a squat. I chuckled at her theatrics as she huffed and pulled her hips back farther. I envied the stretch she had to be feeling in her lats. "What is wrong with me?"

"Not one thing. You are amazing. And everyone should be able to see it." I wanted to shake her. If Paris was dicking her around, keeping her on the hook while she fucked other women or just refused to get serious or whatever...I wanted to punch her. I wasn't violent, but no one fucked with my friends. The shot had also made me braver. I could feel the effects already. I was such a lightweight.

She looked at me around the arm that was still holding onto the edge of the bar. "Thank you. But why am I like this? When she says, 'Maya,' like *that*, why do I just melt and follow her with my tongue hanging out?"

"It says that you're a work in progress. So is she, but you have the right to protect your heart. You don't need her."

"I don't," she said indignantly.

"You're right. What can I do to help you right now?" I couldn't necessarily relate to what she was going through, but I wanted to help however I could.

"Dance with me? I love to dance, and if we go together, I can't dance with the devil."

"Well, I might be the devil, but you're like my sister, so I'll protect you." We smiled and high-fived. Because after one shot, I was feeling a little boozy, and it felt like the right move.

We did one more shot—because why wouldn't we—and hit the dance floor. I wasn't a great dancer, but when in a crowd, I felt free enough to let my hips find the rhythm, and they didn't let me down. I'm sure the tequila didn't hurt. My arms and hips and feet found the music, and we danced. And danced. And danced. Until I couldn't think or feel or care. I forgot about Kinzie and the mess I found myself in.

All the minutes melted together until I was dancing by myself. I was lost in the beat and had no idea how long it had been going on for, but I didn't mind. Well, I didn't mind until some tall, sweaty, white guy was suddenly in front of me. At first, he was just dancing by himself. But he danced closer. And closer. And I tried to step back, but I bumped into a couple behind me. He put his hand on my hip, and I pushed it off.

"Sorry," he breathed on me. I tried not to gag. "I just saw we were both dancing alone and thought maybe you'd like to join me. It's rare that I meet a woman who is almost as tall as me."

I wanted to place a hand on his chest and shove him away. But it was hard to know what to expect from men sometimes, and I didn't want to escalate anything. I sidestepped and tried a more appeasing route. I giggled and hated myself a little for it. "Oh, I'm not alone. I'm just waiting for my friend to come back." I wished I'd said girlfriend; fending off weirdos didn't require full truths. But he might have been *more* interested, so maybe I'd said the right thing.

Also, where had Maya gone? It felt like I'd been dancing with her and Vicky, and then, I wasn't sure. I think Vicky had brought me another shot. Why the fuck was I doing multiple shots? Though it made sense as to why the night had become confusing.

Too much tequila on a stomach barely half-full from a Johnny Rockets Impossible burger hours ago.

"Can't you dance with me while you wait?" he whined and reached for my hip again.

"She doesn't have to wait any longer, friend," Kinzie said as she wrapped her fingers around his wrist and removed it from my hip.

I was a couple of inches taller than her, but she looked intense and intimidating in that moment. He cowered, and I couldn't have been more grateful if I'd tried. I wanted to sink into her arms for saving me from the scene that I'd been afraid I was going to need to cause.

His voice cracked as he said, "Why don't we all just dance together?"

"Thanks, babe," I said and pulled her in for a kiss. I wasn't sure what I meant by it, but it felt natural. So natural that Kinzie's hand wrapped around me and pulled me closer. I'd meant the kiss to be a peck to make sure that the dude got the message and skulked off, but it quickly changed.

I wasn't sure whose mouth opened first, whose tongue entered first, but I dug my fingers into her jean-clad hips and pulled her as close as our clothes would allow. Any concern regarding the interloping guy vanished.

Her thigh slid between my own, and I groaned. Maybe she did too, but I couldn't hear her over the thump of the music. All my senses were consumed by her. All I could feel, smell, and taste was her. Fuck. How had we gone months without this? We kissed. And kissed. And danced. And kissed. My entire body melted into hers as we moved together. Hell, my entire being melted into her. Every inch of skin was on fire for her. My hands danced along her back, up her neck, in her hair. I couldn't feel enough of her. I couldn't pull her close enough.

I had no idea how long we were lost in each other until someone fell into me from behind. My teeth hit Kinzie's, and we both pulled away in surprise. I was ready to spin in anger, but Kinzie must have seen the flash in my eyes.

"Do you want to get out of here?" she asked.

Any anger I felt at the interruption disappeared as I envisioned spending the rest of the night in her bed. Or my own. I wasn't picky. As long as it included us together, and preferably without clothes, I was game.

I nodded and laced my fingers with hers as she led me toward the exit. Just before she hit the push bar on the door out of the club, a female stick figure nearby caught my eye, and the urge to pee was nearly overpowering. I tugged Kinzie's hand, and she paused. "I'm going to hit the restroom quick, okay?"

She nodded and leaned against a column.

I jogged into the restroom, not wanting to waste a second before I got her in my bed. However, as I was flushing, I heard a little gagging followed by retching. I felt bad for whoever it was. Puking always sucked, but it seemed especially sad in a public bathroom at a club on the strip.

My heart went out to her as she continued to throw up as I washed my hands. I wanted to walk away, but I couldn't do it. I couldn't leave another woman in there without checking on her. She might have just overindulged, but someone could have slipped something in her drink. And there were probably a lot of people out there who might take advantage of her. Despite knowing Kinzie was waiting, I knocked on the stall door. "Are you okay in there?"

Only a groan answered me, but the woman flopped back until she was sitting on the floor against the door, and I saw the side of her dress. Shit.

"Vicky? Is that you? Do you need help?"

"Yeah," Vicky answered, her voice rough yet weak. Any lingering buzz I had from those shots and kisses vanished at her distress. "I think I need to go home."

Understatement of the year. "Can you open the door? I'll help you get back to your room."

Sounds of scratching came from the other side, and I envisioned her reaching for the lock but unable to grab it because of her position on the floor. The door to the club opened. and the thump of bass beat louder for a moment, ratcheting up my own heartbeat. I looked over. It was Kinzie. I sighed in relief.

"Are you okay? You were taking a while." She smiled and looked a little uncomfortable.

"Yeah, I'm fine, but Vicky isn't doing well," I said. "I can't leave her."

Kinzie said, "Of course not. How can I help?" just as Vicky said, "Ssh. I don't want anyone on the team to know that I can't handle my alcohol. They'll make fun of me."

I rolled my eyes and chuckled. "It's Kinzie, and I promise. She won't tell anyone."

"You have my word," Kinzie said.

"Oh no, she's not on the team. She's an outsider. That's worse." Vicky's voice was nearly a sob, and I watched Kinzie's face fall.

"She's not an outsider. I promise. She's promoting us and is our biggest cheerleader. She's exactly what you're looking for. Not an outsider but also not a teammate." I smiled at Kinzie so she'd know my words were completely truthful, and she rewarded me with a real smile.

"You promise?" Vicky said from the other side of the stall door.

"Promise," I said, still looking at Kinzie. "Would you get a few bottles of water? I'm about to break into this stall, but she's going to want some water on our walk back to the hotel."

"No problem. I'll be right back."

I nodded and sighed, relieved that I had her help. Not that I couldn't do this by myself, but knowing I had backup eased my stress. Once she left, I said. "Okay, Vicky I'm about to pick the lock to your restroom door. Don't lean too much weight on it, or you're going to fall over."

"How're you gonna do that?" she slurred as I pulled out my room key and used it as a makeshift flat head screwdriver to turn the latch from the outside. Before she finished talking, the stall door sprang open, and she fell over onto my feet. Luckily, she was sitting on the floor, so she didn't fall far. "You're magic," she said as she righted herself with my help.

I laughed but was relieved that she was okay and sitting up without assistance. I hoped that meant she'd be able to walk too. "That's right. A regular magician. What do you think about trying to stand and getting cleaned up a little?" Thankfully, she'd seemed to hit the toilet when she'd been throwing up, but she needed to wash her hands and face. And I was sure she'd feel a lot better if she rinsed her mouth out too.

"You're a magician on the court too. A magician everywhere." She slurred the last word. I would have been embarrassed and maybe a little flattered if she hadn't been sloshed.

"For my next trick, let's see if I can get you off this floor, huh?"

"Ooo, fun."

Dear God, send me strength.

I got her feet situated in front of her and her legs bent at the knees so hopefully as I lifted, she'd plant her feet. "Okay, wrap your arms around my neck. But please don't touch me with your hands if you can help it, okay?" I cringed at the thought of her touching my hair with hands that had just been all over the restroom floor and toilet.

"Okey doke," she said and did as instructed.

I used my legs and lifted, my arms under her pits. She almost helped. "You're pretty too. Did you know that? I had a little crush on you when you first started. I'm over it now." She giggled.

This was becoming a night of revelations. Evidently, tequila was Vicky's truth serum. "Oh really?" I said, just trying to keep her talking.

"Yeah, I got a crush on someone else now."

"And who might that be?" It seemed like she had her feet under her, so I helped her walk to the sink.

"Shh. It's a secret. I can't tell."

"I think you want to tell me. But while you think about it, why don't you wash your hands? Maybe splash some water on your face. Rinse out your mouth. Do you have any gum or mints in your little clutch?" It was a little like pulling teeth, but I finally got both of us washed up, and she thankfully did find a small tin of mints just as Kinzie opened the door again.

"You two ready to get the hell out of here?"

"Let's roll," Vicky said. She tried to do some half dance maneuver and almost knocked us both over, but Kinzie was there to steady us even as she balanced three bottles of water in her other hand.

"Since when did you get so coordinated?" I said.

"Why did you think I'm uncoordinated? Have I ever seemed clumsy to you?" She laughed as she looked at me.

"No, but you said you hate sports. I guess I just thought you weren't coordinated."

She barked another laugh. "That's a little elitist, isn't it?"

I was dumbstruck. I wasn't sure why I'd made that assumption. "Um."

She laughed before she said, "I don't play sports, nor do I enjoy them—or at least, I didn't used to enjoy them—but I do yoga or Pilates every day."

"I'm…sorry," I said weakly, embarrassed and wishing I could take back my silly statement.

"As you can see—and as you should remember—I'm pretty darn coordinated." Her sexy smirk did something to me. I hated feeling foolish, but I'd nearly forgotten it with that gaze.

"Wait, did you two sleep together?" Vicky perked up enough to read between the lines.

"Um, no," I said with more determination than I felt and shrugged at Kinzie in the mirror, hoping Vicky didn't notice. And hoping I didn't hurt Kinzie's feelings, though I certainly wasn't ready for the whole team to know.

"Oh, okay. Can I go to bed now?"

"Yeah, let's go. It's just a short walk, okay? Can you make it?" I said.

"I'm a professional athlete. Of course I can take a short walk." She giggled again. I wasn't sure I believed her, but I was afraid that getting into a car and doing a couple of U-turns on the strip to get back to our hotel would make her get sick again. Plus, the walk might help sober her up.

By the time we poured her into her bed with a couple of bottles of water and aspirin on the nightstand, I expected to feel completely exhausted, but instead, I felt a little wired.

"That isn't exactly how I expected our night to go when we left the dance floor, but I'm glad you found Vicky," Kinzie said as we stepped out into the hall, and the door to Vicky's room clicked behind us.

"Yeah, I worry about what could've happened if I hadn't. I texted Brittany and Mercedes and told them I got her to bed. Apparently, they were supposed to be watching out for each other, but neither realized when Vicky went to the restroom and panicked when they couldn't find her. I think they'd been about to call the National Guard."

"Ah, the kids sticking together. I love it. I hadn't even thought about whether someone might miss you when I was luring you out of the club earlier. Is there anyone you need to text?"

"I didn't promise to check in with anyone, but everyone seems to be heading back to their rooms. I let Maya know I was heading to bed, and I thought you were too."

"Oh, did you?" She looked at me, her brows arched.

"Uh, did I misspeak?"

She bit the side of her lip. "Well I *was* hoping to spend a little more time with you. If you aren't too tired."

"Oh?" was all I managed as my self-doubt vanished, and the need I felt for her surged in my veins again, sending my heart rate through the roof.

"I was going to invite you to my room, but I was afraid you might sneak out in the middle of the night again, so I was trying to figure out how to get myself invited to your room without being too forward." She ran her hand down my arm and interlaced our fingers, pulling me closer.

I'd thought she would have been happy that I'd snuck out of her room when she'd been sleeping last time. No one wanted a one-night stand to stick around for an awkward morning after, did they? But I wasn't going to ignore the electricity flowing between our fingers to ask. Or chance ruining the connection. "You? Too forward?" I laughed and squeezed her hand. "I think you've mentioned that before and never shied away from it. But my room isn't far. Do you want to come up for a nightcap?"

"There is nothing I want more. What floor are you on?" she said as her fingers hovered over the elevator call buttons.

"Thirty."

She pressed the up button. "Nice."

The air felt heavy as we waited for the elevator, and my mouth went dry at her intense gaze. It was that hungry look that Maya and Brittany had been teasing me about the other day, and I wondered why I'd been uncertain not that long ago. Or why I'd been uncertain about her interest at all. We had intense chemistry the one night we'd been together, and if our making out earlier was any indicator, it had only intensified. I wished I could will the elevator to hurry up, but also, standing there looking at each other was building a tension between us that felt so good, I never wanted it to end. I shivered just as the elevator dinged and signaled its arrival.

Chapter Eleven

Kinzie was quiet on our walk from the elevator to my room, but I could feel the intensity of her gaze with every step. Why were these corridors so damn long?

"Your jeans make me feel things, Jane. I don't think I can really describe exactly what, but there's an old country song about hating to see someone go but loving to watch her leave. Walking a step behind you, I understand the sentiment."

Her words started pleasant flutters in my stomach and gave me confidence as I stopped in front of my door. Because the hall was empty and I appreciated her openness, I brushed a light kiss across her lips before I turned and opened the door. "Luckily, I convinced you to leave with me."

She whistled as she walked into my room and looked around. "Nice digs. Also, I would not have guessed you would be this tidy."

"Oh?" I took in my room from an outsider's perspective. Sure, I kept my clothes hanging in the closet or neatly folded. I kept my dirty clothes rolled tightly in half my suitcase. I didn't like a mess, but I didn't think that was strange.

She laughed. "Not that I would expect you to be sloppy, but you don't have a single item of clothing strewn across your bed or hanging over the back of a chair. Did you know exactly what you were going to wear tonight that you didn't have to try on a few things?"

"No, I tried on one other shirt, but I hung it back up. Is that weird?"

She grinned as she took my hand again. "Not weird at all. Endearing. I like learning more about you, Jane Gray."

I loved how we were the same height when she wore heels. Most women I'd dated were shorter than me—quite a bit in some cases—and it was really hot that I could look straight at her. I ran a finger along her jaw, still channeling a boldness that didn't really feel like my own, but I was riding the wave. Fake-confident sexy Jane was back, and I was letting her run the show. "I was going to offer you a drink, but I'd much rather kiss you. If that's okay with you." I intentionally used the same words she'd said to me that first night in her hotel room. I didn't know why, but it felt poetic.

Maybe she felt the same because her eyes flicked to my mouth, but she didn't answer, so I used the last word she'd said to me that first night before I'd kissed her. "Please," I whispered.

She gripped my jeans and pulled me until our bodies were completely flush and kissed me again as though we'd never taken a pause from the dance floor. No hesitating or figuring out how our mouths fit together. Her tongue softly yet confidently stroked mine, and wetness surged between my thighs.

I slid my hands down her back and cupped her ass, squeezing and pulling her infinitesimally closer. Her breath caught, and she pulled back just a little. "What do you do to me, Jane?" she whispered.

She had that completely backward, but I didn't want to get into it right then. I was the one who'd been swearing all season that anything with her would be unprofessional, yet here I was, at the all-star game in Sin City, about to take her to bed. I shrugged and flashed what I thought was my cocky smile. "It's that athlete swagger, I guess. Do you still want to do this?" Since she'd pulled away, I wanted to check in.

Her tongue peeked out, and she sucked her lower lip into her mouth. "If you stop right now, Jane, I might die."

"We certainly can't have that." Rather than taking her mouth again, I pressed a kiss just below her ear and made my way down the delicious column of her neck until I reached her collarbone. When I grazed it with my teeth, she groaned and pulled me as she backed into the wall.

I kissed across her chest until I came to the thin strap of her camisole. I slid two fingers under it and glided it to the edge of her shoulder, but before I pushed it down, I looked up. "Is this okay?"

She nodded, but in case I didn't get the message, she laid her hand atop mine and helped guide it and the strap all the way down her arm until her breast was exposed. It wasn't the first time I'd seen her, but I still paused and marveled at the dusky pink nipple, hard and straining toward me. Her breasts weren't large, but they were perfect.

I was apparently taking too much time because Kinzie took my hand again and brought it to her breast, guiding me to rub my palm lightly back and forth across the hard nipple before pressing firmly into her.

"Sorry, was I moving too slow?" I said, teasing, not at all offended by the guidance.

"Not anymore." She tightened her fingers around mine.

I took that as a hint, so I massaged and squeezed. "Is that what you were looking for?"

Her eyes were heavy with lust as she nodded.

I slid my left hand across her collarbone on the other side until my fingers slid under that strap as well. "Do you want me to do the same thing over here?"

"Please," she said.

I started to slide the strap down, but unlike the other side, I moved excruciatingly slowly, following my hand with my mouth as I kissed her smooth skin, loving the feel of it beneath my lips, and loving it even more when goose bumps erupted along her arm. "You are so sexy," I said right before I captured her nipple with my lips. It was already tight before I touched it, but as I flicked my tongue back and forth, it hardened more.

Kinzie moaned, "Please, Jane."

"Please what?"

Her fingers tightened in my hair until I released her nipple and tipped my head up. "I need you. Now. Please take me to bed."

I almost laughed as those words made it sound like the bedroom was on the other side of the house instead of ten feet away. But with the way she was looking at me, it wasn't that funny.

I stood and kissed her hard but fast. "Your wish is my command." I tugged her toward my bed. When we reached the foot, I reached for her belt buckle and fumbled with it until I realized that buckle and front belt were a ruse. "It's like your pants don't want me to get into them," I said and chuckled.

"I can assure you, that is *not* true. My pants and I both want you in them."

I unclasped the hook of her pants and unzipped them, but I didn't push them off her hips. "You want me in your pants? Or in *you*?" I was amazed at the audaciousness she brought out in me.

She gasped as I ran my thumbs under the elastic of her panties. "They're near the same thing, aren't they?"

"It's a nuanced situation, but shall I take that as an affirmative to both questions?" I was putting on a good show, but my knees were quivering. I was hoping she wasn't looking that far down.

"Yeah," she breathed. "I think that's best. Both of those things."

I couldn't stop my smile as I thought of the implications, remembering how much she liked it when I'd taken her from behind in that Milwaukee hotel room months ago. I gave her wide-legged slacks a slight push, and they slid off her hips and pooled on the floor. She kicked out of them with her foot, still in the high heels that I hadn't been able to appreciate before then.

Every inch of her calves looked amazing flexed by her three-inch shoes.

Standing in nothing but her sparkling silver high heels, black lace panties, and a camisole bunched at her waist, she nearly stopped my heart. I took half a step back just to drink her in. "What did I do to deserve this? Deserve your perfection?" I said without thought.

"I don't know, but I'm going to need to get you out of some of those clothes before you do get lucky. Not that I'm trying to rush you," she said softly and tilted her head side to side. "Well, maybe I am." She reached for the bottom of my flowing V-neck blouse and slid it over my head. I felt like she deliberately slid her fingers along my skin from hips to collarbone. Especially when a couple of her fingers fluttered across my nipple—covered by only a thin cotton bra—as they passed.

I shuddered at the contact, and my eyes slid closed for a long breath.

After tossing my shirt somewhere, she traced her index finger down the center of my abs. That made me shudder again, and I blinked my eyes open. "I thought abs like this didn't exist in real life. It's like they've been airbrushed on."

That made me laugh. "They're not airbrushed. Nor are they easy to maintain." She dropped to her knees in front of me and lightly bit the skin just above my pants. My voice raised an octave or two as I said, "But the way you're staring at me, I'd be willing to do anything to keep your interest."

"Oh I'd be interested even without these beauties, but they don't hurt." She ran her tongue up the center of my abs.

"Holy shit," I said as my knees nearly buckled.

"Language, Jane. What would your fans think?"

I barked a laugh, but it didn't last long as her fingers came to the button on my jeans, flicking it open as though it was a piece of old Velcro. She pulled my pants and underwear down in one quick motion, leaving them pooled at my feet before standing. I helped her out of her camisole as she unclasped my bra.

I was about to push her onto the bed when I remembered that it wasn't that long ago that I'd lifted Vicky off the floor of the restroom, and although I really wanted to get into bed with Kinzie, I wanted to get cleaned up first.

"How would you feel about a shower?" I said.

Her brows were a little furrowed, and her eyes cloudy with lust as she said, "I'm not opposed." She ran the tip of her finger from the hollow at the base of my throat, between my breasts, dipping through my belly button and stopping to tease the top of my trimmed hair. "But I'm also not opposed to dirty sex either. I've mostly only been sweating with you this evening while we danced."

"I'm just afraid I have puke in my hair from Vicky," I blurted, embarrassed at how unromantic that was to say.

Kinzie's head tipped back as she laughed. "That's a lot less sexy than sweat," she said between bouts of laughter. "Let's take a shower. I also like clean sex. Clean sex that turns into dirty sex especially." She grinned at me, and all of my embarrassment evaporated as I tugged her toward my ridiculously large bathroom.

I leaned into my vast walk-in shower and turned on the water. When I stood straight again to let it heat up, Kinzie captured my mouth in a kiss so hot, I was surprised the cool droplets of water ricocheting onto me didn't sizzle. Her fingers dug into my hips as she pulled us close and began to walk us both backward.

We both gasped and broke our kiss at the cool water pouring out of the rain showerhead. "You could have waited another minute," I said.

"I got impatient." Her cocky smile made me laugh. "And anyway, aren't you the queen of the ice baths?"

"I'd never claim to be the queen. I hate those damn things, but they're effective."

Kinzie turned halfway to crank the heat up and get shampoo from the wall dispenser. I thought she was about to wash her own hair, but instead, I hummed in pleasure when her fingers began to knead my scalp. I braced myself by grabbing her hips before I stumbled.

"You're really good at this," I mumbled.

"Fast learner, I guess. I've never done it before."

She rinsed my hair out before massaging conditioner in and grabbing body soap. I was expecting to soap up quickly and get back to bed, but Kinzie had other ideas as she spun me around and massaged my shoulders, her hands slippery. "You're tight in here," she said as her thumbs dug into twin sore areas alongside both my shoulder blades.

"It feels like days ago, but I guess it was just today that I played a basketball game," I said, my voice a near a moan at the pleasure. Not the pleasure I'd been expecting but fantastic nonetheless.

"I think it was yesterday at this point. But it feels like more than a few hours ago." She chuckled as she ran her hands down my chest, across my nipples, under my breasts, and between my legs, but none of those motions were the caresses my body most ached for, even as I angled my hips up, trying to get her to find the spot where I craved her touch most.

"Don't get ahead of yourself," she teased as she pumped conditioner into her hand and started to work it into her hair. "I want you on top of me. Underneath me. And we can't do that until we get out of here."

"If those are the rules…" I pumped body soap into my hands as Kinzie continued to condition her hair and ran my hands all over her body, teasing the same spots where she'd teased me. I laughed when she wiggled her hips for more contact, but I pulled away. "You have to wait." I smirked.

"Luckily," she said as she pulled me into her under the showerhead and kissed me as water poured onto us. "We're basically done." She rubbed our bodies together for good measure and turned the water off.

The bathroom was huge, and without the warm water, I shivered.

"It got cold in here fast, didn't it?" she said as she handed me a towel and wrapped another around herself.

"It really did."

"Guess we need to get dry and get into bed, huh?" She bit her lip as she watched me dry my leg, her hands on her own towel momentarily paused.

"See something you like?" I said.

"Something about how you dry your legs is very sexy. I noticed when I walked in on you in the ice bath."

Heat flooded me, and I dried myself faster. I dropped my towel and pulled hers away to join mine on the floor. "Let's go."

We tumbled onto the bed, and the feel of our skin pressed together had me desperate to hold her closer, yet also move ever so slightly to appreciate the delicate feel. I'd landed on top and used my advantage to slide her legs apart with my knees.

"This feels unfair," she said.

"What part of it?"

"I'm not exclusively a bottom, but for some reason you always seem to top me." She laughed. "Don't get me wrong, it's fantastic. You're fantastic, but I'm not used to it."

"I'm happy to let you top me any time. Okay, almost any time, but not in this second. I need to taste you first. After that, you can top me over and over if you want." I was flexible in bed, but after teasing each other all evening—hell, for months—I had such a need to make her come, I wouldn't have been able to focus if she'd tried to make me come first.

"I will accept this." Her half-smile spurred me on. I slid down her body, leaving a path of light bites on the way.

I nipped at her hip, and she squirmed. "Please don't tease me this time. I need you now, Jane."

"Is this where you want me?" I traced a finger lightly along the outside of her labia. I could see and feel the moisture waiting for me.

"Please. Fuck. Please, now." She ran her fingers through my hair again and scraped her nails along my head, urgent this time rather than caring like they'd been in the shower.

My need to taste her overpowered my desire to tease her, and I spread her open. I could see how wet she was, and my clit pulsed in response. I ran my tongue from her opening up to her clit and circled it a few times before taking her fully into my mouth. I groaned at how amazing she tasted.

I felt the mattress dip as she dug her heels in and angled her hips up a fraction. I brought two fingers to her entrance and pulled my mouth away from her to look up. "Are you okay if I go inside?"

She giggled as she said, "Fuck, please, yes."

I slid my fingers in until her head dropped back onto the bed. When I couldn't watch her anymore, I moved my mouth back to her center. I matched the thrust of my fingers and tongue to the movement of her hips. Her breathing quickened, and I forced myself to keep building and not bring her back down to draw it out. I could feel how frantic she was to come, and I wanted to give her what she wanted.

I knew from the last time that she had plenty of orgasms in her, and I wanted to make her cry out as many times as I possibly could. I didn't know if this was another one-nighter. After all, the saying was, what happens in Vegas, stays in Vegas.

She cried out as the orgasm tore through her, and I didn't even worry if anyone could hear. Normally, that type of expression would have made me uncomfortable, but as she came in my mouth, I didn't think I'd encountered a more perfect sound in my life.

Hours and countless orgasms afterward, I lay on my back with Kinzie's head on my shoulder, running my fingers through her still damp hair. My body was far past relaxation, and I thought I might melt into a puddle. Or maybe it was sublimation as I had felt solid, but now, I felt like I could be floating away. Except that Kinzie was anchoring me in place. "How was that so good again?" I said.

"There's something incendiary here. I've felt it from the second our eyes connected across the bar in Milwaukee. Haven't you?"

"I tried to deny it, but yeah, I guess I have. But I wasn't sure it was real. Or that you felt anything," I said, feeling more vulnerable than I had ever been with her. "I thought it was all in my head. And I thought I could suppress it."

"I don't understand how you ever questioned my feelings for you. Or desire for you." She pushed up on her elbow and looked at me. "I was really sad when I woke up alone the next morning. I wondered if I'd misread your enjoyment of the evening, and you hadn't felt the same things I had."

I tucked a few strands of hair behind her ear. "I'm sorry. I thought you'd want me to be gone when you woke up to avoid any awkwardness. I didn't know why you would want something more with me."

"Because from the moment your eyes met mine, I was enraptured. It took me an eternity to gather the courage to talk to you. Do you not remember me asking you how long you were there for? Even before I took you back to my room, I wanted more. I wanted to have breakfast with you the next morning. See you again. I couldn't explain it, but I just wanted to spend time with you." She tapped my chest and ran her finger slowly over my collarbones. "Stay in touch."

Her words warmed me, yet I didn't understand. "But why? I'm nothing special. Plain Jane."

"Plain Jane? Nothing special?" She sat fully up, tucking her legs under and kneeling, not bothering to cover herself. "Do you really believe that?"

She made me nervous. Par for the course. I swallowed hard. "Yeah, kind of. I'm tall, but I'm not beautiful. Not bad looking, either. Just…plain."

"Oh, Jane." She squeezed my hand, and I couldn't believe she wasn't self-conscious with her body on display. Not that she should have been. Her body was beautiful, but if our positions had been reversed, I would not have been comfortable kneeling in front of her completely naked. "There is nothing plain about you. You have a beautiful face." She placed light kisses across my forehead and cheeks and sighed. "Your body is something most women would kill for. Your arms, your breasts, your stomach, your long legs. I've gotten wet every time I've seen you over the last few months, and images of you lying naked in my bed would pop into my head." She pressed kisses to my nipples, my hip bones, and just above my pubic line.

I wanted to stop her because I'd always felt uncomfortable with compliments, but she climbed over me and straddled my hips, kissing my mouth before I could.

"And more than all that, your heart." She placed her palm over where my heart beat wildly against my ribcage. "You have more heart than anyone I've ever met. The fact that you stuck with a game that hurt you. That hurt you over and over again and still came back year after year and figured out a way to become a dominant player? I am in awe of that courage and determination. You're also kind to your friends and your teammates. You're supportive and caring, and I've never met anyone like you. I was hot for you when I didn't know you at all, and now that I know more of you, I like all of you. I just want to be in your orbit."

I didn't feel courageous, but I didn't want to disagree with her. I didn't want to be so unsure. I knew lacking self-confidence wasn't sexy. But I didn't know how else to be. I'd never been particularly confident unless I was in the groove on the court.

"Okay, you don't have to believe my words. You don't have to tell me what happened to you that makes you unsure of yourself. But believe me when I tell you how attracted I am to you. When I tell you how much I want you. How much I've wanted you from the moment our eyes met across the bar and every moment since then. If you don't believe my words, believe my body."

She grabbed my wrist and slid my fingers into her hot wet folds. I groaned when she shifted back and forth across them.

Her eyes bored into me as she spoke. "You did this to me. Even after a few orgasms, I still want *you*. I've *always* wanted you."

I didn't expect her to get so serious after what I was expecting to be a lighthearted bout of sex, but I needed to hold her close after that. No one had ever made me feel beautiful before. No one had ever made me feel this wanted and desired.

I pulled her down with the hand not buried between her legs and kissed her. I might not have believed everything she said, even though I wanted to. Badly. But I needed her to know how much I appreciated it. How much I cherished her vulnerability with me. I slipped two fingers into her, and we both groaned as I applied pressure to her clit with my palm.

She pushed up as she continued to ride my hand, and watching her move with abandon, eyes closed, breasts swaying over me, was fucking hot. I bit my lip hard to keep from coming as my clit ached with need.

Without opening her eyes and while still moving against me, she scooted away a couple of inches without moving out of reach. I didn't understand until she sat up fully and slid her hand between my thighs, slowly tracing up and down my folds.

I slid my legs apart, needing her touch, which had the added benefit of widening her legs farther for me. My fingers went a little deeper, and I tested out adding a third that she easily took. "Just like that," she whispered.

I had a hard time focusing as her fingers found my clit and started moving. Our hips circled together, steadily picking up speed until I felt her walls tighten around me, and she cried out my name as she came, continuing to grind against me as several waves of aftershocks seemed to roll through her. Those involuntary movements of pleasure sent me over the edge right behind her.

"Fuck," she breathed as she collapsed on top of me. "Do you see what you do to me?"

"I guess. But you do the same to me." My voice was barely a croak.

I would have lay there with her on top of me forever, but she shimmied her hips off mine. I tightened my arms around her, irrationally afraid for a second that she was going to leave. "I'm not going anywhere. I just like to sleep like a flamingo."

I understood what she meant when I felt her thigh slide up my legs until it was across my hips. I instinctively held on to it, tracing small circles with my thumb on her thigh.

"Promise me you'll still be here in the morning," she said.

A twinge of guilt hit my chest. "I'll be here when you wake up. I promise."

"Okay, me too," she said and released a sigh.

I was only awake for minutes before slipping off to sleep, but in those minutes, an unfamiliar sensation that I later recognized as contentment blanketed me for perhaps the first time in my life.

Chapter Twelve

I felt disoriented when I awoke. Sunlight was creeping around my curtains. I was pretty sure it was late, but there was no clock in the room that I could see—fucking Vegas—and my phone was apparently dead since I hadn't remembered to plug it in when I was busy getting Kinzie out of her clothes. I was sure we still had time before the van picked us up, so I plugged in my phone and slid out of bed to use the bathroom while it charged enough to at least let me know what time it was.

I focused on not waking Kinzie; she looked amazing. Her hair fanned across the pillow and the top of her back. The white hotel duvet was mostly covering her, except for her right leg that curled out from under the covers and back across it. Her flamingo leg.

I loved her legs. I would never try to deny it. I didn't know if it was from wearing heels all the time or the yoga, but that leg made my mouth water and wetness flood my pussy. I'd been thinking about ordering room service for breakfast—or whatever meal it was—but a new idea was taking hold.

First, I needed to verify we weren't about to miss our flight. God help me if Maya showed up pounding on my door wondering where I was and why I wasn't answering my phone and found me and Kinzie in bed together. I might have died. Not because I wouldn't tell her—I knew I would—but out of sheer embarrassment that as grown women, we'd gone out, gotten so drunk that we'd forgotten to set alarms or even plug in our phones, and fucked all night.

Happiness surged through me as I checked the time. We still had hours. I'd order room service in a bit.

I peeled back the covers and slid on top of Kinzie, straddling her left leg, the one not up in the flamingo stance. I chuckled thinking about her sleeping like that. I was pretty sure I'd get a horrible cramp in my glute or hurt my knee if I lay in that position. Thinking back to that first night, I had been kind of spooning her when I'd woken up, but I think she had been sleeping like this too. Since she had been the little spoon, however, her knee was up on a pillow.

I traced a finger down her spine, across her hip, and over her thigh. She stirred slightly but didn't wake. I traced that finger up the same path I'd just gone down, and she wiggled and let out an "Mmm," but still didn't wake up.

I ran my fingertips down her back again, but this time, instead of going down her leg, I traced a path down and around her hip until I could flutter my fingers just above her heat. She groaned and pressed her pelvis into my hand, shimmying it from side to side. She didn't open her eyes, but with that encouragement, I kept going.

I caressed up her hip and around her butt cheek until I found her wetness. I ran two fingers from her entrance up to the top of her clit, and when she ground her hips down into my hand again, I found her entrance with my thumb and pressed inside a fraction of an inch. She moaned and pushed back into my thumb to help it.

She had to be awake, right? I pressed kisses to her back and neck.

"Good morning, Jane," she said, her voice still rough from sleep. "Are you going to keep teasing me, or are you going to give me what I want?"

The thin beams of sunlight around the black-out drapes made me feel playful. Also, it was ten a.m., and we were still in bed, making me even more playful. "And what is it that you want, Kinzie Lancaster? I don't think you've said yet." I slid my heat up and down her thigh, showing her how much I was enjoying this.

"Fuck, Jane. Touch my clit. Please." As if to emphasize her point, she ground against my hand harder this time.

I shifted my fingers to her clit, but an idea struck me. "Will you do it?" I whispered.

"Do what?" Her voice was still gravelly.

"Fuck my hand."

Wordlessly, she began to rock her hips, pushing herself back until my thumb was fully inside her. Her body moving against mine, the pressure of her thigh against my center was delicious, and my entire body tingled.

I didn't know if it was because she'd just woken up, or maybe the position was really good for her too, but she surprised me with how fast she came. What also surprised me was that she bit my forearm where I'd curled it under shoulders to hold her close. Not only that she bit me, but how much I'd liked it. It was the bite that sent me coming right behind her without her ever touching me directly as I rubbed myself along the inside of her thigh.

Before I'd even had a chance to catch my breath, Kinzie pushed up and flipped me onto my back and climbed on top. "You ambushed me."

"Only because you were asleep, sleeping beauty." All of her hair draping my face like a curtain made her look like a princess.

"Most definitely the best way I've ever woken up. Can I hire you to be my daily alarm clock?" Before I could react, however, she bent forward and kissed my nipple before lightly biting it.

"Fuck," I said as my hips twitched up, seeking her.

She rolled over until she was under me again. "Slide up here."

"Um, what?"

"Come up here and sit on my face. Please." She smiled a Cheshire Cat smile.

I hadn't ever done that before, but the idea of it made me hot. And wet. So very wet. I crawled up until I was straddling her shoulders. "Are you sure?"

Her brows furrowed, and her lips pursed. "Yes. Do you not like this?"

"No, it's not that," I said as I moved forward until I was hovering over her mouth. I didn't want to hurt her, so I let her guide me into place. "Like this?" I said.

"Exactly like this." She pulled down firmly until my sex was pressed against her mouth, and her tongue was tracing delicious patterns along my center that desperately needed her.

I tried to be cautious and not put too much weight on her, but it wasn't long before my orgasm started to build within me, and I started moving my hips faster and faster. I reached up and palmed my own breast, squeezing my nipple. My hips moved faster, and I pinched harder, tugging my nipple until her free hand pushed mine out of the way and took over.

She lifted me slightly to say, "Your nipples are perfect. Textbook perfect."

I wanted to tease her about owning a textbook about breasts, but everything in *my life* felt completely perfect in that moment, so I didn't spend any time on it, and I couldn't think rational thoughts as she pulled me back down onto her mouth.

She slid one finger into me, and that was all it took to allow my orgasm to rip free. Sensation concentrated in my chest, and my clit erupted, the pleasure rippling out through my fingertips.

I lifted my hips and collapsed forward into the headboard, too tired to keep holding myself up but afraid of suffocating her as I caught my breath. "Holy shit," I panted.

"Yeah, that," Kinzie said as she massaged my thighs.

Sweat dripped along my hairline as I rested my head against the wall. I swiped at it with my wrist even as my heart continued to thunder so loudly, I could feel it in my ears.

"Come down here," she whispered. "I want to hold you."

In an inelegant move, I shimmied my hips until I could lie down. I tried to lie on my side next to Kinzie, but she pulled me right on top of her.

"I don't want to smush you," I said, again worried about my weight.

Her chest bounced beneath me with laughter as she said, "I'm not a fragile flower."

"Obviously not, but I'm also not thin. I have a lot of muscle, which is—"

"Oh, I know you have a lot of muscle." She fluttered her fingertips over the muscles of my deltoids and then down my back to my lats, which jolted as she tickled me. She giggled. "I didn't know you were ticklish. This could be fun."

She tried to tickle me again, but I had enough warning to steel myself against her onslaught. When I didn't squirm or laugh, she said, "Are you really able to control your body's response that way?"

I pushed up onto my elbow to look down at her and nodded.

"This is bullshit."

"Sorry. Yet not sorry. It's all mind over matter."

"But if I catch you off guard…" She tried tickling me again, but I was still ready for it.

"You're going to have to try harder than that. Not to change the subject, but do you want breakfast? Or brunch? I'm kind of starving. I feel like I haven't eaten in days."

Her eyes went wide. "That sounds amazing. Pancakes, maybe? No, waffles with fresh fruit."

"What kind of a monster are you that you would choose waffles over pancakes?" I said in mock horror, which was ironic because I didn't eat either other than on very special occasions. But I had always preferred pancakes.

She pushed me off her as she sat up. I was surprised at how easily she moved me. "I didn't realize that you erroneously believed that pancakes are superior to waffles. I am rethinking everything right now."

I really didn't have strong feelings, but her reaction was hilarious. "You are aware that they're basically the same, right? Same batter cooked differently."

"Sacrilege. That's like saying vodka and french fries are the same thing because they both come from potatoes. I'm not sure if I'm going to be able to get past this, but if you want to try to make me see that you aren't just one bad belief, I'm going to need you to order some waffles with fruit and join me in the shower while we wait." She smirked as she pressed a light kiss to one nipple, then the other, and one more at the top of my vulva. "Shower sexy times are the only way you can possibly make this up to me."

"While I am amenable to proving my worth in the shower, aren't you worried about the room service arriving while we're in there?"

She hopped out of bed and padded naked into the bathroom. Before she closed the door she said, "Room service always takes forever. We have plenty of time. But you should hurry." She winked at me, and seconds later, I heard the shower running.

The thought of ordering room service and not getting dressed to receive it right away just in case it was fast gave me anxiety, but the vision of Kinzie in there alone, soaping herself, conquered my fears, and I quickly ordered her waffles and myself avocado toast with a side of black beans. Although I'd gone a little wild with the tequila the night before—and with all the food and drinks in general while in Vegas—I needed to get back into my real dietary habits. I needed to get back to reality.

But before I did, I was going to join Kinzie in the shower. At the last second, I grabbed the two robes from the hotel closet and took them into the bathroom with me.

The silhouette of Kinzie in the shower behind the steamy glass took my breath away more than the warm humid air did. She was washing her hair, and I felt like I'd walked into an old movie where the tease of what I didn't see was more sensuous than what I did.

She leaned around the shower wall and stuck her head out. "Are you planning to join me in here, or are you just going to watch?"

I swallowed hard to relieve my dry mouth. "Oh, I'm definitely coming." And I did. Twice.

It also turned out to be a good move bringing the robes as the food did arrive as we were finally rinsing all the soap off. I was too embarrassed at the thought of opening the door in a robe, so Kinzie pulled one on while she was still dripping and went to grab the food while I hid in the bathroom.

"My hero," I said as I came out when I heard the door click closed.

Kinzie looked adorable with her hair still dripping as she pushed the room service cart to the windows. Thankfully, the robe was a thick terrycloth, so it didn't look like she was wearing a wet T-shirt, which would have been sexy but awkward for the room service deliverer. Plus, it would have been distracting for me, and I was starving. And we needed to start thinking about packing to avoid being late. "Anytime. I have no shame. I did tip him really well, pretending to be you since he had to wait so long. I hope that's okay."

"I'm a firm believer in tipping well," I said as I helped her position the cart beside the two overstuffed chairs that faced each other in front of the window. "Especially in this day and age."

"Me too, and if he was put off by the fact that I was dripping, he didn't give any indication, which earned him a little more. Let me just wrap my hair in a towel, and I'll be right back."

Kinzie was quick, and we dug into our brunch. She cut off a corner of her waffle and speared a strawberry before putting it into her mouth. She groaned as she bit down. "Oh my God, this is delicious."

Not feeling optimistic that I was going to be in love with my food the way that she was, I cut off a piece of toast. "Eh."

"You should've gotten the waffles, Jane. Do you want to try a bite?"

I knew I should have said no. I needed to get back into a training mindset, but she loaded her fork with waffle, a strawberry, and a blueberry and held it out at me. I couldn't refuse. It was enough of a special occasion to break my vegan rules, right? There were berries. They were healthy. I took the bite from her fork and suppressed my groan. "Oh my God is right. This is fantastic. The avocado toast is fine but nothing special."

"It doesn't even have a fried egg or feta cheese. Why would you bother with such a boring piece of toast? It doesn't even make sense."

"It has pickled onions and tomatoes," I said. At her disbelieving gaze, I sighed. "And it's still the middle of the season, so I need to get back on track after this holiday. And other than special occasions, I don't eat those types of non-vegan things."

"Well, I'm happy to share more of this with you if this morning is enough of a special occasion. How much time to we have before we have to all meet downstairs?"

"I think about an hour," I said, sadness coating my words. I didn't want our bubble to burst, but it was going to soon.

"Ugh. That's soon. Too soon." She looked around my room and chuckled. "I'm pretty sure it's going to take you ten minutes to pack—maybe less—but I'm going to need a little more time. I should probably head back to my room once we finish eating." She sighed as she took another bite. "How do you see this going once we get back to Milwaukee?"

"Um, what do you mean?" I'd assumed that, even though it wasn't a one-night stand since she'd stayed for breakfast, this was just a little Vegas interlude.

"I just mean that I'd prefer it if this isn't the last time we do this. Our connection is intense. I'd like to keep seeing you if you're interested. No pressure. I know you're busy." Her face looked unsure, not a look I'd seen on her often.

I weighed her words, feeling torn because although I'd really enjoyed last night, anything more felt ill-advised. "I don't know how much time I'll really have. Plus, you live in New York, and I live in Milwaukee."

"True, but we're in the same city pretty frequently, even if it isn't every day."

"Fair. But I also really can't afford any distractions. I'm playing really well right now, and I'm in a groove. I don't want to mess anything up and lose my mojo." After just skating by for eight years, my greatest fear was everything disappearing again. I'd started to picture playing for a few more years. Hell, Diana Taurasi was well into her forties and was still playing. I could have another decade. Now that I knew what success felt like, I was even more afraid to lose it.

"Hmm." She tapped her lips. "What if we keep it light? If we both have time, we go out occasionally. If you feel like it's detrimental to your play, we'll call it quits. No strings. Just fun."

I let the idea marinate and couldn't see a downside. Regular sex could definitely be a stress reliever, which would probably help my game. If I felt like it was taking up too much of my free time, I'd step back, but otherwise...I really was starting to enjoy Kinzie's company. "Okay."

"Okay?" Her smile grew brighter.

"Yeah, let's do it." Remembering the possible appearance of being unprofessional, I added, "Can we keep things quiet, though? I don't want anything to seem inappropriate to the team, you know?"

The corners of her mouth turned down nearly imperceptibly, but I'd been studying her for months, so I didn't miss it. "You're not embarrassed, are you?"

"No! I'm just worried about the appearance of something inappropriate. I don't want anyone to think I'm getting special attention or anything. I'm kind of in a weird spot."

"I really don't think it's inappropriate, but I get it, I guess. We can keep it quiet. But will you tell me if you do let someone else know?"

"Of course. You can assume Maya is going to figure it out. She's really perceptive, and she already knows about how we met." I laughed.

Her jaw dropped. "Wait. Maya has known about us this whole time? How'd that come up?"

"She saw how we looked at each other at that post-practice team meeting where they introduced you. We were apparently fairly obvious." I shrugged.

I wasn't embarrassed of Kinzie at all. She was gorgeous, and I was lucky to date her, even casually, but I was uncomfortable with myself. I was playing well for the first time in eight long years. Was I really going to risk it all for my libido?

But I didn't think I really had a choice. I couldn't force myself to stop seeing Kinzie when the pull toward her was undeniable, and she was clearly interested.

I loaned Kinzie a pair of my team warmups to wear back to her room to make it slightly less obvious that she hadn't gone back there last night, though it would've been less conspicuous if I'd had anything *without* the team's name on it. After a lengthy good-bye involving lots of kissing, I took another luxurious shower, delighting in every deliciously sore muscle Kinzie left me with.

I was an athlete. Sore muscles were the norm for me, but the slight stiffness in my inner thighs hit differently from Kinzie rather than lateral moving squats. I ran my fingers over a small love bite that I could see over my left breast, smiling as I remembered when Kinzie had made it. I was pretty sure it'd be covered by my sports bra. I hoped.

After I packed up, I texted Maya to ask if she wanted to meet up and head downstairs together. Given how much I hated flying, I was filled with anxiety the moment I got out of the shower, and I obsessively packed quickly and was ready to leave extra early. I wanted someone to talk to in order to take my mind off the upcoming flight, and spilling everything to Maya about the previous night seemed a lovely way to do that.

Sadly, however, she was running late, so I headed downstairs to wander and people watch. Other than playing—and the activities Kinzie and I had engaged in the previous night, of course—people watching in Vegas was my favorite part. I wandered, looking at the bleary-eyed gamblers who might have been at their tables for hours without a break. The groups of guys who looked like they were at a bachelor party. The couples meandering arm in arm, fawning over each other. Some looked a little panicked, but others looked in love. One couple was sitting at a casino-side café table with sparkling rings on their left fingers. A young Black man with short hair held out a fork twirled with pasta to a giggling young white man with coiffed blond hair sitting across from him. Judging by how they both played with their bands, I suspected they were new and foreign, and I wondered if they'd just eloped. Or maybe they'd married somewhere else and were honeymooning there. They were so cute together, I really hoped they had a forever love.

I wasn't sure if I'd ever find my true love—I wasn't really sure I deserved one—but I wanted to believe the concept existed. I'd never really felt like I belonged anywhere other than on a basketball court, so I didn't have a strong belief that I'd ever find one person with whom I clicked and wanted to spend the rest of my life with. The one person who wanted to spend the rest of her life with me. Maybe that was the bigger issue. I couldn't understand why anyone would.

I wandered around with my unfortunately maudlin thoughts, surprised that the rest of the team still wasn't downstairs. I paused and leaned up against the side of a vacant slot machine to pull out my phone and see if I had a text stating the meeting time had changed.

"Are you lost, ma'am?" a seductive voice said, her mouth so close to my ear, I could feel the heat of her breath. Kinzie.

I couldn't help but smile. She was my sunshine in a bottle all of the sudden. I turned. "No, just wondering where everyone else is." How could she look like she'd just had a full night's sleep when I knew for a fact that she had been up more than half the night? It wasn't fair. I was as presentable as I could make myself, but I knew my eyes still looked tired.

"You didn't see the text?"

I waved my phone in the air. "I was just looking now before you startled me."

"Well, I'll save you looking. There are some nasty thunderstorms moving across the Great Plains right now, so our charter departure time is delayed for two hours. I was going to grab some coffee and happen to be in the neighborhood of your room, but...here you are. Your bag in tow."

"Yep, here I am." I finally got into my app and saw the text from Coach Brandy about the flight and another one from Maya asking if I'd seen Coach Brandy's text and saying she was going back to bed. "And I'm already checked out, which is unfortunate. Shit."

"Well...you could come back to my room with me," she said with a twinkle in her eye. "Or do you know what I'd really like to do?"

I wondered what on Earth she was going to suggest that would be the root of her mischievous expression that didn't involve going back to her bed. "What?"

She stepped into my space and tucked a lock of hair that had slipped out of my ponytail behind my ear. She was a couple of inches shorter than me in tennis shoes, but it didn't feel like it with the big energy she was radiating. She ran a finger from the inside of my elbow to my wrist as she leaned in and whispered, "I'd really like you to drop your bag with the bellhop and come to the aquarium with me."

That was…unexpected. "Really? The aquarium?" I'd been all in on going back up to her room and spending another hour and a half in bed, and the last thing I'd been expecting was Kinzie to want to go to an aquarium. Or any tourist attraction.

"Yeah. I like sharks. And they apparently have a lot of them here. Fourteen kinds or something." Her earnest expression was adorable, and I wanted to give her whatever she wanted. "And I'd really love to share it with you."

"Okay," I said, feeling more excitement than I'd been expecting at the prospect of sharing something that Kinzie really enjoyed.

Dropping my bag at the bellhop desk was quick, though the walk to the aquarium took a while as we had to pass the basketball courts and the rest of the convention center. It felt like a mile. Hell, it might have been. Everything in Vegas was far. Luckily, we still had a lot of time to kill before our flight, and we filled the walk with a lot of getting-to-know each other chatter but delved into some deeper topics too.

"How's your dad doing?" I said.

"He's good. He's pretty much back to normal, though he swears he's working fewer hours and is cutting back on the steak dinners in favor of seafood. The last time we took a client to dinner together, he picked Gallaghers Steakhouse, and although he got a fillet mignon rather than a porterhouse, the better choice would have been the grilled salmon." She sighed, and a look of fondness flashed across her face.

"Do you miss your parents since you've been in Milwaukee and with the team more than home this summer?" I said.

"I do. Dad and I have always been really close. You already know I work for him, and he's grooming me to be the third generation to run Lancaster Consulting, so I'm used to seeing him every day. But my mom?" Kinzie looked away and scratched the side of her neck. "She passed away when I was young. Brain cancer. It's always been only me and him."

"Oh God, I'm so sorry. That must have been really difficult. How old were you?"

"Nine. Sometimes, I have a hard time remembering much about her other than the love I always felt with her, but my dad kept her memory alive. And we have home movies from vacations that we watch sometimes." She shrugged. "Her birthday and stuff like that."

I took her hand and squeezed, but when I tried to let go, she held tight and interlaced our fingers. "That's nice that you can rewatch those happy memories."

"I know. But without Mom, I think it made Dad and me extra close. I hated not being there for him when he was recovering, especially since he didn't have anyone else to care for him at home, but he was insistent that I still take this assignment for him. But in his order of priorities, I think I come first, the company second, and his health third. I've tried to convince him that he needs to take better care of himself, but he's hardheaded." She shook her head with an expression that was a mix of love and exasperation that one would use with an ornery toddler.

"Maybe he focuses on the company because he sees it as your financial security. Your future."

"Probably. I've always known I could do whatever I wanted for a career, but all I've ever wanted was to take over the Lancaster empire." She laughed before she continued, "Not that it's some massive enterprise, but it's a decent-sized company."

When we got to the Shark Reef entrance, I tried to pull out my wallet to pay for my ticket, but Kinzie shooed my hands away.

"I asked you on this little adventure. I'm not going to let you pay for our date."

Date?

I gulped.

"Okay," I squeaked. I was pretty sure she didn't mean *date* date. We'd just talked about keeping things casual and light a few hours before.

Though as Kinzie held my hand and dragged me through the aquarium, it did feel like a date. I could have pulled away, but I didn't want to. Her hand was warm and soft and radiated comfort. Kinzie brushed her lips against mine as we stepped onto an escalator and rode it into what looked like a temple. Dates could still be casual, right?

"Wow. So far, this is the best themed aquarium I've ever been to." Kinzie said.

My knees shouldn't have felt weak at that barely-a-kiss kiss, but they did. At her words, however, I noticed more of our surroundings, including the intricate details of the faux stones of the temple walls and all the lush greenery. "I'm not sure why the aquatic life lives in a temple of some sort, but yeah. This is really neat."

The crocodiles and Komodo dragon were exotic, and some kind of snake slithering out of the water was cool if horrifying. The piranhas were actually a little bit of a letdown, but I was awestruck when we entered the reef tunnel. The shimmering blue-green water around us made me feel like we were walking along the bottom of the ocean in a bubble.

Kinzie gasped and pointed up. "Look at that."

A shark was passing overhead, but in looking up, I moved closer to Kinzie, and she wrapped her arms around me, pulling my back to her chest.

"This is amazing. Thank you for humoring me," she said, her lips just below my ear. "I'm having a good time."

She pressed a kiss to my neck, and although I wasn't normally a PDA person, I still turned in her arms and kissed her. Not an I-want-to-rip-your-clothes-off-now sort of kiss, but more of an I'm-happy-we're-here sort of kiss. "Me too. Although, this wouldn't have been high on my list of must-sees, I'm having fun."

"Good," she said.

I thought she might release her hold, but she didn't, and instead, we stood there in each other's arms watching sea turtles, fish, and sharks swim all around us. Fully immersed in the romance of the afternoon, the romance of being in Kinzie's arms while underwater creatures floated all around, I allowed myself to pretend that this could be real. That there could be something between us more than a casual fling.

"Do you want to check out the shipwreck?" she finally said. "I think that's the last exhibit down here."

I didn't want to break the spell, but we didn't have all day since at some point, we would have to go to the airport. "Sure."

It was surprisingly dark in the shipwreck. It probably shouldn't have been a surprise, since if we'd been in a real shipwreck, there wouldn't have been a lot of light, but it still surprised me. Kinzie pulled us to the glass, nearly pressing her face against it. "Did you see that?"

"What?"

"A shark ray. Look there." She pointed at an animal that looked like a stingray had mated with a small shark and had a baby that looked like a stingray in front but with the back end of a shark.

"It's...cute." I wasn't sure what to say. Cute didn't seem right, but given her excitement, I didn't want to say it was kind of ugly. Though it moved beautifully as it glided through the water and turned to come back at us. "Its eyes are so human," I said, not realizing I was speaking my thoughts aloud until I heard myself.

"I know." Excited Kinzie was the most adorable thing I'd ever seen. She always seemed cool and untouchable at the gym or at games, but her genuine excitement at seeing the shark ray made her more human.

Kinzie continued to marvel at the different sharks that swam by the windows of the fake ship as we slowly moved around the small space. The scene the casino had set when creating this aquarium was pretty amazing for how small it was, but it had nothing on how breathtaking Kinzie was, fascinated as she watched all the marine life swimming around us. I couldn't take my eyes off her. Reminding myself that this was supposed to be casual might be harder than I'd been expecting.

Unable and unwilling to resist any longer, I ended up pulling her into a dark alcove and making out with her until her cell phone buzzed in her pocket, telling us our flight had been further delayed due to high winds. The team had managed to secure extra late checkouts for everyone, and that prompted us to head back to her room. We spent several more blissful hours in her bed before we finally had to head to the airport. All of this weekend felt a little overwhelming and surreal, but I reveled in every second of it.

CHAPTER THIRTEEN

Maya flopped into the seat on the plane next to me with a heavy sigh. Although I'd seen her in the van, I was already in the back when she'd climbed in at the last minute. Then at the airport, she'd run into the restroom while we were boarding, so this was the first I'd really seen of her since the club, and she was looking a little rough, with tired red eyes and a slightly pale face.

"You doing okay?" I asked.

She shook her head as she said, "I don't know, really. I might have just made a huge mistake. Or maybe I didn't. I'm not sure, but I'm exhausted. I didn't get much sleep last night."

Intrigued, I turned in my seat and asked, "What maybe mistake did you make?"

She closed her eyes and quietly said, "I spent last night with Paris." Each word was a staccato bullet. Disjointed but fast, as though she felt disconnected from them.

My jaw dropped. "Paris? Paris, whom I *saved* you from last night? Bleach and ammonia Paris?"

Maya tipped her head back onto the seat behind her and exhaled wearily. "That's the Paris."

"Why? How? What?" The surprise made me eloquent.

"I don't know…I don't know who was pushing all that fucking tequila last night, but I hate them. We were dancing, and you ended up dancing with Kinzie. You were looking friendly, and I was feeling a little lonely. It's been a long time since I've dated anyone, and Paris danced up to me. She started complimenting me again. On how I looked, on my play, and I don't know… I just…got sucked in. She was fucking hot in those black skintight pants of hers and that crop top. God, her abs and hips have always been my Kryptonite…" She trailed off as she stared dreamily at the plain bulkhead in front of us. When I cleared my throat, she continued, "I was barely keeping my hands to myself when you'd broken the tension earlier. After a couple more shots… Fuck."

I laid my hand on her arm and squeezed. "Do you feel like she took advantage of you?" I consciously loosened my jaw. I was livid that Paris would get Maya drunk to soften her defenses and take advantage of her. I knew it was possible that wasn't how it had played out, but that was how it sounded.

"No, nothing like that. I made my own decisions. She convinced me to leave with her, but I told her I wasn't going to just fuck without talking and clearing the air, so we walked around for hours up and down the strip, just talking about everything. She apologized for being horrible. She told me her biggest regret was cheating on me and tossing me aside. There were tears, there was laughing. I don't know. Then, we did go back to her room. And we did fuck. And it was fantastic. So fantastic. But I barely slept, and now my sleep-addled brain is having a meltdown about it all. And the tequila hangover isn't helping." She rolled her head against the seat until she was looking at me rather than the bulkhead in front of her. Her eyes were pleading. "What do you think? She begged me to try again, and I gave in and said I would. Did I make a mistake?"

"I…I'm not sure how to answer that. I hate how she's made you feel in the past, but I don't know. Maybe she's changed? Matured?" I didn't really believe that. There was something snakelike about Paris that made me not like her from the moment I met her, but I didn't want Maya obsessing about it when it was perhaps too soon to tell if Paris was being genuine in her regret.

Also, I hadn't known Maya when she was with Paris, so I hadn't seen firsthand how they were together.

Maya made a growling sound in her throat, but movement in the aisle caught my eye.

Kinzie.

It wasn't like I hadn't seen her in those clothes already today. She'd been dressed when we'd shared one last searing kiss before I'd left her room so we could head downstairs separately. Yet, seeing her walk toward me in those sexy jeans had my heart rate kicking up.

Her lips fluttered into a smile, and a bouquet of butterflies took flight in my stomach.

Maya hit me in the arm once Kinzie had passed. "Oh. My. God. I'm not the only one. You slept with her last night." Neither of those were questions. "You sneaky minx." She smiled for the first time since getting on the plane, and I decided to not play with her or be coy.

"I did." Even if she wasn't sure about whether being with Paris was a mistake for herself, she'd always been in camp Kinzie for me.

"Tell. Me. Everything. Was the first time a fluke, or was it just as good last night?"

I shushed her. "We're keeping it on the DL for now. And it's nothing serious. I'm too busy for serious. But, yes, it was fantastic."

Maya squealed, and I shushed her again.

"Please be cool and not gush like a schoolchild. I don't want Kinzie to know we're talking about her when she comes back through."

Maya said, "Sorry," as Kinzie came even with our seats and leaned down.

Fuck. Of course Kinzie was there.

"It might be a little too late for that." She smirked. "But I don't mind. I like knowing I'm in your thoughts." She gave me a sly smile and brushed her fingers across my shoulder before standing fully and heading back to her seat with Coach near the front of the plane.

Kinzie and I had made the decision to head to the lobby separately and sit apart on both the van ride and the flight home, but I did feel a pang of regret that I wouldn't have her hand to hold while we were taxiing and taking off. That had made the flight much more pleasant on the way to Vegas, but it was the right move.

Even if it only took one look for Maya to know what was going on, I didn't think everyone else would figure it out that quickly. I hoped they didn't anyway.

Even when I wasn't playing much, the time after the all-star break felt like it moved twice as fast as the beginning of the season; each successive game felt like it meant more than the last. And since I was now in the starting rotation, the time seemed to go even faster. The Pitbulls were in fifth place in the league. We were going to make the playoffs as long as we didn't fall apart, but now it had become about jockeying for position.

No one wanted to face Vegas, New York, or Indiana in the first round, so holding on to the number five spot was important. Or if we could climb into the number four spot, we would secure home court advantage for at least the first round of the playoffs.

Our practices were still fun, but they were a little more intense as everyone knew what was at stake over the next few short weeks. My mind wandered as I saw Kinzie enter the gym, and I flashed back to a few nights ago in her hotel room when I had her on her hands and knees while I fucked her with the strap-on she was bold enough to put in her carry-on luggage. We had both come so hard that I was surprised none of the neighbors had heard us and called the hotel's front desk to complain.

In that moment of inattention, I lost Vicky, who I was supposed to be guarding, and when I didn't get around the screen the way I should have, she popped up for an easy midrange jumper.

"Come on, Gray," Coach Carr yelled. "Head in the game. That was a piss-poor screen you should've easily run around. And, Ruby, your feet weren't set. Vicky, you've got to cut closer to Ruby on the screen. You two got lucky there. If this was a game, you wouldn't have gotten free, or that would have been a foul on Ruby."

"Sorry, Coach," the three of us all yelled.

"Run it again, and everyone, focus like you want to win," Coach yelled.

I gave myself one more brief second to check out Kinzie's legs in that skirt suit and heels before forcing my concentration back onto the court. I knew I was going to be seeing those legs up close and personal later. Kinzie had been in New York for the last five days, but she was back, and I was going to her hotel after Maya and I had smoothies, so I needed to focus on the present moment as Brigitte always reminded me and think about those legs wrapped around me later. I swallowed hard and huffed on my exhale while I got set to defend again.

"I'm gonna burn you again, Jane," Vicky said with pretend heat. Since that night in Vegas when Kinzie and I had taken care of her and tucked her into bed, we'd become friends. "Especially if you keep your eyes on Kinzie the whole time."

"Bring it, Vlack. I got your number," I said. Sometimes, she teased me a little about Kinzie, but I never confirmed nor denied anything. I wasn't even really sure what she remembered from that night since we'd never talked about it, so I assumed all of her shit was her trying to figure out exactly what was going on. But at least she hadn't said anything to the rest of the team. I was pretty sure she hadn't, anyway.

Regardless, I stuck closer and got around the screen faster that time, denying Vicky the open look. I mouthed "boom" to her after, and she surreptitiously shot me the bird.

I had a good time with Maya at smoothies, and she caught me up on the Paris drama. There wasn't much drama—yet—but I was still worried about her. Next week, we were going down to Indiana for back-to-back games against the Fever on Friday night and Sunday afternoon.

Maya was planning to spend time with Paris after the game and when we weren't practicing on Saturday. She asked if I'd cover for her, which felt kind of icky, but I understood her not wanting to tell the team she'd started dating Paris again. And it wasn't like I could judge since I was secretly sleeping with Kinzie.

Kinzie, who yanked opened the hotel room door the second I knocked. Kinzie, who looked fantastic in nothing but the hotel's plush robe that was gaping enough to give me a tantalizing view of her cleavage.

"What if I'd been room service? Or housekeeping with extra towels?" I said as I took her in my arms and walked her backward into the room, kicking the door closed behind me.

"Luckily for me, I haven't ordered either of those things. I was just getting ready for you to get here," she said, reaching for the zipper on my hoodie, having already slid my duffel bag from my shoulder and allowing it to hit the ground with a thud.

Hours later, we lay in bed, Kinzie's back to my front, her hips pressed into mine, catching our breath. I'd just made her come again in that position, my right hand between her thighs, my left hand massaging her breast and toying with the nipple. I'd never been one to be a spoon sleeper, but feeling entirely content, there was no way I was going to let go of her. I wished I'd remembered to bring the strap-on she'd left in my possession last time, but I'd forgotten it in my hurry to make it on time to practice that morning.

"You are something else, Jane Gray." Kinzie's voice was a near purr.

"I could say the same thing about you, Ms. Lancaster." I traced my right hand along the firm line of her hip. "I missed you this week." I couldn't believe I'd just said that. I blamed my blissfully relaxed brain after my most recent orgasm. Riding Kinzie's face had recently become my favorite position, which was strange because I'd never been able to relax enough before, but she just made me comfortable in a way I never could with past girlfriends.

Before I could backpedal or rephrase it as missing all the orgasms or something, Kinzie said, "I missed you too. It was a long week in New York. I'm happy you were free tonight."

She wiggled her ass against me, and another surge of arousal coursed through my veins as I pulled her infinitesimally closer. I sighed in relief as I figured that gesture meant she'd mostly missed the sex and must have thought I meant the same thing. I *had* meant it as I missed her company, but I didn't want to embarrass myself by admitting that.

But I didn't know what to say when she said, "I missed seeing you and talking to you too. Not just that I missed this." She squeezed my ass. "Why does just being near you feel so good, Jane?"

Thrown off-balance, I said, "I don't know, but it feels good to me too. I'm not sure if I've ever felt this comfortable with anyone."

"Really?"

I couldn't believe I was about to share all this with her, but not being able to see Kinzie's face made it a little easier to be open. Vulnerable. "I've always struggled with fitting in. In high school, I was always this tall weirdo freak. I never dated, but I also wasn't out back then. I was friendly with a couple of my teammates, but we weren't close. They played basketball because their parents had put them in it at a young age, but none of them were that into it. I don't know why they still played. We went to state all four years when I was on the team but only because of me."

Kinzie laughed, and I realized what I'd said.

"Shit that sounds really horrible."

"It doesn't. I laughed because, honestly, it's the first thing I've heard you say that almost sounded like a brag. It was a little sexy." She laughed again, and it was disarming even as I was sure I was blushing furiously. I was happy she was facing away from me and couldn't see it.

"I was one of the best basketball players in the state. It's a fact, not a brag. But Vermont isn't a huge state, so take that with a grain of salt about my abilities." I could keep talking as long as I didn't look at her, though I was unsure why I was sharing this much except that it felt…good. "I played because I loved it, even if it made me even more of a freak, and I was hoping I'd be able to use it to get my degree for free. But I tried to minimize my height off the court to fit in. I made myself as small as I could. I didn't want everyone to think of me as an oaf. I tried to make myself Plain Jane—"

"Jane," Kinzie said, what sounded a lot like pity infusing that one word, and tried to roll in my arms, but I tightened my grip and held her as she was, facing away from me.

"All of that to say that I'm not great at making friends. Or at fitting in. But I feel like I belong when we're together."

She interlaced her fingers with mine. "I'm glad." She caught me off guard and peeled my fingers off her shoulder, quickly rolling as she pushed me onto my back. She straddled my hips and pushed my hands over my head.

I probably could have broken her grip if I'd tried, but I was frozen. It felt like her eyes were boring into me. She said, "But I want you to hear me when I tell you, you're not an oaf, and you're certainly not plain. I'm sorry asshole kids made you think that, but my God, you are the sexiest woman I've ever dated. Ever been with. You're like Artemis. A tall, beautiful, graceful goddess."

I felt my face flame. I wasn't good at receiving compliments and didn't know how to get more comfortable with it. I opened my mouth to speak without a clue what I was about to say.

"I know, I know. You're the worst at taking a compliment gracefully. I'm sorry to embarrass you." She pressed a kiss to my nose. "Thank you for sharing some of your insecurities with me. As I told you in Vegas, I won't press you for more, but please know I am here for you. And you are...I wish I were a poet. I would write sonnets about how beautiful you are. But since I'm not, I'll just have to show you."

Before I could respond, she captured my lips with her own, her mouth urgent and full of need. Her passion carried me away, my last coherent thought was that I needed to stop letting myself be emotionally vulnerable with her when we were in bed. I really didn't want her always feeling like she was responsible for shoring up my pathetic self-confidence.

Seeing my agent's face appear on my phone, I tapped the side of my earbuds to answer her call while in my Uber heading to some charity golf outing. "Hey, Nelly. To what do I owe the pleasure?"

I'd gone through a dry spell where Nelly hadn't called me at all. A lot of that was last year when I wasn't even on a WNBA team and barely had any playing time on my French FIBA team. Seeing her on my screen now made my heart jump: worried something bad had happened and also worried something good might be happening.

"Jane." Her sultry voice was like hot honey coating every word. I didn't think I'd enjoyed anyone saying my name more than Nelly. Maybe Kinzie, but I wasn't going there. "I just had a *very* interesting call with Emma Braun about you."

"Emma Braun?" I racked my brain trying to match the name with the job position. Were they a GM somewhere? A marketing executive?

"The GM of the London Lions."

"Oh. Didn't they just win the EuroCup last year?"

"That's them. Anyway, Emma's been following you this season and wants you to come play with them in October. And the offer is generous. The best I've received for you. I know you said you were done playing overseas. But you said you were done playing in the W too, and here we are with you playing the best basketball of your life, even as you're on the wrong side of thirty."

"Way to make me feel old. I'm going to remember this in your Christmas bonus," I said, hoping to get a rise out of her.

"Don't start with me, Jane. Anyway, I think it's worth entertaining, even if you decided to retire from the WNBA before next season. But I highly doubt that's happening."

"As of today, I'm planning to play again next year. Though as a geriatric player, who knows what next year holds?" Despite my words, I didn't feel nearly as old as I felt last year. Or even three years ago.

"Ha. If you're geriatric, I'm extinct, so watch your language there, pipsqueak."

I scoffed. "If you ever call me pipsqueak again, I'm going to be forced to fire you."

"Hold off on firing me until you see this deal I've negotiated on your behalf. I think you'll be sending me a thank-you card."

"Thanks, Nelly. I'll take a look as soon as we hang up."

"I also received a call from Ekaterinburg, but I—"

"I hope you said absolutely not." There was no amount of money that could get me to play in Russia after the past few years.

"I told them I'd talk to you but that I highly doubted you'd have any interest."

"Good. The truth is, I'd never touch a basketball again before I'd go to that country and play for them."

Nelly laughed on the other end of the line. "I figured, but I'll be more diplomatic when I talk to their GM. You never know where he'll land, but I'm not sad that you're against playing in Russia again. Nothing good could come of that, other than more money."

When I hung up, I was on cloud nine, but at the same time, a little sadness hung around my heart. I really thought I was done playing overseas, but as I looked over the London Lions's offer, I knew it was way too good to even consider rejecting. While I wasn't poor by any means, it was an impossible number to turn my back on. I'd been saving plenty over the years, but I'd have a lot more flexibility if I took that payday.

Except that I was tired of playing overseas. It was exhausting playing nearly year-round. But the Lions wanted to repeat their win and apparently wanted me as one of the faces of their team. At least London was one of the easiest European cities to get back and forth from.

But a little slice of me had been hoping Kinzie and I would keep up our casual arrangement over the winter, but it wasn't like Kinzie would be interested in waiting for me.

I wasn't interested in that either, I tried to tell myself.

As my Uber pulled in, I saw Kinzie standing outside the clubhouse. How had she beat me? I left her hotel before she had. But seeing her made me smile. "Good morning," I said, just in case anyone was within earshot.

"Good morning, Jane." She extended her hand to shake. "I don't know why I'm being formal," she said as she leaned in. "We're the first ones here, so we really could've ridden out here together."

Her smile made my legs feel like Jell-O, which was embarrassing. "You never know when someone is watching though, I guess, right?"

She cleared her throat. "Definitely," she said, though her smile looked forced, and I wondered if keeping our arrangement private was wearing on her already. "Anyway, how'd your Lyft bring you? I can't believe I beat you."

"I honestly don't even know. I was a little distracted."

"Oh?" She arched an eyebrow at me and gave me a lascivious look that made my panties damp. "By what? Memories of your sizzling hot *lover* whose bed you just jumped out of?"

"Almost, Romeo." I laughed when she pursed her lips into a pout. "Fine, I was at first, but my agent called."

Her smile brightened. "Oh really? Something good on the horizon?"

"I guess, yeah. The London Lions want me for the offseason." I looked at the ground as I spoke.

"You guess it's good news? That's fantastic, Jane. London is such an amazing city. I'm excited for you."

"Thanks," I said, though my heart fell a little bit at her enthusiasm for me to leave the country.

"Seriously, I'm not surprised that you're in demand. Do you want to celebrate tonight? I know you probably still have to work out this afternoon since I'm monopolizing you, Maya, and Vicky at this celebrity golf tournament and that you won't want to do a fancy dinner because you're in season, but what about a lakefront picnic with salads and sparkling water?"

That sounded incredibly romantic. I wanted to say yes, but I was worried about developing romantic feelings for Kinzie, so I hesitated.

"Come on, Jane. I'll take care of all the details while you're working out, and I'll text you where to meet me. Just let me know when you're heading back to your place to shower." Her voice was pleading, and I couldn't resist. I didn't think I'd ever resisted her when she directly asked me anything, going back to the night we'd met.

"Okay."

Her smile bloomed full and filled my heart. I tried to silence it, but it seemed to have a mind of its own.

The golf tournament was an unmitigated disaster. I tried telling them I hadn't played golf in a decade, but I'd held a club before, and apparently, the tournament sponsors really wanted me. Thus, I got roped in. However, even in a scramble where each member of the foursome played the best ball on every stroke, I spent most of the day looking for my ball in the rough. My play looked even worse because Vicky was apparently a few swings on the driving range away from being a pro. While I climbed through knee-high grass hoping a snake wouldn't eat me, she stood on the course, leaning against the golf cart, chatting with the lesbian couple, Dorothy and Amy, who'd placed the winning bid on us in the fundraiser.

It was pathetic really, except for the highlight of the day when Kinzie zipped up in her golf cart, looking sexy in her preppy golf attire. Who knew a white pleated skirt and collared sleeveless shirt with a sun visor would get my heart pumping, but it did.

Okay, it wasn't just the clothes. She was riding with Jada, who was wearing a similar outfit and did nothing to my sympathetic nervous system. It was Kinzie. They were bouncing back and forth on the course, checking on all the foursomes as well as taking photos and videos they needed for marketing and branding. Today, when I was nearly up to my armpits in tall grass or traipsing through sandpits, I found the camera particularly annoying.

But how could I be annoyed when on the other side of the camera, Kinzie was smiling at me?

After eighteen agonizingly slow holes of golf and an hour of lunch with Dorothy and Amy—where they were surprisingly complimentary about my golf game—I was able to slip away and get to the gym. Despite my desire to rush through it and meet up with Kinzie again, I forced myself to take my time and not skip anything. I ran my seven miles, lifted weights, and didn't skip a shot in my shooting practice. If I missed a shot, I restarted the count as I'd been doing for a few weeks.

To make up for it, I took the fastest shower ever. The level of my desire to be with Kinzie was a little embarrassing, but it was sweet that she'd planned a picnic for us to celebrate my contract, even though it made me feel awkward.

Kinzie had texted me to meet her at Veteran's Park and dropped a pin to help me find which tree she was lounging under.

The park was surprisingly empty given what a beautiful late summer night it was.

"There's the woman of the hour," she said as I approached.

I felt myself blushing and wished I could control it, but Kinzie's smile grew wider the closer I got.

She had a blue and white checkered blanket spread across the grass close to the lake, with a wicker picnic basket sitting on one corner. She patted the spot next to her. and I sank onto it, my knees popping on the way down.

She winced. "Ouch, did that hurt?"

"No, that was nothing. You clearly haven't heard my knees first thing in the morning."

"I'm glad they don't hurt, and I probably would have heard them in the morning if you weren't such a late sleeper." She rested her hand behind my hip and leaned in and kissed me on the top of my nose.

"Hey, I'm an athlete. I have to get rest so my body can heal. And someone." I tapped the top of her chest. "Has been keeping me up a little late."

"You have no one to blame but yourself for that. You're irresistible." She leaned in again, but rather than a sweet kiss to my nose, she brought her lips to mine.

I forgot we were in a public park when her tongue lightly brushed my own. I groaned softly when her fingers grazed my cheek.

"I really am proud of you. Though selfishly, I wish you were staying in the States through the winter."

My skin felt prickly, and I wasn't sure what to say. "I hadn't planned to play overseas this year, but it was hard to refuse the offer they made." I bit my lip. "Honestly, I know my play has been solid this year, but I'm worried it's a fluke. That I'm going to go and be terrible in London with a different team. My agent is negotiating with the Pitbulls for a new contract next year, but I worry it's all going to collapse."

She squeezed my hand and scooted closer. "Hey."

"God, I'm sorry. I don't mean to dump on you. You're not my therapist, yet I feel like every time we're together, I'm spilling all of my pathetic insecurities on you." I buried my face in my hands in embarrassment, wishing I could crawl into a hole. Wishing I could have pumped myself up before I'd sat down so I would've been able to act more confident. To feel more confident.

"You're fine." She pulled one of my hands away from my face. "And solid is an understatement. You're kicking ass this season. And I'm always willing to be your biggest cheerleader. Even if I can only do it privately. You're amazing, Jane Gray, and I'm happy to call you a friend. I'm especially happy to call you a sexy friend." She nudged me with her shoulder.

"Thanks." I gave her a smile, but it felt weak as I was still embarrassed.

"No one is confident about everything all the time."

"I know. You seem to be, though."

"Ha! Have I got you fooled. You remember that first night? At the hotel, when I propositioned you in the elevator lobby?"

"I don't know if propositioned is the right word, but it's not like I could forget that night." Goose bumps broke out on my arms thinking back to it. And the nights we'd shared since.

"Propositioned is *exactly* the right word. But I was scared to death chasing after you. But I just knew I'd regret it if I never saw you again. I could tell that you'd be special to me. So I summoned all my courage and chased after you. Because sometimes, the risk is worth the fear. Sometimes, being too forward"—she ran her index finger down my forearm—"and going after the right thing is worth the possibility of getting shot down."

I shivered at her touch. "I don't think I've ever been accused of being too forward anywhere."

"You were pretty forward with me a few times in Vegas." I felt myself blush. "And I've seen you play. You're pretty damn forward on the court."

"I *am* a forward. Being forward there is my job."

"Do you always feel confident when you walk out there?"

"Of course not," I said, though I knew a lot of players were confident at all times.

"Then, what do you do to find your confidence?"

"Honestly, I pretend to be someone else." I blushed, remembering our first time. "I kind of did that the first night."

Kinzie's eyes went wide. "You pretended to be someone else?"

I looked away, hoping I hadn't hurt her feelings. "Yeah, I'd never done something like that in my entire life. I'm painfully shy, and I overcome it on the court when I'm playing, but to say yes to you, to get naked with you—a stranger—took much more confidence than I think I've ever had. But something about you spoke to something in me, and I didn't *want* to say no to you, so I channeled someone else. Someone bolder. Someone more confident. I might have done that in Vegas too."

"I'm awfully glad you did. Because I like this a lot." She wagged a finger between us. "And without that first night, I don't think we'd be here."

My instincts told me to brush her words off, but something in them rang true. I liked what was going on between us too. "I think you're right."

"I've enjoyed flirting with you all season, but I never would have been that forward with you at work if we didn't have a history." I loved her teasing smile but didn't believe her words.

"You haven't been flirting with me all season."

"I can assure you, I have been. Flirting with my words. With my looks. I tried to hide it at first, but I've grown bolder as the season has come along. You really haven't noticed?"

"I...no."

"You're so oblivious it's cute. Or it would be if it wasn't maddeningly frustrating. I think we would have found our way here sooner if you'd noticed. Or maybe believed what you were experiencing is a better way to phrase it."

I rolled my eyes and decided it was time for a subject change. "How was New York this week? Did you spend all of your time there in meetings?"

"I did," Kinzie said and sighed. "It was a little tedious, really. I used to eat that shit up, and now…I don't know. I just wanted to get out of there and get back here. I feel like I'm making a difference here. I don't think I told you, but I've signed the softball and NWSL teams down in Chicago and am working on their branding now. I just hop on the Amtrak down there on days I need to meet with those teams."

I laughed. "That's an interesting twist from a woman who told me she didn't even like sports the first night we met."

"How about that, huh? All kinds of things have been changing for me."

Although my natural instincts pushed me toward disbelief and assuming Kinzie was just trying to make me feel better, looking back, maybe she was telling me the truth, and she actually had been flirting with me. But that didn't really change anything, did it?

I was still going to be traveling and didn't want to distract myself from my game. Yet, sitting there, on a picnic blanket, drinking sparkling apple juice and eating carrots and hummus, I gave myself permission to imagine, just for a few minutes, what it might be like if it did.

Chapter Fourteen

"Okay. Give me all the deets about what's going on with you and Kinzie," Maya said as we slid into the booth. We had a game that evening and were grabbing lunch before we went home to nap.

I took a deep breath as we'd had such a busy travel schedule that Maya and I really hadn't had a chance to catch up.

"Stop being coy with me. You know I can't take it. And I know she's the reason you've been busy when we aren't on the road."

I picked up the menu even though I knew what I was going to order—stir-fried veggies with brown rice and crispy tofu—because I knew the longer I made Maya wait, the more impatient she'd get, and for some reason, that brought me glee. She really was like the little sister I'd never had. "Maybe I'm holding out, waiting to hear about what's going on with you and Paris."

"We're still seeing each other. But that's all you're getting until you tell me about Kinzie. While I've been spending my nights on the phone, I know you've been with Kinzie. You haven't even come over to visit Francesca."

"Because you've been on FaceTime every night."

She leveled a disbelieving gaze at me.

"Okay, fine. Yes, I've been with Kinzie most nights when she's in town. I've been going to her hotel to avoid any speculation from the team since I still live in the team apartments."

"Hotel trysts." She pursed her lips. "Sounds tawdry, yet glamorous."

"Oh my God. She lives in a hotel when she's here. Though, I guess I've made it a little more illicit than it would otherwise be by insisting on secrecy."

"It just sounds like a little role-playing. Oh wait, you met each other in an activity other couples might try as role-playing." Maya laughed hard enough that that she smacked herself in the chest a few times trying to catch her breath while tears rolled down her face. "Have you re-role-played that night yet?"

"It's a little funny but not that funny, and no, we haven't. I mostly just meet her in her room. Except for last night. She took me on a picnic to celebrate my contract with the Lions."

"How romantic. Where'd you go?"

"Some park right on the lake. And it was romantic. Kind of. We stayed there until it got dark, staring at the night sky and looking at the stars we could see through the light pollution."

"That doesn't sound quite as light and fun and carefree as you've described your relationship. Are you two growing real feelings?"

"No, of course not. She just wanted to help me celebrate. That's all." But even as I said the words, they didn't ring entirely true. Something felt different inside me recently, but I couldn't explain it. Or even put my finger on it.

Maya gasped. "Oh my God. You're falling for her. I knew it."

"I…no," I denied, but it was futile.

"I can see it on your face. And I think it's perfect because I'm very certain she's already fallen for you."

"No way. She lives in New York. I'm about to live in London. She's too practical for that." I wanted to believe her, but I was afraid.

"She's not that practical. She's been flirting with you all season—"

"She's in sales and marketing. She flirts with everyone. It's part of her personality," I tried to object. That was what I'd told myself the previous night when I'd finally had to admit that Kinzie had been flirting with me all season. I'd just been oblivious.

"Bullshit. She's never once flirted with me—and let's be serious, I'm super cute if a little short—nor anyone else that I've seen. And in Vegas, you said she hadn't been flirting with you all season. You can't claim you don't see her flirting with you while you do see her flirting with the rest of the team. She's wanted you all season. And not in the 'one more night of fun' way. I'm fairly certain you're the reason she's spending all this time in Milwaukee and at our games. People don't do that if it's just fucking."

I opened my mouth to deny her words, but the server placed our food in front of us, and the sweet yet spicy scent of my stir-fry distracted me.

"And another thing." She cut off a piece of her salmon with a fork and pointed it at me as she spoke. "You told me you were afraid of your game going to shit if you started seeing her, which is why you wanted to keep it light. I'm not sure if you've noticed, but your game has gotten *better* since the all-star break, you know, like with your thirty-five points the other night?"

"Okay, yes, that was one game that was amazing," I said, not wanting to let her conflagrate one game into a pattern.

"Look at the stats, Jane. I think you're playing better because falling for someone inspires you, and regular sex relaxes you. Could be unrelated but I believe there's some correlation there. Now me? My game's been going to hell since Vegas."

"That is not true," I said.

"It is. I had a game the other night with more turnovers than assists. I'm distracted, and I don't know what to do." She huffed as she put her fork down with a clank.

"Okay, yes, that one game against Vegas, but they have really fast hands."

"Agreed, but we played them twice earlier in the season, and I had one turnover in each game. I'm just having a hard time focusing sometimes. Fucking Paris. Unlike you, I never play well when I'm falling."

I wanted Maya to be happy, but Paris just seemed like such a bad fit for her. "Are you FaceTiming with her at night?"

"When she can. And when I can. Obviously, we both have games. And are busy with stuff." She took another bite and chewed, but it seemed like maybe she wanted to say something more, so I waited. "At least she is," Maya mumbled without making eye contact.

That bitch.

I wasn't sure what to say because I'd questioned Paris's intentions the whole time, but I didn't want to hurt Maya. "Is she doing extra practices or something?" I finally said.

"I don't know. Maybe. Probably. We do talk some every day. And have had some yummy phone sex. FaceTime sex." She turned a little red, and I couldn't imagine having sex over FaceTime. Being on display like that. Jesus.

"Then why are you distracted?"

"I don't know. She seems like she's interested, yet she's busy a lot. And she's burned me before. And it's not like I'm thinking about her during games, per se. I'm just having a little trouble focusing occasionally. And I just make dumb mistakes. I'm frustrated with myself."

"What about focus breathing? Have you ever tried that or gotten that lesson from Brigitte?" It had really helped me take my game to the next level earlier in the season and was probably the reason I'd been voted an all-star, honestly.

"I don't think so. I've never had a focus problem before. What do I do?"

I was a little shocked there was something I could teach Maya. "It's really easy. You just focus on your breath. How it feels in your lungs. How it feels in your nose. How it sounds.

And then, once you've blocked everything else out, you can focus on the game."

"Huh. And you've been doing that all season?"

I nodded. "Starting right about when I turned the corner from playing fairly well to playing amazing."

"Oh my God, Jane."

"What?" I panicked a little.

"You just said you played amazing. I didn't know if you were ever going to truly believe it."

I thought about it for a second. "I didn't know I had it in me, but it's true, right? I feel like it's true."

She flashed a big smile. "It's true. You're playing amazing, and I'm just happy you've finally seen it. Even if it's taken you nearly the whole season."

I wasn't sure if it was playing better that was making me more confident in the game and with Kinzie or if Kinzie's faith in me was making me more confident elsewhere. Or if Coach's and Maya's and the rest of the team's faith in me helped me both on and off the court—maybe it was a combination of all of those things—but things were feeling different in my life all of the sudden. Different, but good for a change.

I used the towel one of the assistants handed me to wipe sweat off my forehead and focused on my breathing during the final time-out while the coaches huddled and drew up a play. There were forty seconds left, and we were down by one with no time-outs left. Seattle had called this one, which was a gift. I was sure that Coach was drawing up a plan both for defense as well as on our next possession since it wasn't like they would take another time-out to give us time to plan.

The arena was rocking, which was amazing. The energy coursing through the sold-out crowd was feeding all of us. It was the second to last game before the playoffs, and at the all-star break, we weren't expecting to have a shot at securing the third slot in the playoffs. Yet, here we were, and if we lost tonight, we'd still have one more chance to grab the third spot, and even if we landed in fourth, we'd still have home court in the first round, which, if the crowd was like this every game, would be a huge advantage. No one had predicted this for us preseason. Hell, I'd never predicted this for myself period.

But I needed to stop focusing on all of that. Breathe, I reminded myself.

I followed the technique I'd just taught Maya a few days ago. Inhaling, I focused on the sensation of my lungs expanding, the feel of my nostrils flaring to allow more air in. Exhaling, I felt the slight tickle in my nose. I did that a couple of more times and focused on the feel in my body when I made a perfect jumper and the way I could feel from the second the ball left my fingertips that it would find the bottom of the net. I immediately felt more centered. I looked over and saw Vicky saying something to Maya, but the coaches came back and gathered us in our huddle.

Coach leaned in and gave us our defensive assignments. I would stay with Brenna North, but unlike the rest of the game, we would switch on any screens to give them a different look. If we were able to get an offensive possession, I'd inbound to Maya and help her break a press if needed. They wouldn't want to foul because they were in the bonus already, so we weren't anticipating a full-court press…maybe just an extra defender to be a nuisance. But if they did, Brittany would also be on standby for a high pass.

Once we got across the half-court, Maya was to eat the clock until there were about ten seconds left, provided they hadn't scored. I would initiate movement by cutting across the top of the key while Ruby moved to the elbow to give Maya a screen. Once clear, she was supposed to pass to me to drive where I could shoot or pass depending on what my look was.

We'd drilled all of this countless times, but a touch of nerves tingled in my fingers. I wiggled them. We stood. Everything moved fast.

Maya yelled, "Together on three, family on six. One, two, three."

The whole team and I shouted, "Together."

"Four, five, six," Maya said.

"Family," we all answered.

"Let's fucking go," Maya said and hit me on the ass as we walked onto the court.

"We got this," I said, feeling it. We did have it. I swung my arms, giving myself a bear hug, then swung them behind me with my arms bent like chicken wings. It probably looked silly, but it was my routine. It grounded me and stretched out the tightest areas of my body.

Maya, Brittany, Ruby, Mercedes, and I circled together on the court waiting for Seattle to come out of their huddle.

"We have plenty of time here. Brittany, Ruby, whoever ends up underneath, focus on boxing out. We need that board. Looks like their two rookies are still going to be on the floor, and although they're good, you're going to be able to get position on them."

"You know I'm a rookie, right?" Brittany said as she laughed.

"Yeah, but you're better. You've got this. Let's do it."

We bumped fists and spread out to defend. North was inbounding. I took my place in front of her to guard and make inbounding a little harder. The ref hadn't blown the whistle or tossed the ball to her yet, so I looked up and saw Kinzie leaning against the side of the bleachers in the tunnel, arms crossed, staring at me.

A few months ago, that probably would have made me so nervous, I would have blown this assignment, but instead, I felt warm. Her confidence in me gave me a boost in my own confidence, and I smiled back. She winked at me, and I felt happy flutters low in my belly. I thought I'd been convinced we were going to win before, but certainty flooded me after seeing her.

If I'd had more time, I probably would have overanalyzed it, but the ref blew the whistle, and it was game time. I gave North my most intimidating glare as I spread my arms and legs in what I always thought of as my starfish pose. I was about an inch taller than she was, but to make myself bigger and block her view as much as I could, I jumped up and down.

Just before the ref got to five, she was able to pass the ball in to their center. I didn't think that was her first choice, but it didn't matter. The center passed the ball out to their point guard, and I stayed with North as she cut crosscourt. North tried to jockey for position, but I stayed on her and kept her from getting an open look.

When I saw one of their guards go up to shoot from my peripheral, I spun and watched for the rebound, keeping North behind me as best as I could to keep her out of position for the rebound. The resounding ring as the ball hit the rim was music to my ears, and I was in great position as I jumped and snagged the ball before North even had a chance.

We were still only down by one. They pressed harder than I'd been expecting after I passed the ball back to Maya, so I ran and cut until she had a clear pass to me. After we broke their press, I passed the ball back to Maya, who dribbled it near the logo to burn a little time off the clock. She signaled me, and I initiated the play by cutting across the court.

Coach Carr believed in player movement and ball movement. Everyone seemed like they were in motion. I saw Ruby get in position to screen Maya's defender. Three point five seconds. She had a clear line to me but not the basket, so she passed me the ball. Three seconds. I started to drive, but I didn't love the look. Their center and a forward were between me and the basket, but that meant someone had to be wide open. It was Maya in the corner with no defender on her. Two seconds. I couldn't believe it. I slowed a little to put my defender off, and rather than go up for a jumper, I sent a hard no-look bounce pass to Maya between defenders.

She caught it, gathered her feet, and went up for the three. It was a thing of beauty as it sailed through the net just as the buzzer went off.

Everyone screamed as though it was the championship. I charged at Maya to hug her, happy she hit the buzzer beater to lock us into the number three spot. When we collided, however, Maya yelled, "You did it!"

"Me?" What the hell was she talking about? She'd just nailed the final shot.

"A triple-double."

"What?"

"That last board at the other end and that last assist to me. That's going to get you a triple-double! You were at twenty-four points, nine boards, and nine assists coming out of that last time-out. Vicky told me." Maya pointed up to the screen where Pitbulls win was flashing across it, but beside that was one of my promo shots where I was smirking with a ball spinning on my finger and the words *Triple-Double* bouncing below me.

I couldn't believe what I was seeing. I had no idea that I was even close to a triple-double. I just stood staring until Vicky ran into me. Then Brittany and Ruby.

I couldn't focus on anything because never in my wildest dreams did I think I'd get close to a triple-double. Only a handful of players had ever achieved it, and now I was among them. Kinzie was walking toward me, smiling. She placed a hand on my shoulder. "Congrats, Jane. That was a hell of a game."

I smiled back even as my teammates jostled me around. "Thanks."

"I'll catch up with you later. I've got a CEO sitting up in a suite that I need to go woo with Jada and Owen." She winked again—I swear she'd never done that before the last ten minutes, but it sent my already racing pulse into the stratosphere—and walked away. I knew she was going to catch up with me later because I was going to her hotel after getting cleaned up, but I liked hearing her say it all nonchalantly.

Someone from ESPN tapped me to do an on-court interview with Dolly French. They gave me headphones, and before I could even take a breath, the light was flashing that we were on air.

"Jane, did you have any idea that you'd have such a solid performance today against the strong defense of Seattle?" Dolly said.

"We all felt pretty confident coming into the game. We've been on a roll, and with the momentum behind us, I think everyone was hoping to play well," I said.

"From the opening layup off that no-look pass from Maya through that board and beautiful pass to Maya to win the game, you played with fire and exuded confidence tonight. What gave you that little extra push to take your play to the next level?"

My hands shook, and my palms were sweaty with nerves, but I tried to keep my face calm. "I think my confidence has been building all season, Dolly. I think everyone knows, Coach Carr and I go way back, and I think she could see something in me that I honestly had forgotten I had. Um, and the whole team has been a huge support to me. Maya's and Brittany's and Vicky's and everyone's faith in me has made me a believer in myself again, I guess. Also, Maya is such a dynamic PG who makes opportunities happen. I'm a beneficiary of her amazing play. That first layup came off her steal, and I made the pass on her last shot, but it was all her directing traffic that got her open in the corner. Playing alongside the best PG in the league is an opportunity I appreciate every day." I didn't care that I probably sounded a little gushy about Maya. I really loved playing with her. She was undoubtedly the best PG in the league and contributed to my success.

"In every courtside interview I do with the Pitbulls, everyone is overwhelmingly complimentary of each other. It seems like y'all really are a family. Does it feel like that on the inside too?"

I laughed because that was an odd way to phrase it. "Yeah, I guess we really are. I don't think I've ever played on a team that felt like this. Like I belong, really."

"That's amazing. Now that you've secured the third spot in the playoffs, you have home court advantage in the first round, and you're likely to face off against Indiana after your final regular season game against Atlanta in a few days. Indiana had some success against you in the early part of the season, but you took the last two games you played each other. How do you feel facing off against them?"

"The post season is a reset of the clock. They've been playing amazing, so we have our work cut out for us." Truthfully, I felt really good about our chances of taking the series because they were on a four-game losing streak, but I didn't want to sound cocky or jinx us.

Also, I was worried about Maya. She was struggling with Paris, and I couldn't help but worry Paris would not take it well if Maya was the one who sent them home in the playoffs, given how rocky their relationship was already.

"Well, congrats on the win and hope you have at least a little time to enjoy the glow of the triple-double before you have to get back at it to prepare for Atlanta this week and likely Indiana next week in the first round of the playoffs."

I jogged up the tunnel, grateful for the win, grateful for the relatively painless interview, and grateful that I was that much closer to seeing Kinzie. Even if I had another dreaded ice bath in between.

Chapter Fifteen

After the post-game interview, Coach presenting me with the game ball, the ice bath and the showers, I headed to Kinzie's hotel room, as had become the routine while she was in town. But when the elevator doors slid open on her floor, Kinzie was leaning against the hallway in the lobby typing on her phone.

"You're escorting me to your room tonight?" I said, feeling confused. She'd never done that before.

"Yes, because we have a slight change of plans."

My chest felt a little tight at a change of plans. I didn't like change, but I could see her vibrating with eagerness. I couldn't say no. "Oh really?"

"Yeah." She held out her hand for mine and pulled us to the elevator buttons, but rather than pushing down, which was where I was assuming our change of plans would take us, she hit up.

"Where are we going?"

"My room."

Relieved but still confused, I said, "But this is the floor you were on last night?"

"I moved." She shrugged as we walked out of the elevator as if it was normal for her to move hotel rooms mid-stay.

"Why?"

She tapped her card against the reader, and it beeped. As Kinzie opened the door she said, "Today called for some celebration. I pulled a string or two and upgraded."

The door swung into a huge suite that was illuminated by flickering candles on every surface. I gasped. "W…why?"

"To celebrate you, Miss First Triple-Double of her career. If that doesn't need celebrating, I don't know what does."

I didn't realize I'd barely made it through the door until Kinzie's gentle hands at my hips encouraged me farther into the room. She slid my duffel bag off my shoulder and dropped it onto the floor.

"I don't know what to say." I was feeling a little embarrassed which I recognized was ridiculous. I was also incredibly flattered. I felt…cherished…for the first time in my life maybe.

"Rather than saying something, why don't we do this?" She brushed her lips across mine, but that wasn't enough contact for me. I pulled her hips into mine. She groaned.

She guided us around the corner and a hot tub came into view, also with several candles lit around the edge. "You are aware that this is quite a fire hazard, right? Especially leaving them burning while you came to meet me?"

"Yes, but it was a calculated risk that paid off and was worth it to see your face." She shrugged. "And it was only for two minutes since you shared your Uber's location with me."

"Well, thank you. Even if I can't condone this risky behavior." I pursed my lips as I looked at her.

Her eyes flashed. "Perhaps I deserve a little punishing later."

"You probably do." I smirked. "But first, I want to get in this hot tub with you. It will be a nice contrast to the ice bath." I shivered just remembering it.

"Well, then, let's get you out of these and into the tub." Her fingers wandered quite a bit in the process, but she managed to relieve me of my clothes quickly. And I certainly didn't mind the casual swipes across my thighs and torso, though my knees nearly buckled when she raked a fingernail across my nipple.

She *tsked*. "For a professional athlete, I thought you'd have better balance."

I laughed. "My balance is just fine when you aren't trying to have your way with me."

"Just in case, let me help you into the tub." She held out her hand as support as I stepped in.

I took her hand but still said, "I'm a lot bigger than you are, you know? What do you think you're going to do if I do slip."

"Catch you," she whispered before pointing at the tub. "Now sit and turn on the bubbles."

Watching Kinzie strip for me was a true delight. As was the foot massage she gave me that led to my first orgasm in a hot tub.

When I opened my eyes again, Kinzie said, "I hadn't meant that massage to lead there, but I can't say I'm sorry. I love watching you let go. Come undone." She reached behind her and grabbed a bottle from an ice bucket I hadn't noticed. "Now let's have some sparkling apple juice."

She handed me a champagne flute, and I took a sip, savoring the effervescent bubbles exploding in my mouth. "Thank you."

"I can honestly say, absolutely anytime." She smirked.

I shook my head, trying to figure out how to explain how I was feeling. "No, not for that. For making me feel…cherished? Desired? I don't know."

"Jane, I can promise you, it's my pleasure." She interlaced our fingers under the water.

"I know. I'm actually starting to believe that, and…that's new for me. I've never been terribly confident…I think maybe feeling like a gangly outsider growing up is the root of all my insecurity issues. I don't know. I was good at basketball, but being from a small town in a small state, I didn't think that meant a lot. It wasn't like Dawn Staley was knocking on my door. But when I got to Duke and started playing with a team full of other full ride, athletic scholarship kids, I started to gain attention because Coach Carr ran a program that I integrated into seamlessly and played to my strengths. And that made me more confident. I played better. I felt better. Inside, I never felt like I deserved any of it, but with all of their support and the fan base down there, I felt good, but I still never believed it. I fed off their enthusiasm, but for the first time in my life, I'm finally starting to *believe* in myself both on and off the court. I don't know what's different, but something is. And it's weird and wonderful."

"I am so happy for you, Jane. Watching you bloom over the past few months has been amazing."

"I haven't watched it, but even looking back at how unsure I was only a few months ago is bizarre. Working with Brigitte has been amazing for me mentally, and Aaron helping me strengthen my legs has me trusting my knee again, but I'm thinking about getting a therapist once the season is over. Brigitte has been encouraging me to even as I make progress with her. She says that although I feel good, slipping back into my old mindset is normal, but having a therapist to work with year-round consistently will be better." Saying the words "see a therapist" out loud made me cringe a little bit. The old me would have felt like that was admitting failure, though the new me knew it was nothing to be ashamed of.

"That's great, Jane. My therapist has helped me work through a lot of stuff with losing my mom as a child, my dad, decisions that I make that, even in the moment, don't make sense."

"Wait, you see a therapist? But you seem so…composed?" I couldn't believe it. How did someone like Kinzie need a therapist? But as I thought it, I realized my bias was showing again. Needing a little help was nothing to be ashamed of. Intellectually, I knew that it was true, but it was hard to remind myself to believe it.

She laughed as she said, "I don't see her as often as I used to, but why do you think I'm able to be so composed? It's because I know talking to someone helps. I've actually talked to her about you quite a bit."

"Me? Why?" I knew logically it was a little silly to be uncomfortable with Kinzie talking to her therapist about me, but it still made my gut churn.

"I had a lot to work through with you." She ran her fingers up my arm and massaged my shoulder. "I'd never had a one-night stand before, but I had a lot of feelings about it. It was reckless, which is *very* out of character for me. I also really wanted to see you again, and I needed to work through what that might mean. I wasn't sure if it was because I felt guilty for doing something I believed unethical or if it was because I really was drawn to you."

She moved to massaging my other shoulder, and I groaned and leaned toward her. "And then, I ran into you, and that really threw me through a loop. I won't bore you with the details, but talking to her about you is really talking to her about *my* reaction to you."

"Well, that makes sense, I guess." We adjusted in the tub until I was sitting between Kinzie's legs, and she started digging into my shoulders in earnest with both thumbs.

I could only blame the elevated level of relaxation the tub brought out—combined with Kinzie's magical hands on my shoulders—that led me to say, "For me, getting hurt was the worst thing that ever happened to me. I'd always felt like an outsider, and then, for three and a half short years in college, I felt like I belonged, but I got hurt in my second professional game, and everything was stolen from me. The woman I'd been dating for two years decided she'd rather date some stockbroker who had a *real future* that wasn't dependent upon the body's fickle health."

"I'm sorry you had to go through all that," Kinzie said as she moved one of her hands up to my neck while the other continued to dig into a gnarly knot along my shoulder blade.

"And now I feel like everything is coming together, but I'm afraid that it's all going to collapse again. Am I the brick house you suggested I build a few weeks ago, or am I still a house of cards? Today, after such a big win, I think I'm made of brick for maybe the first time ever, but I'm afraid. What if it's still nothing but a house of cards with a brick pattern? What if my confidence fades, and I realize I've been made of paper this whole time?"

She took my glass and set it on the side of the tub as she shimmied around until she was straddling my lap. I didn't think I was ready to go again after my last orgasm, but the feel of her breasts pressing down on mine told me I was wrong. So very wrong.

"Here's the thing. My therapist also reminds me regularly that it's okay to give myself a little grace, which I don't excel at. I was kind of bitter about taking this assignment in the beginning. I've told you about that before."

I laughed. "I do, in fact, remember that."

"I almost died when I saw you there in the gym. I was ridiculously excited to see you, but also, holy shit. I'd confessed how much I didn't want the assignment—how much I didn't like sports—to a player on the team that I was hired to help market. Yet my heart soared a little at seeing you too. I told my therapist about all of it, and she reminded me that I was doing the best that I could with all the knowledge I had. And that I had to stop being self-critical."

"Huh."

"And as I was able to break down your walls, convince you to believe—I think—that I wanted you, I worked through a lot of my own shit. So as a reminder." She wiggled her center against my thighs. "If you do slip at remembering that you're pretty fucking amazing, a therapist can be there to catch you and remind you of what is important. And if you let me, I'll be there to remind you too."

I was afraid to believe her words. I still had a hard time believing that she wanted someone like me, but I was starting to. I slid two fingers between her legs and along both sides of her clit. She groaned and dropped her head to my shoulder. "I want to," I said.

"Then do. I'm here for you, Jane. More than my job, more than anything else. I'm here for *you*."

As she rode my fingers in that hot tub, there was nothing more in the world that I wanted to be open to. To believe in.

CHAPTER SIXTEEN

Game days were starting to feel like they did when I was a kid. I was actually excited for them. And I was finding out that waking up on game days in Kinzie's bed was also a delight. Especially on a weekend when she didn't have to run off to early morning meetings and could sleep in with me.

On the morning of our last game of the regular season, I woke up to Kinzie's fingers between my thighs, perhaps my most favorite way to wake up. We had room service together for breakfast, and I headed off to our game-day film and light practice, walking on a cloud. It seemed like nothing could go wrong until the game scratched the needle right off my happiness record.

The sweat was pouring off my face as I guarded Smith, Atlanta's best forward. This shouldn't have been so hard. Atlanta didn't have a chance to make the playoffs. It was supposed to be a throwaway game. After starting the season strong, Atlanta was on a seven game losing streak after their center had torn her meniscus and ended her season. But Smith didn't get the memo that this game wasn't supposed to be that competitive as she aggressively pushed back against me while dribbling. It was the third quarter, and we were down by two.

I was guarding her as though my life depended on it. The sweat poured into my eyes as I struggled to stay with her. I wondered if I was playing poorly—and feeling fatigued—because I was tired after a great night—and morning—with Kinzie. I hated the idea of her seeing me play this way. For some reason, all the fans didn't concern me, but I didn't want Kinzie to see any weaknesses.

The pressure against me disappeared, and I stumbled. How could I have been caught off guard like that? She took a step forward, spun, and went into a jumper that wasn't her typical shot. I didn't even have my hand in her face. She never took shots from that distance, yet she did now. I hoped Kinzie hadn't seen my lapse on defense. I tried to recover.

My gut told me she was going to miss, and I was proven right as the metal plink of the ball hitting the rim twice resonated through the arena, and I turned toward the basket. I wasn't sure where it was going to bounce to, but I got into the best position I could and tried to box Smith out. I jockeyed for position. Smith shimmied. Someone else hip checked me.

I stumbled to my left and slammed into the court, and the pain in my knee was excruciating. Did I bounce? It felt like I was an ancient sequoia falling to the ground. I wanted to pull my knee in, but the pain was too much. I was crying, and I hated knowing I was on ESPN. Or maybe it was ABC. The things my mind went to were bizarre. Who gave a shit if it was ABC or ESPN? But my mind revolved around that question even as the trainer asked me where it hurt.

My head spun even as they asked if I could stand. I nodded, but I didn't know if it was true. I was defensively occupying my mind with something that didn't matter one shit in that moment because the pain in my knee was blinding as Aaron helped me off the court. I tried putting a little weight on that leg and almost passed out, and the only thing going through my head was the overwhelming fear that it was all over.

There was no way I was going to be able to come back from a second ACL—or any other ligament—tear. I didn't have time. I was too old. Terror seized my heart, and I tried to hope for the best. To stay positive. The training staff packed my knee with ice packs, and Aaron squeezed my shoulder and promised to be back shortly. As the training room door clicked closed behind him, I flopped back on the table and draped my arm across my face.

My eyes burned with tears that I refused to let fall now that I'd gotten them under control, yet my mind spiraled around the idea that all of this was over. The pain in my knee felt like when I'd torn my ACL years ago. I couldn't believe that this was how my career was going to end. Kinzie was going to leave me. I'd always known forever was a pipe dream, but my body was reminding me that I was a loser. No one wanted to be with a loser.

I'd already learned that lesson the hard way.

The room was completely silent as the game was still in progress on the court, though I could occasionally hear the roar of the crowd. It was hard to wrap my head around how the world could keep going while I was there with my life falling apart. Neither the silence nor the noise of the crowd helped. There was nothing to distract me from every doomsday scenario that played out in my mind.

I lifted my head when the door slammed into the wall.

"Oh my God, are you okay?" Kinzie said, her heels echoing as she nearly ran to my side.

She took my face in her hands, her skin cool against mine, and all I could do was raise my brows. "Okay, dumb question. You're not okay. Do they know how serious it is yet?"

I swallowed around the lump in my throat and shook my head. Her casual touch was calming, but having her there solidified in my mind that this relationship could never work. "No, I'll get an MRI first thing in the morning. For tonight, I'll just ice, keep my leg elevated, and try to pretend like my career isn't crumbling around me."

"You can't think like that. Whatever it is, we'll get through it. I know it."

"I'm not dying," I quipped. "But my career almost certainly is."

I didn't realize my hand was balled in a fist on my stomach until Kinzie's wrapped around it and coaxed it into relaxing. "I know you're upset and scared, but you have so many people in your corner. This isn't the end for you, I know it."

I hated myself as her words made me angry. "How would you know? What do you know about sports or injuries?"

"Absolutely nothing. But I know you. And you have a lot of fight in you. I've seen it all season. You've had it for the last eight years, or you never would have made a comeback this year. You have much more fight in you than you realize. And your team, your friends, your coach, will be here with you every step of the way. *I'll* be here with you every step of the way." Her eyes were earnest, but I knew it was only a matter of time before she would tire of me. I was already tired of myself. And her insistence that I would be fine proved that she only wanted to be with me if I *was* fine. Just like my college girlfriend had. And thoughts of her distracted me seconds before my injury. If I hadn't been thinking about her, maybe I wouldn't have…

I squeezed my eyes shut and said what needed to be said, knowing it was probably going to hurt as badly as my knee did. "I appreciate the offer, but I need to focus on me and my recovery now. I'll have the team and the trainers. I don't have time for any distractions."

"I get it. But I'm not a distraction. I know you were worried at first, but I think I've proved to you I can fit into your life without distracting you, haven't I?"

I couldn't bring myself to look at her face. "That was different. I was in a groove then. Things were clicking. Now… nothing is going to click for a while. No matter what is going on with my knee."

"I don't accept that, Jane. Just because you're going through something—and, you don't even know what that's going to look like yet—doesn't mean I'm suddenly a distraction. This might be something. I think it *is* something."

There was a pleading in her voice that was stabbing me in the heart, but I couldn't let that stop me. "But you *were* a distraction. You were in my thoughts when I missed coverage on Smith. I'm lying here because I couldn't keep my mind on what I was doing. I can't let—"

She stopped me with a squeeze of my hand. "Just stop, Jane. Please don't do or say anything in the heat of the moment that you can't take back. I'm going to leave now and give you some time to cool off. Reassess, okay?"

I blinked my eyes open for the first time in minutes and saw tears pooling in hers. I nodded, self-loathing coursing through me, but I wasn't sure what I hated more: how I was hurting her or how I didn't have the strength to just end things completely. Sever them cleanly so we could both start to heal.

She cupped my cheek. "My heart is with you. I believe in you. I believe that you are going to be fine and bounce back. No matter how long it takes." She brushed her lips lightly against mine, then across my forehead before turning and walking away. She opened the door a lot more quietly on her way out than she had when she'd come in. Before the door closed, however, I heard a cheer race through the arena. It sounded like we'd just won the game, which was amazing.

Yet, I was consumed with dread, a weight pinning me to the table, leaving me without an ounce of joy. I wished I could feel like celebrating, but I couldn't.

"How does this feel?" the orthopedic doctor asked as he sadistically poked a finger into the outside of my knee. It felt like he was driving an ice pick into me, even though I could see that he wasn't even pressing that hard.

"Not great," I managed to get out through my clenched jaw.

I was particularly irritable because on top of my career being thrown into jeopardy, I'd also had a terrible night's sleep.

I'd been planning to spend last night at Kinzie's hotel before she flew home to New York today. Instead, I lay in bed in my own apartment, staring at the ceiling, counting down the hours until I learned whether my life would be fundamentally shifted again.

I had no desire to eat breakfast. All I'd done since Kinzie walked out was obsess about my career. And Kinzie herself if I was being honest, though I'd tried to avoid the topic, even with myself.

"How about here?"

I yelped as he found a new, incredibly sensitive spot.

"I'll take that as a yes. How much do you recall of the injury?"

I wanted to growl at him, but his eyes were kind and guilted me into answering without it. "Not much," I admitted. "It all happened really fast."

"That's not a surprise. Do you remember feeling a pop or a crunch or anything that you can describe in your knee at impact last night?"

I strained to think but struggled to remember. "I'm not sure. It was fast, and I think I'm merging my ACL tear from almost a decade ago with last night. That time, there was definitely a pop, but it was loud in the arena, and I'm just not sure." I sighed in frustration as I watched him continue to manipulate my knee. "There was impact and then just blinding pain."

"You have a lot of swelling here, but the tenderness is mostly isolated to the outside of your knee, which is potentially good news. I am going to watch the film of the injury while we get you into the MRI machine to confirm what's going on. Do you have any questions for me?"

"How bad do you think it is?" I said, dread festering in my stomach like dirty uniforms in a gym bag forgotten in a hot car for months.

"It's too soon to say," he said, a compassionate smile on his face. I felt my shoulders fall before he said, "Don't start building things up in your head. It could be minor. Or it could be something. But until we know, just breathe."

"Fine," I mumbled. I hated MRI machines. Even though my head and chest were not in the machine, and I had headphones on, it was still miserable lying still for more than an hour. Especially being a little stiff after the incident the night before. Yes, my knee hurt, but my hip and elbow were also sore as hell and aching.

The machine clicked and beeped. *Breathe in.* Banged and clanked. *Breathe out. Don't let the uncertainty, the pessimism, creep in.* It was going to be fine. *Or was it?*

My favorite Billie Eilish song for the ice bath came on. I wasn't sure if it was better or worse because I knew exactly how long that song was. I normally listened to it during torture, so perhaps it was fitting.

After what felt like hours lying on my back for that shit, I found myself back in Doctor Clayborn's office waiting for him. It felt like torture having to continue waiting to find out my fate. Aaron was trying to keep me talking and distracted, but I was too wrapped up in my own thoughts to focus on what he was saying. I think I was probably still in a bit of shock and not fully processing everything.

The door swung open, and Doctor Clayborn had a small smile on his face. *That has to be good news, right?*

I couldn't wait. "Give it to me straight. Am I going to play again this season?" I swallowed. "Or ever?" I squeezed the fingers of my left hand hard enough with my right that my hands ached, but I couldn't make myself stop.

His smile grew. "Yes, to both."

I let out a huge sigh of breath I hadn't realized had been trapped in my lungs.

"You sprained your LCL, but it's not career threatening. It's a fairly mild sprain. Looks like a grade one, and the timing is going to be tight, but I think if your team makes it, we should have you back in the lineup by the finals."

It was like my chest was released from a vise. I took my first deep breath since I'd fallen to the floor the night before. "Thank you," I said, my voice barely above a whisper as I, again, tried not to cry. I'd just gotten the absolute best news I could have received, and I still wanted to cry. I wanted to share this news with Kinzie but that wasn't a possibility, and the fear of a career-ending injury was replaced with fears of not being able to trust my knee again. I was kind of pathetic.

"That's great news, Doc," Aaron said. He and Doctor Clayborn went through my recovery plan, starting with RICE but also other exercises and stretches I could do while recovering to not lose any of my current fitness. I was in the best shape of my life, and I didn't want to let any of that go.

As we exited the office, I tried not to hobble in my hinged knee brace and crutches, and Aaron said, "Strictly rest for the next week, and we'll go from there. Only exercises to maintain your fitness without further injuring your knee."

"You can't keep me out of practice," I said, knowing he damn well could. And knowing that my knee needed to heal.

He leveled his gaze at me. "Wanna bet?"

"Okay, fine, yes you can keep me from *practicing*, but what I meant was I need to be there with the team. At practice, on the sidelines watching, still a part of the team." Even though I feared losing my groove, I also feared the team moving on without me. Replacing me and forgetting that I'd ever existed.

"That's fine. But no practice for a *full week*. That's a full week from today, by the way. Today, we're going to take you home, and you're going to put your leg up and ice it. Tomorrow morning, Coach wants you to spend a little time talking to Brigitte."

"Of course. I will."

Aaron opened the door to let me crutch-walk my way out, and I blinked into the bright sunlight. The brightness felt like it was burning into my soul. I paused and balanced on one leg, holding my crutches as I tried to find my sunglasses. Fuck, where were they?

I was startled by a horn honk and shielded my eyes as I tried to see the source and who was honking at me.

"Get in the truck, babe."

My heart swelled as I wondered if it was Kinzie but dismissed it immediately. I knew she was back in New York already, and that wasn't her voice. Plus, with the way I'd callously pushed her away, there was no way she'd want to see me. Which was for the best, but it hurt a lot more than I thought it would.

Apparently, I stood staring too long without moving because she said, "Come on, Jane. We gotta get out of here."

Maya. That made sense, except she should have been at practice. I finally found my sunglasses and put them on. "Aaron's giving me a ride home, and shouldn't you be at practice?" I said, though I did want to go with her. If anyone could cheer me up, it would be Maya.

"Practice, schmactice. Who cares? My bestie needs my cheery disposition, so here I am." She looked past me to Aaron and said, "I got this, Aaron, okay?"

"Can I trust you to take her home and help get her settled, get her ice?"

"I'm perfectly capable of taking care of myself, Aaron," I grumbled.

"Of course," Maya said to him, ignoring that I'd said anything at all. "As the captain, I'm the most responsible person on the team." Maya smiled cheekily, and Aaron relented as everyone did when Maya turned on her charm.

"Okay, but no shenanigans. Either of you." He pointed a finger between us. "I'm trusting you. And I'm trusting that Coach released you from practice." He pointed at Maya still sitting in her car.

She saluted him. "Now, let's go, Hopalong. We've got resting and icing to do."

I shook my head but smiled as I maneuvered to her car and managed to shove my crutches in before doing a single leg squat in what probably looked incredibly ungraceful to passersby but that I was pretty proud of since I was able to do it without tweaking my bad knee at all. Balance, grace, poise, I clearly had them all.

"Hopalong, huh? Is that really politically correct?" I said.

"Eh. To-may-to, to-mah-to." She shrugged, but said, "But sorry if I offended you."

"You didn't, but thank you." I elbowed her.

She slid her car into gear and squealed the tires as she pulled away, which I was certain was just for Aaron's benefit. "Well, you aren't crying, so not bad news, huh?"

"Not bad news. The best possible news, given how bad my knee hurts. It's just a sprain, probably grade one." For some reason, saying the words to Maya made me feel lighter. The fear of not being good enough when I could come back didn't seize me like it had in the doctor's office.

"When do you come back?"

"I don't know for sure. He said it would be tight, but I could probably return in time for finals."

Maya punched the air and hooted. "Yas, girl."

"You're a little overly confident, aren't you?"

Maya signaled that she was turning but slammed on the brakes in the parking lane so hard that the seat belt caught against my chest. She looked at me. "*Overly?* No. We are going to make it to the finals, where we are going to kick someone's ass, though only time will tell whose ass that will be. And you are going to be back in time for it because you are amazing. You are a fighter. I'm calling all of it now. Because it's true. *Boom.*" She mimed explosions with both her hands.

"Thank you, my friend. I don't know what I'd do without you. I'm sorry you're always the one here for me, and I never return the favor." My plan to get a real therapist was feeling more and more necessary. I felt like an emotional burden on my friends, and I hated it. Brigitte was helping, but I knew I needed more.

"*Psh.* What about with Paris? You've been my rock as we've had our ups and downs."

I actually hated Paris and thought she was horrible to Maya. But I would never say that to her. At least not outright and not while Maya was happy. But, God, it was hard. "I'm always here for you." I squeezed her hand.

Even if I didn't think I provided much support for Maya, I was incredibly thankful for her friendship and encouragement. I really couldn't do any of this without her and was beyond grateful I'd have her by my side over the coming weeks as I tried to heal my body and get back into shape. I feared healing my heart was going to take more than I'd been expecting.

Chapter Seventeen

As it turned out, Dr. Clayton was right. I made it back in time for game one of the finals. It was a stressful few weeks. I spent a lot of time with Brigitte talking about my fears, and she continued to remind me that I could trust myself and my body. I worked with Aaron with a knee brace on to maintain my fitness, and we determined which brace I felt the most comfortable in.

Through it all, I did everything I could to keep my mind off Kinzie and how I'd completely fucked things up. My heart hurt, but I was still certain it had been the right move. I'd been distracted by thoughts of her seconds before my injury, and I couldn't afford that. The next time, I might not be so lucky to only have a sprain. So I focused on the team. I traveled with them and cheered them on from the sidelines while also analyzing their play. I surprised myself with how much I saw—I'd never done that when riding the bench before, but I'd also never been as invested—and I helped Coach see a few patterns she'd missed with Connecticut's defense. That pumped up my confidence, and I felt pretty darn good going into the game, which made my abysmal performance even worse. I had been sure I'd jump back in like I hadn't missed a few weeks, and yet, things fell apart. Fuck.

I sat, staring into my locker in the visitor's locker room, replaying every single missed shot. Every time I didn't cut when I should have. A towel snapping against my back drew my attention back to the room. "Come on, broody. Let's hit the ice bath," Maya said.

I really didn't want to talk to anyone right then. "I don't—"

"No excuses. Your body will thank you. And I want company. I hate the damn polar plunge." She grabbed my hand and pulled until I relented and stood.

"Fine," I said, grumbling. I wanted to be left alone to brood and obsess over whether my career was over, but it wasn't a productive use of my time, and I knew it.

"I'm going to need you to buck up a little bit. We won the game. The first game of the finals. On the road. In front of a sold-out crowd in New York City. It doesn't get much better than this." She shouldered me.

"Our win was in spite of me. I had nothing to do with it."

"You're allowed to have a bad game. It's why it's a team sport. You'll bounce back."

I wanted to believe her, but I was having a hard time. Everything just felt...insurmountable.

"Stop nodding like you believe me when I can see it written across your face that you don't. Your game wasn't that terrible. You're coming back from injury, and it takes time to get that explosiveness in your drives. You'll get it back by next game. You'll talk to Brigitte tomorrow morning, you'll get a massage, you'll work with Aaron, we'll watch some film, and by Wednesday night, you'll be ready to tear up the court, and we'll go home with a two to nothing lead over New York."

I really wanted to believe she was right, but I didn't. Yet. I hoped that talking to Brigitte the next morning would help. "We'll see," was the only thing I could manage that was only semi-pessimistic.

She sighed. "You're infuriating. Speaking of which, have you talked to Kinzie yet?"

"Pouring lemon juice in all the wounds tonight, aren't you?"

"We're in New York. Which happens to be where Kinzie lives. Seems like a sign that you should go talk to her."

The ice baths were ready for us when we walked in and looked horribly cold. "What I need to do is work on my game. And my confidence. Getting more distracted by spending time with Kinzie is not at all what I need. Signs be damned."

"Does that mean you haven't talked to her at all since the night of your injury?"

I started to strip down to my sports bra and spandex shorts. "She texted me a few times. I responded but didn't really engage. She called me once, but I didn't pick up. We were about to board a plane. I couldn't."

Maya put her hand on my shoulder and looked at me with sadness in her eyes, and I was surprised as she said, "Why are you being such a coward?"

"What?"

"You really don't see the parallels between your play tonight and your avoidance of Kinzie since you got hurt?"

"What? The two things have nothing to do with each other. I was never good enough for Kinzie, and she doesn't need me dragging her down. She lives in New York. I live in Milwaukee five months a year and London for the other seven. How can we make that work? We can't. That's the answer. As far as my play tonight…my knee didn't feel strong. I couldn't find a groove. I don't see how they're related."

"Bullshit."

I climbed over the edge into my tub as Maya got into hers, and the needles of pain assaulted my body as Maya continued to assault my mind.

"You're afraid to commit. You're afraid to commit to Kinzie even though she clearly wants you. And you're afraid to commit to the game. I think it's because if you refuse to commit one hundred percent and things don't work out, you can say that you weren't trying anyway. Or it was never going to work anyway. The reason you've been playing so beautifully this season is because you finally put yourself all in. Tonight, you didn't do that. With Kinzie, you didn't do that. Distance doesn't matter if you want to make a relationship work. She practically lived in Milwaukee this summer to be close to you. Clearly, she has a flexible work schedule. London is an easy flight from New York. I'm sure two intelligent women can figure it out. Paris and I are doing it. Even though we just beat her team in the playoffs two weeks ago. But she's going to get over it. And we're going to be fine."

Maya looked sad as she spoke about Paris, and it pissed me off that Paris was bitter about us knocking them out. It was a part of the game when you dated a player from an opposing team. I didn't say anything. I didn't think Maya was in a place to hear something negative about her.

"You deserve love and happiness and a successful career." The water splashed as she turned, and my skin felt cold knowing she'd just brought fresh icy water against her skin. "You know it. You just don't *know* it. You need to *know* it again. In your bones. I think you felt it four weeks ago, but getting hurt made you forget."

"She's a distraction. I need to focus on the game."

"I don't for a second believe you. You were playing inspired basketball when you were dating her."

"I was distracted by her when I got hurt."

"So what? You lost focus for a second and thought of Kinzie? It can happen to anyone. You can lose focus because your shoe is tied a little too tight, or a fan screams too loud and catches you off guard. You can't put that on Kinzie."

Instinctively, I said, "It's on me, but I can't focus—"

Maya's phone alarm interrupted me, and with relief, I hopped out of the tub and wrapped myself in a large but unfortunately scratchy towel.

"Bullshit. Jane, it's time to stop lying to yourself," Maya said as she got out of the tub and into a towel. "Now hurry up, or you're going to miss the bus."

I tried not to shiver as I watched Maya walk away, still dripping. Her words, harsher and colder than she'd ever spoken to me, stuck with me as I dried off alone, showered alone, and boarded the team bus and sat alone. I thought she was full of shit about my being afraid to commit. I was committed to the team. I was giving them everything that I had. The problem was, I was no longer sure that my best was good enough.

She might have had a point about Kinzie, however. I hadn't realized it earlier, but I hadn't fully committed to her because I had always been waiting for her to decide that she was tired of me. Or for my career to pull us apart. And wasn't that what had happened? My career made it impossible for us to be together because without focus, I couldn't play. But I couldn't get the idea out of my head that maybe if I had committed, things could have been different. Would I be so certain that she was a distraction? Would I have been so worried about her seeing my subpar play if I had accepted her feelings for me as genuine?

I wasn't sure of the answers to any of those questions, but they kept me tossing and turning all night wondering if I'd made a mistake.

❖

Brigitte's face filled up half my computer screen the next morning. "How'd you sleep last night, Jane?"

I rubbed at my left eye and adjusted the hotel robe. "Not great. I had a hard time wanting to get up this morning. Luckily, I know you still like me when I'm barely awake and haven't gotten dressed."

She laughed. "You're right. I see you in warm-ups and uniforms, and that's not much different from a robe. But what I really want to talk about is the game last night. Tell me how you're feeling."

"Like shit."

"Why? It was your first game in three weeks."

"Because I'd convinced myself that this injury wasn't going to hold me back. Because I'd convinced myself that I was going to bounce right back like I'd never been gone. I thought that was what I was supposed to do." I flung my hands up and suppressed a growl.

"Jane, there is no supposed to. You have to give yourself a little grace after having been out for nearly a month. Even the greatest players have off nights. Especially given what you've been through the last few weeks."

"It was three weeks, not three months, and I had a slightly sprained ligament, nothing major. And I've been with the team nonstop this whole time. The chemistry should have stayed intact. I should've been able to slide back in seamlessly." My skin prickled, and I wasn't sure if it was irritation or embarrassment, but either way, I hated the feeling.

"For someone who has been pessimistic her entire life but is working on it," she added when I glared at her. "That is pretty damn optimistic. However, do you think demanding an unrealistic standard is a fair way to treat yourself?"

"When you put it that way, I guess not. But am I really that unrealistic?" I said, though I already realized that I probably had been. She stared at me, and I squirmed. Finally, I relented. "Okay, yes, fine, it was a *little* unrealistic."

She nodded. "You need to give yourself time. Do you think *maybe* you're carrying a little extra baggage around this injury?"

"Probably." When she just stared again, I gave in and said, "Fine, yes, I definitely am."

"Given the baggage that you're lugging around, do you think it's *possible* that you're not treating yourself with kindness or giving yourself the grace we've been talking about all season? Especially in this particular situation."

I opened my mouth and closed it. I really hadn't considered it like that, but it felt like I'd forgotten everything we'd been talking about all season. While I kind of hated that she was right, I was also incredibly relieved. Because it meant that maybe I was being too hard on myself. "Yes," I finally said with unexpected confidence. "I'm not treating myself with the kindness I show others. With the kindness that I deserve."

"Does that make you feel differently about practice today and the game tomorrow?"

"Yes. A lot better." I smiled a real smile for the first time since tip-off the night before.

"Great." Her smile looked real too, but it probably had been the whole time. I just hadn't believed her confidence in me. "Jane, every day doesn't have to be perfect for you to be successful. Your team won last night. You're a part of that team, and even if it doesn't feel like it, you were a part of the win. Remember that every game is part of the bigger journey, but no game, no win, no loss, no performance in a vacuum defines that journey. It is up to *you* to commit to the long game."

"Thank you. I needed to see this game in that perspective. One blip. Not a reversion to a self that I swore I would never be again."

She nodded.

Kinzie's words about how much her therapist had been helping her echoed in my mind again, and before I could talk myself out of it, I said, "You'd mentioned getting a therapist was something I should consider. I think you're right. Do you have anyone you can recommend?"

"I do. I'll shoot you a few names."

By the time I closed my laptop and stood to stretch, it felt like a massive load had been taken off me. I pulled out my yoga mat and did fifteen minutes of sun salutations, envisioning my negativity being wrung out of me with every fold, every twist, every compression. With every breath, the words I'd spoken with Brigitte took root and grew. The realization that I'd gone from toxically negative to toxically positive dawned on me, and I realized I'd done exactly what I committed to not doing.

I lost my confidence at the first sign of adversity.

I briefly wondered if that was what was happening with Kinzie too, but I pushed the thought away. I really couldn't deal with both my game and Kinzie at the same time. I needed to focus on my game, even though I missed Kinzie fiercely. I hated that I hadn't seen her in three weeks. I hated how badly I missed her. Her quiet confidence. Her kind soul. Her legs.

Thinking about her legs made me feel shallow, but her legs were divine beneath those pencil skirts. Or wrapped around my hips.

Those thoughts were exactly the reason why now wasn't the right time to try to figure out things with Kinzie. I couldn't handle that distraction too. God, I wanted to, though. I ached for her. She made me feel cherished in a way I hadn't known existed. I hated myself for how I'd treated her, but I also couldn't see a future for us, so I knew I still wouldn't call her. Even if I was in her city. Our last game there was tomorrow night, but it didn't make sense for me to try to see her despite desperately wanting to.

Watching film that afternoon was painful, but I could see the moments where I'd given up on myself rather than went for it. It was weird watching that. It was like a light bulb switched on. In the moment, I didn't feel like I was in control, but watching film, it was clear to me that I would have been fine had I just gone for it. The few times I did commit, I was totally fine.

I felt a mix of embarrassment and anger in the hotel conference room surrounded by my teammates, but rather than getting down on myself, I felt motivated. I knew in my soul that the film I watched wasn't me. Last night, I'd forgotten who I was. Who I'd become. That was not the person I was anymore. That old version of Jane Gray, the cautious version who was afraid to commit, could fuck right the fuck off.

"I like the look on your face right now, Gray. It tells me you're going to bring it tomorrow night," Maya said as I was going through my shooting drills after practice.

"It's because I am. Watching that film made me disgusted, angry, and frustrated with myself."

"You bring your small forward speed with that power forward swagger, and New York isn't going to know what hit them. Except every lesbian in the house is going to want to hate-fuck you when their team comes back to Milwaukee down two games in two days. If you weren't my sister, I'd be really turned on right now." She fanned herself as she walked toward me.

"Stop it, weirdo." I gathered my feet as I took another jumper from the elbow and watched as the ball swished. Maya grabbed the ball and passed it back to me.

"Who's a weirdo? It's a fact. You're lighting up WNBA sapphic Twitter."

"I try to not go on Twitter. It's toxic, and I don't need that negativity in my life. I bring enough negativity to the table without any help." I chuckled as I sank another shot from the elbow.

"That's a fair decision."

I sank another shot.

"What about Kinzie?" Maya asked.

The last topic I wanted to discuss in that moment. I took another shot, and it rimmed out. "See what you made me do?"

"Me? You did that to yourself. But I guess that answers my question. You don't want to talk about it." She tossed the ball back to me. "But I really think you need to think about it."

I didn't want to think about it. I wanted to focus on the game. I had something to prove. That I still had game and wasn't washed up. Yet I didn't know how I could prove that to myself let alone anyone else if all I was doing was obsessing about Kinzie and how much I missed her. How much I wanted to see her standing in the tunnel with her arms crossed, watching me play with that sexy little smirk of hers.

Despite not being able to get Kinzie off my mind, the evening went quickly as I went to bed early, dreamt of Kinzie, and got thirteen hours of sleep in preparation for the game the next day. I needed it. In what felt like a blink of an eye, we were back at Barclays warming up. I felt like I'd found my groove again and was feeling confident without the unrealistic expectations. Everything felt like it was clicking as Coach gave us our final pep talk, as the "The Imperial March" played, as I was announced back on the starting lineup, as I chest bumped Brittany, as I high-fived Ruby, as I huddled up with the team as they announced the Liberty, and as Ellie the elephant danced around, right up until the point where the lights came back up.

"Um," Maya said as she pulled me a step away from the team.

"What's up?"

Her lips were pressed in a thin line. "I don't want you to be blindsided, but guess who just walked in and sat courtside over there?" She tilted her head to the right.

"What? Who?" I said, scanning the courtside seats. There sat Kinzie in my jersey, dress pants, and heels, holding a beer as she leaned over talking to an older man beside her. Given their strong resemblance, he was almost certainly her dad. "Fuck," I said, my voice inaudible over the noise in the arena.

Maya must have read my lips because she said, "Not fuck. This is going to be great. You are going to play great. You're going to nail it. Big time. All the Way Gray."

"All the Way Gray? Since when is that a thing?"

"Oh right, I forgot you don't Twitter. It's been your tagline on there as designated by the fans for the last few weeks. It's good, right? Though they might not just use it in a basketball context." Her eyes widened as she laughed.

I wasn't sure how I felt about that, but I didn't have time to process it because it was time for tip-off. I jockeyed for position as Brittany squared off against Stewart. Maya got possession, and I sprinted up the court before anyone had a chance to react in time for a perfect pass that I put through the hoop on an easy layup.

I couldn't help but look at Kinzie, who had jumped out of her seat and was cheering, much to her neighbors' chagrin. She smiled at me and screamed, "All the Way Gray!" as I ran by to get back on defense.

I rolled my eyes but smiled on the inside. I couldn't help it. She looked amazing, if a little ridiculous, in her outfit, and God,

I'd missed her. But as I took my position on the left wing on our zone defense, I pushed her out of my mind. The support was amazing, but she couldn't be anything more than a fan to me for the rest of the night. Miraculously, neither her presence nor her yelling or cheers every time I scored, got a steal, did practically anything, took my focus off the game.

I was in the zone. Every shot felt amazing. I was battling and getting boards. I thought about my knee the first time I made a hard cut, but when it held, I didn't think about it again. I used my breathing techniques when I was on the bench or in time-outs if I felt myself start to slip out of the moment, and it worked perfectly.

The game was one where, if you weren't a fan of either team, it would have been great because it was really up-tempo, and the score was close the entire game. I couldn't keep track of how many lead changes there were. We would go on a little run, and then, they would answer with a run of their own.

In the end, despite Maya and I both getting double-doubles, we fell one point short. What made it worse was that I missed the last shot. The ref should have called a foul when Stewart hit my hand rather than the ball when she went for the block, but she didn't. I tried to plead my case, but the ref threatened to T me up, and Maya pulled me away. It was bullshit, but that was the game.

I might have been giving her a death stare as Maya pulled me toward the tunnel, but movement from where Kinzie had been sitting caught my eye. "Great game, Jane," she yelled when I looked over.

I smiled at her and then laughed as two people sitting in the row behind her booed her. She seemed unfazed by them as she just stared at me, smiling and looking amazing. I looked at her looking at me and resisted the urge to run to her as every fiber of my being wanted to do, but I needed to get off the court.

"Come on, lover girl," Maya said as she pulled me toward the tunnel in earnest. "Just wait until Twitter gets the photo of you and Kinzie eye fucking. They're going to be insanely disappointed."

I laughed and said, "No way."

She stopped in her tracks in the tunnel and leveled her gaze at me, brows raised. "I guarantee it will be up before you're even out of the shower."

"Oh God. The team doesn't even know we've been dating."

"You believe they haven't figured it out? You two haven't really been subtle."

My stomach dropped. I thought we'd been pretty clandestine. Yet, the thought of the team knowing didn't scare me the way it had before. Being a topic of chatter and speculation on social media made me uncomfortable, but I couldn't control that, which I reminded myself as we walked into the locker room.

The room was muted. Losing a game in the finals tended to do that. But my mental state was much better than two nights ago when we'd won. That night, I'd thought my career might be over. But tonight felt full of possibility despite the loss.

"Nice of you to finally join us," Coach said.

"Sorry, Coach. Jane here was about to go to blows with that ref. It just took a minute to calm her down."

Once we sat, Coach said, "Losing sucks, especially when you all played your damn hearts out. But it happens, and we lost well. We fought hard and didn't give up. We held the lead for half the game in front of an unfriendly, sold-out crowd that was decided on a bullshit call. I am fucking proud of each and every one of you. And it's only game two. We're one and one. It's a clean slate. And we're going home for the next two games. It's okay to be frustrated, but we're going to keep our chins high, watch film, and prepare to do battle again in a few nights. It's still a long series ahead of us. This is only act one."

Maya clapped, and the whole room joined in. The feel of the room was strange after such a big loss. But we really were a family, and I was grateful to be a part of it.

Chapter Eighteen

When I walked out of the locker room, Kinzie was standing on the far side of the hallway, her arms crossed. I jumped, startled to see her.

"I'll see you on the bus. It leaves in nine minutes, and Coach will be *pissed* if you aren't there," Maya said loudly, and then barely loud enough for me to hear, "Don't let her slip through your fingers."

"Hey, you," Kinzie said, still leaning against the wall.

"Hey, yourself," I said, rooted in place. Afraid to get too close. It was bizarre, but I was frozen, as if my feet had sunk into the floor. When I was showering, I'd nearly talked myself into calling her before we headed home tomorrow, but now I was nervous that she was there. I didn't know what to say. The fact I'd been able to play well even with here there cheering for me had me reconsidering her as a distraction. In my panic, I'd somehow forgotten how many games I'd played with her on the sidelines with no ill effect on my playing.

"You were amazing tonight."

"We lost." *Why couldn't I just say thank you?*

"Yes, but *you* were amazing. Unfortunately, New York was too. But I've never watched you courtside like that. It was…" She bit her lip, and heat flooded to my core as she looked me up and down. "Delicious. I liked it. I hope to do more of it. This season. Next year. Every year. If you'll let me."

"I want…" I wanted to run into her arms, but I couldn't move my feet. I don't know if it was fatigue or if my emotions had overridden my motor skills. Regardless, I didn't move. I cleared my throat. I didn't have time to figure things out in that moment, but I knew I needed to say more. Apologize. Tell her I'd been an asshole, but in that tunnel with the team bus waiting for me wasn't the time. "Can I see you later? I have to go catch the bus, but we don't fly home until tomorrow. Can I come by later?"

"Of course. I'll text you my address. You're welcome anytime."

I nodded. Swallowed. Nodded again. "Okay. I'll see you in a little bit, okay?"

She took the step that I couldn't and squeezed my arm. She reached up, and I thought she was going to touch my face, but she let her hand fall, and it felt like something was taken from me, even though I'd never had it. Okay, that wasn't true. I'd had it. But it had been weeks, and I'd thrown it away. Nothing had been taken from me. I'd made the decision not to accept it. The realization churned in my gut.

I squeezed her hand, and her smile grew to megawatt voltage. "Perfect."

She squeezed my hand and left me staring at her heels click-clacking down the cold tunnel as she walked away. Every instinct I had screamed at me to go after her, but I had responsibilities to the team. But after, I was going to go to her. And I was going to…I didn't know, but I needed to figure it out because what I did know was that I needed *her* too.

I tried to tamp down on my impatience, but it was frustrating as hell once I googled how much closer I'd been to Kinzie's Tribeca apartment from Barclay's. It would have been like fifteen minutes. Instead, the Uber from my hotel was an hour in traffic.

I was already walking a razor's edge of stress going to see her, not knowing what I was going to say. By the time I stood outside her building and pressed the intercom for her apartment, I was sweating, and my hands were shaking. I wiped my palms on my jeans and tapped on the vibrant screen until I found her in the short directory, uncomfortable with the video of myself that popped up.

It worked, though, as in less than two seconds, Kinzie's crackly voice said, "Come on up, Jane. Penthouse."

I'd always known she came from money. Her grandfather had founded their company, and it wasn't like Kinzie stayed at the Holiday Inn when she was in town, but she wasn't in the Presidential Suite, either, except for the celebration night after my triple-double. But holy hell, this building was…imposing.

When the doors slid open right in front of Kinzie's door, I was surprised. When she opened the door and the entire wall behind her was glass that looked out at the night sky, I was flabbergasted. I was *almost* distracted from how amazing she looked in her joggers and delightfully low V-neck shirt. But it was still Kinzie who captured my attention.

Always Kinzie.

"Do you want to come in?" she said as I stared.

When I didn't respond, she grabbed my hand and pulled me into her apartment.

"Do you want something to drink?" She took a sip of the red wine she was holding. "I'm guessing you don't want alcohol, but I have water, sparkling water, juice?"

"Sparkling water would be great." I thought maybe the bubbles would give me a little courage, like champagne bubbles.

"What flavor would you like?" It looked like she had the same fancy ass machine as Maya.

"Um, just plain?" I'd made the decision to come over here and see Kinzie, but that took up pretty much all of my decision-making power.

"As you wish." She filled the bottle, attached it to the machine, and pressed a button on the top. For a minute, the only sounds in the apartment were soft jazz music and the gurgling and hissing as the machine carbonated the water.

She handed me a glass with a lime wedge on the rim, and we sat on her soft leather couch, buttery and cool against my hand.

I wasn't sure where to start, but I appreciated Kinzie giving me a moment to think. As I watched the bubbles flit in the glass, their frantic movements seemed to calm my mind. Kinzie interlacing her fingers with mine didn't hurt, either, and I knew I needed to tell her everything in my heart and in my mind, even the parts that hurt.

"I'm sorry for a few weeks ago and for boxing you out since then. I'm sorry I never called you back. After my injury, I was in kind of a dark place. That Jane, with her doomsday outlook and zero self-confidence, isn't the person I want to be, but she took over, and I didn't feel worthy of you, of love, of a playing career." I took a sip and held it in my mouth, appreciating the swirling fizz while I steeled myself to finish telling her the truth. "Of anything good."

Kinzie squeezed my fingers and didn't pull her hand away. "What changed?"

"I talked to Brigitte. I worked with Aaron. I was able to snap myself out of the super negative self-talk and remembered that I am successful. I am worthy. I am deserving of good things. I'm embarrassed with how long that took, but I'm here. And I'm sorrier than you will ever know. I clung to this notion of not being able to handle you as a distraction, but I've played better this season than I ever have, and my play after the all-star break—coincidentally after we started seeing each other—was exponentially better than ever. I was afraid. I'm not proud of it, but I'm sorry I was the worst. I'm still not sure how it'll work with living in different cities one-third of the year and different countries for the other two-thirds, but I've missed you so much. I had to see you and apologize and see if we can figure it out."

"Working out long-distance challenges is not a problem. I have a lot of frequent flier miles and hotel points, and there are about seventy direct flights from New York airports to London airports daily. I have a fairly flexible work schedule—my name *is* on the door to the office after all. There is FaceTime and Zoom and phone calls when we can't be together. Distance is not an obstacle unless you let it be."

She sounded incredibly confident. I loved to hear it, but I also worried she didn't realize what she was getting into with me. "Are you sure? Being with a professional athlete is hard."

"How do you know? Have you ever been in a relationship with one?"

"Well, no. I just see all of my teammates have issues. Especially in the offseason of the W, when we're all playing overseas. Ruby is dating a wide receiver for the Cheetahs, and they struggle to find time to spend together."

She ran her thumb over the top of my hand. "I don't care if they have issues. You aren't them, and I'm not *their* significant others. I want to be *yours*." She sat her glass down and scooted closer to me. "The only thing that has come between us this season has been you. Call me forward if you want, but I'm pretty sure you like me."

I laughed at her words, reminding me of our first night together. "I do."

"And I'm pretty sure you have feelings for me. Real feelings." I opened my mouth to agree, but the words froze in my throat. "For the record, I have feelings—strong ones—for you. You do know that, right?"

"I didn't recognize it a few weeks ago, but I know it now. I have feelings for you too."

"And not just fling ones?"

I laughed. "No, not just fling feelings. Don't get me wrong, I want you. But it's much more than that."

"Have I convinced you that we can make long distance work?"

I swallowed, a little self-doubt still lingering as to whether I was enough. "I mean, I think we can, I'm just worried about the long term. What if I get hurt? What if something happens, and we can't see each other for months?"

"Did I run away when you got hurt this time?"

"You didn't come to Milwaukee the whole time I was injured. I'm sorry, that sounded whiny, I just…the last time I got hurt, I got my heart broken." I sounded like a petulant child, and I hated it, but for some reason, I needed to understand why she'd stayed away.

"Jane," Kinzie said, her voice laced with exasperation. "You wouldn't take my calls. I didn't think you wanted to see me, and you accused me of distracting you when I'd seen you last. I didn't want you to say I distracted you from getting well. I was giving you the space you'd asked for." She didn't pull her hand away, but it tensed against mine. I felt like she wanted to pull back but was fighting it.

"I…I'm sorry. I was a shit. That was a ridiculous question."

"It was pretty fucked-up, Jane. I can't be responsible for reassuring you all the time that you are worthy, regardless of the feelings I have for you. It isn't fair to me. I want to be with you, but at the same time, I'm afraid that you aren't ready for a mature relationship."

Her words nearly sucked the life out of me. My palms went clammy. I felt queasy. I sat my glass on her side table and took her hand in both of mine. I'd done everything I could to push her away, but I realized what a mistake I'd made, and I needed to figure out how to undo it. I couldn't lose her just when I realized maybe I could have it all. "I'm sorry, I shouldn't have said that. You did exactly what I asked. I'm working on myself, but I'm still a work in progress. I'm better than I was, but I'm not perfect. So far from it. But I'm trying." I took a sip of water. "I'm trying to be better. I swear. I'm going to be better." I brought her hand to my mouth and kissed it without breaking eye contact. "I promise you."

"No one is perfect, but you can't always feel like you're not worthy of me. You are fucking amazing." Her eye contact was intense and turned my insides to jelly when combined with her words. "You deserve someone amazing too. I hope I'm that person, but even if you were to walk out of here today and never talk to me again, you would still be worthy of someone special. And not someone you feel inferior to. You are not inferior to *anyone*. You deserve someone who appreciates you. But I worry you don't really believe that for yourself."

I jumped in. "No, I do. I do know that in my bones, but sometimes, my head gets in the way." I paused, trying to collect my thoughts and gather my arguments. "Brigitte gave me the names of a few therapists. I know I need help, and sometimes I might slip, but I commit to you, I will do whatever it takes to not forget who I am. I love you, but I want you to know that I'm going to see a therapist for me. And it's because I want to be the person who truly deserves you. I think seeing a therapist regularly will help me stay in the right headspace and remember that I am worthy and that I deserve happiness and a career. And to not be afraid of any of that." I prayed that would be enough. That she would believe the words and the intention behind them.

"You *love*, love me?"

This wasn't how I'd envisioned telling her, but it was true, even if I hadn't fully admitted it to myself. "I do."

"That's the best news I've heard in a while." The corners of her lips turned up. "Because I love you too."

My heart swelled, and even though there was a tiny sliver of doubt, I told it to shut the fuck up. "You really love me back?"

"I do. Every infuriating inch of you." She set her wine on the glass coffee table with a plink and tucked a lock of hair that had come out of my bun behind my ear as she said, "Can I kiss you now?"

"Please," I said, barely a whisper.

Her lips grazed mine, tentative at first, but the pent-up need in me didn't allow the gentleness to last long. My lips were hungry for her as I deepened the kiss and slid my fingers into her hair.

She moaned and pushed me onto my back on the couch. When her leg slid between my thighs, I sank my fingers into her hips and pulled her more tightly against me, finally realizing home was a feeling, not a place, and Kinzie was my home.

❖

I hated having to crawl out of Kinzie's bed at three a.m., but we had a flight at nine, and I needed time to get back to my hotel, pack my bag, and meet up for the team bus at six.

However, the fifteen-minute detour that I took with Kinzie against her kitchen counter, was fifteen minutes of my life that I would never regret. Even if it caused my anxiety to spike about being late. Unfoundedly.

I made it back early enough that I even had enough time to do some yoga in my room and meditate, envisioning myself in a groove in our next game until a knock sounded at my door and pulled me out of my Zen.

"I was wondering if you'd even be here this morning," Maya said when I opened the door.

"Why wouldn't I be?"

She didn't say anything as she stared. I squirmed but didn't break as she slid past me into my room. "No Kinzie?"

"Why would she be here?" I said, feigning innocence.

"I know you two made some kind of plans at the arena, and then you slipped off to 'bed' as soon as we got back. Super sus. You snuck off to her place, then?"

"As if anyone would trade this generic hotel room for her gorgeous condo," I scoffed.

"Gorgeous condo, huh? What time did you get back?"

"About four."

"My favorite lovebirds patched things up?" Maya said.

"I think you could safely say that." I tried not to blush.

She whooped and pumped her fist. "I'm happy for you," she said before pulling me into a hug.

I struggled to not jump around with her. I was dignified, after all. "Me too."

"What's the plan now?" Maya asked.

"We don't have anything completely firmed up, but she's going to come to Milwaukee tomorrow and stay for our two home games. And then, I don't know. She says she has a lot of frequent flier miles and some pull with her boss, aka her dad, to be able to work remote while I'm in Europe, and I guess we just play it by ear from there."

Maya fanned her face. "I love this for you so hard. And don't mind me living vicariously through you as things fall apart with fucking Paris." She flopped on the bed.

"Ugh. What happened with her last night?" I dropped next to her on my stomach.

"She called me and seemed like she was going to be sympathetic about our loss, but she got kind of mean."

"Mean how?" I really didn't understand why Maya seemed content to stay with her, and maybe today was the day I should say something about it. I hated the idea, but fucking Paris seemed toxic.

"She made a couple of comments that *I* didn't bring my A game. It was like a backhanded compliment though because she said something like, 'but I'm sure you'll play better next game, more like yourself.'"

"What a bitch," I said before I could sensor myself.

"That's what I thought too. I don't know where we stand. I hung up on her after we got into it. But I'm just done with her shit. I'm pretty amazing, and I don't need her making me feel bad about myself all the time. But it's easier for me to think and say these things when she's not around. My resolve weakens when we're in the same room."

"You're right, though. You deserve someone who makes you feel good about yourself. Someone who builds you up without cutting you down in the next breath. She's manipulative as fuck, but I haven't known how to say that to you."

"Thank you. You're a good friend." She pushed my arm.

"I try."

"Will you help me keep my resolve?"

"Of course."

Chapter Nineteen

In game three, it felt like New York hadn't come to Milwaukee to play basketball at all. We blew them out of the water, and I went back to Kinzie's hotel and had some of the most amazing sex of my life.

That was not the case in game four. Brondello must have shaken something into them, or maybe they'd all had the stomach flu in game three and bounced back fiercely, because they played with a passion that knocked us back on our heels. We kept it close, but we ended up losing by five, which sucked, even though it felt like we were playing well. I went back to Kinzie's hotel and had a wound-licking hot tub soak and unbelievable sex. My wounds were not the only things licked, and it was fantastic.

None of that was on my mind, however, as I wiped sweat from my forehead and shook out my legs during our final time-out in game five back in New York. We were down by two, and there were thirteen seconds left. These next thirteen seconds were going to determine who would be crowned the next WNBA champions. I tried to push the nerves away. It was just another game. But also, the most important one of my career. I'd never been on a team that had won a championship. I focused on my breath and the sensation of the air.

Coach came over and drew the play out on the clipboard as she said, "Jane, you've had a hot hand today, and they're having a hard time when you drive. We're running a play for you. If they collapse in, look to kick it back out to either Maya or Mercedes in the corners, which will leave you in position to go after the board if we need it."

We all nodded and put a hand in.

Maya inbounded the ball to Ruby, who swung it over to Brittany at the high post. I got free off Maya's screen and checked the time when Brittany passed it to me near the top of the key. With eight seconds left, I faked right and made a hard crossover move to the left.

It was almost like Coach could read New Yorks' minds. When I drove to the basket, the defender on Maya dropped in to double-team me. I sent a hard no-look pass out to her and continued to charge forward to get in position for the board.

I saw in my peripheral that Maya caught the ball and went up, her toes just outside the arc. If this went through, we'd be up by one with about two seconds left. I heard Kinzie cheering my name from her courtside seat, but it was just background noise as I stayed focused on the game in the hostile arena.

Maya's shot was a fraction of an inch off, the ping of the ball hitting the rim echoed, and I jumped for the board. I muscled the ball away from my defender, who also had a hand on it. I didn't have time to dribble and went straight up with the defender's hand in my face, shooting the ball just as the clock expired.

The ball bounced once. Twice. Rolled around the top of the rim for an eternity before rolling out and falling benignly to the floor. The arena erupted in cheers for New York as their whole team surged onto the floor in a scrum, jumping up and down.

To be so close to winning the championship and having it snatched from my grasp hurt. But not as bad as I thought it would. As I stood there, watching the basketball bounce across the floor toward the press, even as tears pricked the backs of my eyes, I understood that this game wasn't the most important thing. It wasn't the end of anything.

I looked to the courtside seats right by the tunnel where Kinzie had been sitting, knowing she'd still be there. She was staring at me. I could see in her eyes that she wanted to come to me but wouldn't come out onto the court. I wanted to grab her and hug her, but I settled for walking over and squeezing her hand.

She leaned in and whispered in my ear, "I'll wait for you, okay? Will you come back to my place tonight rather than going back to the hotel?"

"Yeah," I said. I nonchalantly kissed her on the cheek.

Maya wrapped her arm around my shoulders as aqua colored confetti swirled around us. "Hey, Kinzie. Sorry to interrupt, but it's time to get outta here and let these damn New Yorkers have their fun. If we don't run soon, Dolly might come over here and ask us questions about the loss, and God knows that would be horrible."

"Yeah, yeah," I said. To Kinzie, I said, "I'll text you when we're almost done? You don't have to wait. I can Uber."

"I know I don't *have to* wait, but I will. Now get out of here before Dolly sees you over here looking at me like you love me."

Expecting an embarrassment that never came gave me the courage to say, "Well, I do love you, and I'm not ashamed of it."

"Good." Kinzie smiled, and I probably would have given her a kiss on the mouth except Maya made a gagging sound.

"You're going to need to break this up, lovebirds. She'll see you later, Kinzie. I promise, we won't keep her too late."

Kinzie mouthed, "I love you," just before Maya turned me away and guided me toward the tunnel with her arm still around my shoulder.

"You two are really cute. Even if it's a little gross."

"Sorry, not sorry," I said and shrugged.

"Yeah. This blows. I can't believe we both missed our shots."

Surprising myself, I said, "It's all part of the game." I'd expected to feel like I let down the team missing the final shot like that, but I didn't. It wasn't the first shot I'd missed that day.

It wouldn't be the last shot I missed in my life. But I was proud of myself for being willing to *take* the shot, and that was what was different about me now. And it gave me an amazing foundation to build on.

❖

I texted Kinzie when I thought I'd be about fifteen more minutes. Time after a loss always moved at a glacial pace. The team meeting, the post-game interview, stretching, icing, the minutes just dragged on, and after that finals loss, time was practically moving in reverse, so it felt like it'd been an eternity by the time I finally caught up with Kinzie.

"Your arena privileges in Milwaukee don't translate to New York, huh? You couldn't get in and surprise me in the ice bath again?" I said, genuinely curious.

"I probably could've gotten back there. My dad is friends with the owner of the team, and we've done work for them in other ventures. It's how I got courtside tickets to a sold-out game. But it felt weird creeping back there as your girlfriend. When you have home games, I work for the team and have nearly full access. I'm just trying to color within the lines. I don't want to make you uncomfortable."

I took her hand and smiled. "I appreciate that. I'm done hiding us, but yeah, we should still be appropriate. But talking to you while I was in the ice bath actually made it go faster last time."

"You just tell me when and where, and I'll be there." She squeezed my hand before letting go to allow us to both get into the town car she'd ordered for the night. "You don't seem as sad as I was expecting. Are you really okay?"

"It sucks, and it's horrible, and it hurts, and I might have a good cry when we get back to your place, but, yeah, I'm okay. Coach Carr reminded us that while this is a setback, at the start of the year, the preseason polls had us ranked to finish eighth in the league, and we finished second. That's pretty impressive. And we played incredibly well in all five games. And honestly, I realized that winning this championship isn't everything. I wanted to win. I wanted to stick it to every GM, coach, and team that gave up on me. But what does that matter? I'm here now. I have you. I have a team that is a family. I am really lucky. So while I'm disappointed, we're going to come back stronger next year and win this whole thing."

I'd never felt as certain of anything else in my life. Next year, the Pitbulls were going to win the championship, and I'd have Kinzie by my side when we did.

Epilogue

Six Months Later

I straightened Kinzie's collar peeking out from her suit jacket. "Have I told you how much I love you in a suit?"

She laughed. "Maybe just once or twice. But I always love to hear it. I also love to see the way you look at me when I wear it."

I ran a fingertip down her chest and between her breasts, the skin exposed by several undone buttons on her blouse. "Although...I also love to see it on the floor." She shivered, and heat flooded my core, but rather than let me take us on a small detour, she wrapped her fingers around my wrist and brought my hand to her mouth.

She kissed the tip of my index finger. "While I love that idea." She kissed the tip of my middle finger. "We have a grand opening party to attend." She kissed the tip of my ring finger. "And since it's my party." She kissed the tip of my pinkie finger. "I really can't be late. As much as I'd love to throw caution to the wind, it's not really an option."

"I can't believe you're opening a satellite office of Lancaster Consulting in Milwaukee that's focused on advancing women's sports." I was giddy with excitement that we'd be living in the same city. When I wasn't on the road anyway. But still, it would be amazing.

"Me either. It was one of the things I was working on in the fall."

"My, my, how far you've come. From someone who told me the first night that she hated sports to creating a new division in your company solely focused on advancing women's sports? I don't know, Kinzie. I think you've gone soft."

"Perhaps. But only because of you." She kissed me. "I'm glad you're able to be here with me."

"I was going to be here either way. But the Lions losing in the Euroleague quarterfinals was convenient because I was able to come back to the States, and I've loved living with you before the W's season starts. Not that I like losing, but if I have to lose, I like it when it makes my life more convenient."

"Are you excited for training camp to start in a few weeks?"

"Of course. But this year, the season is going to end differently. We're going to go all the way. I guarantee it." And I was totally committed to making it happen. I'd been working out like I was possessed while in London, increasing my strength and fitness as well as doing more basketball drills after every practice. "And having you by my side makes me even more confident."

"It doesn't matter to me if you win or lose. I love you no matter what."

"I love you no matter what too. I'm glad you were so forward that first night and came over to talk to me."

"I'm not sure if you're aware, but we're coming up on our one-year anniversary." She gave me a sly smile.

"You're counting our anniversary as the first night we slept together? Even though I snuck out in the middle of the night while you were still asleep?" I said, a little surprised.

"It's been exactly a year since I met you, and my life changed forever. That's what I'm counting."

"You're sweet. You changed my life too. Everything about my life is different from what it was last year, but I love it. I thought I couldn't have love and basketball, but here we are. Thank you for holding my hand while I worked on myself to figure it all out."

"I'm here for you always," Kinzie said and pulled me close. I didn't know what the future held. But I did know that I was ready to face any and all of it, with Kinzie by my side.

About the Author

Krystina has been a lover of romance novels since she was probably too young to read them and developed an affinity for sapphic romance after she found her first one on a shelf in a used bookstore in 2001. Despite a lifelong desire, she never made the time to write her own until the COVID-19 pandemic struck, and she had extra time with no daily commute or work travel.

Krystina grew up in Florida but, after spending six years in the military, finds herself now calling Chicago home—though she frequently travels so often for work that she forgets what city she's in. She works in real estate and lives with her wife and their two rescue pit bulls. When not working, traveling, or writing, Krystina is most often found reading with a glass of wine in hand, doing yoga (occasionally with a glass of wine in hand), snuggling with her fur-babies, or trying to convince herself that it's not too cold to go for a jog outside.

Books Available from Bold Strokes Books

Across the Enchanted Border by Crin Claxton. Magic, telepathy, swordsmanship, tyranny, and tenderness abound in a tale of two lands separated by the enchanted border. (978-1-63679-804-2)

Deep Cover by Kara A. McLeod. Running from your problems by pretending to be someone else only works if the person you're pretending to be doesn't have even bigger problems. (978-1-63679-808-0)

Good Game by Suzanne Lenoir. Even though Lauren has sworn off dating gamers, it's becoming hard to resist the multifaceted Sam. An opposites attract lesbian romance. (978-1-63679-764-9)

Innocence of the Maiden by Ileandra Young. Three powerful women. Two covens at war. One horrifying murder. When mighty and powerful witches begin to butt heads, who out there is strong enough to mediate? (978-1-63679-765-6)

Protection in Paradise by Julia Underwood. When arson forces them together, the flames between chief of police Eve Maguire and librarian Shaye Hayden aren't that easy to extinguish. (978-1-63679-847-9)

Too Forward by Krystina Rivers. Just as professional basketball player Jane May's career finally starts heating up, a new relationship with her team's brand consultant could derail the success and happiness she's struggled so long to find. (978-1-63679-717-5)

Worth Waiting For by Kristin Keppler. For Peyton and Hanna, reliving the past is painful, but looking back might be the only way to move forward. (978-1-63679-773-1)

Flowers and Gemstones by Alaina Erdell. Caught between past loves and present secrets, Hannah and Vanessa must each decide if the other is worth making difficult changes for a shot at happiness. (978-1-63679-745-8)

Foul Play by Erin Kaste. Music librarian Kirsten Lindquist knows someone is stalking the symphony musicians, but can she prove that a string of murders and suspicious accidents are connected, all without becoming a victim herself? (978-1-63679-689-5)

Hollywood Hearts by Toni Logan. What happens when an A-list actress falls for a paparazzo, having no idea her love interest is the one responsible for the photos in a troublesome tabloid scandal targeting her? (978-1-63679-695-6)

Ride It Out by Jenna Jarvis. When the COVID-19 lockdown traps Mick and Katy in situations they'd convinced themselves were temporary, they're forced to face what they really want from their lives, and who they want to share them with. (978-1-63679-709-0)

Scarlet Love by Gun Brooke. Felicienne de Montagne is content with her hybrid flowers and greenhouses—until she finds adventurer Puck Aston on her doorstep and realizes nothing will ever be the same. (978-1-63679-721-2)

The Hard Stuff by Ana Hartnett. When Hannah, the sales manager for a big liquor brand, moves to Alexandra's hometown and rivals her local distillery, sparks of friction and attraction fly. It turns out the liquor is the least of the hard stuff. (978-1-63679-599-7)

The Hunter and Her Witch by Rachel Sullivan. When an ex-witch-hunter falls for a witch, buried pasts are unearthed, and love is placed on trial. (978-1-63679-830-1)

Trustfall by Patricia Evans. Devri and Shiv never expect their feelings for each other to linger, but sometimes what you've always wanted has a way of leading you to who you've always needed. (978-1-63679-705-2)

All For Her: Forbidden Romance Novellas by Gun Brooke, J.J. Hale, Aurora Rey. Explore the angst and excitement of forbidden love few would dare in this heart-stopping novella collection. (978-1-63679-713-7)

Finding Harmony by CF Frizzell. Rock star Harper Cushing has to rearrange her grandmother's future and sell the family store out from under her, but she reassesses everything because Gram's helper, Frankie, could be offering the harmony her heart has been missing. (978-1-63679-741-0)

Gaze by Kris Bryant. Love at first sight is for dreamers, but the more time Lucky and Brianna spend together, the more they realize the chemistry of a gaze can make anything possible. (978-1-63679-711-3)

Laying of Hands by Patricia Evans. The mysterious new writing instructor at camp makes Grace Waters brave enough to wonder what would happen if she dared to write her own story. (978-1-63679-782-3)

Seducing the Widow by Jane Walsh. Former rival debutantes have a second chance at love after fifteen years apart when a spinster persuades her ex-lover to help save her family business. (978-1-63679-747-2)

The Naked Truth by Sandy Lowe. How far are Rowan and Genevieve willing to go and how much will they risk to make their most captivating and forbidden fantasies a reality? (978-1-63679-426-6)

The Roommate by Claire Forsythe. Jess Black's boyfriend is handsome and successful. That's why it comes as a shock when she meets a woman on the train who makes her pulse race. (978-1-63679-757-1)